"Range me."

Larquette took a deep breath and settled on her elbows. "Tell me what to do."

Bolan pointed across the hills. "Do you see that man out there with the binoculars?"

She nodded slightly, not taking her eyes off him. "Yes."

Bolan settled into a prone firing position. "Now, press the button above your right finger. There should be a red-colored readout in the bottom left-hand corner of your view. What does it say?"

"Eight hundred and seventy-three M. Now what?"

"There's a little ravine behind us about thirty yards. When I give the word, get into it fast."

The Executioner pushed off the safety and began to slowly take up the trigger's slack. In his scope he saw the Russian's jaw drop as he came face-to-face with Bolan's rifle through his binoculars.

Larquette flinched as the huge weapon boomed beside her, then she whipped her binoculars around. All through the rocks, the Russians were scurrying for cover. And sudden aiming their assault ri

MACK BOLAN ®

The Executioner

#152 Combat Stretch
#153 Firebase Florida
#154 Night Hit
#155 Hawaiian Heat
#156 Phantom Force
#157 Cayman Strike
#158 Firing Line
#159 Steel and Flame
#160 Storm Warning
#161 Eye of the Storm
#162 Colors of Hell
#163 Warrior's Edge
#164 Death Trail
#165 Fire Sweep
#166 Assassin's Creed
#167 Double Action
#168 Blood Price
#169 White Heat
#170 Baja Blitz
#171 Deadly Force
#172 Fast Strike
#173 Capitol Hit
#174 Battle Plan
#175 Battle Ground
#176 Ransom Run
#177 Evil Code
#178 Black Hand
#179 War Hammer
#180 Force Down
#181 Shifting Target
#182 Lethal Agent
#183 Clean Sweep
#184 Death Warrant
#185 Sudden Fury
#186 Fire Burst
#187 Cleansing Flame

#188 War Paint
#189 Wellfire
#190 Killing Range
#191 Extreme Force
#192 Maximum Impact
#193 Hostile Action
#194 Deadly Contest
#195 Select Fire
#196 Triburst
#197 Armed Force
#198 Shoot Down
#199 Rogue Agent
#200 Crisis Point
#201 Prime Target
#202 Combat Zone
#203 Hard Contact
#204 Rescue Run
#205 Hell Road
#206 Hunting Cry
#207 Freedom Strike
#208 Death Whisper

DON PENDLETON'S
THE EXECUTIONER®
DEATH WHISPER

A GOLD EAGLE BOOK FROM
WORLDWIDE.

TORONTO • NEW YORK • LONDON
AMSTERDAM • PARIS • SYDNEY • HAMBURG
STOCKHOLM • ATHENS • TOKYO • MILAN
MADRID • WARSAW • BUDAPEST • AUCKLAND

First edition April 1996
ISBN 0-373-64208-3

Special thanks and acknowledgment to
Chuck Rogers for his contribution to this work.

DEATH WHISPER

Printed in U.S.A.

Men rise from one ambition to another; first they seek to secure themselves from attack, and then they attack others.

—Niccolò Machiavelli
Discorsi, 1531

Aggression unchallenged is aggression unleashed.

—Lyndon B. Johnson
August 4, 1964

You have to fight fire with fire, give as good as you get. When America's enemies attempt to gain a foothold, my response will be scorched earth all the way.

—Mack Bolan

THE
MACK BOLAN®
LEGEND

Nothing less than a war could have fashioned the destiny of the man called Mack Bolan. Bolan earned the Executioner title in the jungle hell of Vietnam.

But this soldier also wore another name—Sergeant Mercy. He was so tagged because of the compassion he showed to wounded comrades-in-arms and Vietnamese civilians.

Mack Bolan's second tour of duty ended prematurely when he was given emergency leave to return home and bury his family, victims of the Mob. Then he declared a one-man war against the Mafia.

He confronted the Families head-on from coast to coast, and soon a hope of victory began to appear. But Bolan had broken society's every rule. That same society started gunning for this elusive warrior—to no avail.

So Bolan was offered amnesty to work within the system against terrorism. This time, as an employee of Uncle Sam, Bolan became Colonel John Phoenix. With a command center at Stony Man Farm in Virginia, he and his new allies—Able Team and Phoenix Force—waged relentless war on a new adversary: the KGB.

But when his one true love, April Rose, died at the hands of the Soviet terror machine, Bolan severed all ties with Establishment authority.

Now, after a lengthy lone-wolf struggle and much soul-searching, the Executioner has agreed to enter an "arm's-length" alliance with his government once more, reserving the right to pursue personal missions in his Everlasting War.

PROLOGUE

Within the corrugated steel walls of the shack the phone rang once. There were no greetings. None was expected.

"You have succeeded," a woman's voice said coldly. It was a statement, not a question.

The man snorted. "Of course."

"How?"

There was a pause, and the man's voice hinted at insult as he answered. "I thought you said you did not wish to know of these things."

The woman's tone became irritated. "Tell me. Now."

"Very well. It was done by the roadside. He never expected it. It will appear to be a random killing, and I am sure with your influence you can have the case open and shut very quickly. Oh, you will also be pleased to know our new friend was extremely helpful in the matter."

"Can we trust him?"

The man laughed. "Of course not, but, let us say that his help was indispensable. Evidence of his indispensability in this matter is in our hands, and he has been made very well aware of this. He has also been very generously paid for his services." The man shrugged. "Do you wish him killed?"

For a moment there was silence. "No, I believe he can be of further use to us. You are sure there will be no trouble? I understand this man Beckett was well liked in the community."

"We have Crucible—" the man wrapped his mind around the American phrase "—in our pocket. He was well liked, yes, but even those in the community we do not own are too scared to act. Besides, there is no proof that it was anything other than a random, roadside killing. These things happen in America. One reads about them all the time, and Crucible is a small town, and the people are scared. There will be no local reprisals. However—''

The woman cut in angrily. "I do not like, 'however.' ''

"However, he was the chief of police. I agree his death was necessary, but it could attract unwanted attention outside of Crucible.''

"Leave that to me," the woman snapped.

"I am informed he was once a United States Marshal.''

The woman sneered. "That was decades ago. He was long retired. No connection he had could lead to reprisal, and even if it could, I could stop it. You just worry about what happens inside of town. I will take care of the rest.''

"As you say. But there is one other thing.''

The woman sighed irritably. "And just what is that?''

"Beckett's daughter has returned.''

"A daughter?''

"I did not know of this either until she arrived.''

"What does this mean to us?''

"It appears she is a lawyer, with an FBI background. She is poking around, speaking with this citizens' committee, but she will find nothing. There is only one thing of interest.''

"What is that?''

"There is talk in town that she will replace her father as chief of police.''

"Unacceptable.''

"I disagree. Our new friend can help us keep a close eye on her. With her father gone she has little influence, and she has no recent experience, apparently, in law enforcement. I say it is better we keep a devil we know than risk having one we do not. Besides, I believe there have been too many killings. The chief is dead. Now you wish the daughter dead, as well. I tell you this will not look good.''

"It will give their little citizens' committee something to think about.''

"You are sure? This could cause more problems than it would solve.''

"Kill her. That is an order. But listen to me. Choose your moment well. I don't want her murdered on the street. This must be subtle." There was a moment of grim silence. "I want you to make her disappear."

1

The Executioner waited in darkness. He knew they were coming. He had beaten the grass to see what would come out and had picked up two tails during the day. Now, the question of the evening was, just who were they?

The heat in the adobe bungalow was oppressive. Many deserts were bitterly cold at night, but along the border of Mexico, the Sonoran Desert of Arizona held the burning heat of the day and radiated it back into the moonless night. Mack Bolan stood in the inky stillness and waited. It was nearly 4:00 a.m., the deadest time of night, when a sleeper was in his deepest phase of slumber, when metabolism slowed and the mind was in the most vivid depths of its dreams. In waking, reaction times would be at their slowest—the ideal time of assassination.

The Executioner stood motionless against the central wall of the house. The old adobe was shuttered against even the dim starlight of the moonless night. Wearing a combat blacksuit, and with his body armor and web gear as black as the night itself, Bolan was a shadow among shadows.

His finger slid around the trigger of the 9 mm Beretta 93-R. In his left ear he wore a plug that ran to a receiver in the shoulder of his web gear. The receiver was attuned to a number of simple trip sensors attached to the bungalow's windows and doors, and it now chirped in Bolan's ear for the second time.

Someone was at the back door.

Bolan waited several long seconds to see if any other part of the house was being breached. For a moment all was silent, then the transmitter on the back door peeped plaintively as its connection was cut. The door had been opened.

Someone was inside.

He slid his night-vision goggles off his forehead and fitted them over his eyes. With a flick of a tiny switch the goggles powered up, and the interior of the bungalow lit up in eerie hues of gray and green. He slid the Beretta's fire selector to 3-round-burst mode and began to move. His rubber soled shoes were silent on the stone floor as he glided along the wall of the small house. The back door led to the kitchen, and from the kitchen the intruder could move only in two directions. One was through the kitchen and into the living room, where Bolan was now. The other way led through a tiny hallway to the bedroom, where presumably the Executioner lay sleeping.

He moved along the wall to flank the assassin. It was utterly still inside the house. Whoever was in the bungalow was moving as silently as Bolan. The soldier slowly released half a breath, slid around the corner and entered the kitchen.

In the flat monochrome light of his night vision goggles, he saw a man in dark, close-fitting coveralls carefully moving toward the rear hallway. The man held a small automatic pistol with both hands before him in the combat entry position. Protruding from the pistol's barrel was the long, thin tube of a sound suppressor. Bolan leveled the Beretta's muzzle squarely between the man's shoulder blades, his voice sounding unnaturally loud as he spoke in the heavy silence.

"Freeze."

The man whipped around with the oiled speed of a professional. His upper body swung like a turret as he leveled his pistol and pulled the trigger in rapid semiautomatic fire. Bolan took a slanting step to the side as the silenced pistol spit at him, then put a 3-round burst into the man's chest. His adversary staggered back from the trip hammer blows but didn't fall. Night vision equipment much like Bolan's protruded from the man's face, and the lenses goggled at the Executioner like the eyes of a giant insect as the man adjusted his aim.

A second burst into the man's chest also had no effect. The man was wearing armor, and he was still firing. The

Executioner flinched as a bullet punched into his own armored vest and spoiled his head shot. The assassin's pistol
clicked open on empty, and without hesitation he hurled it
at Bolan's head. As the soldier dodged the flying gun, the
man lunged at him.

Fingers clamped onto Bolan's night-vision goggles, and
the world plunged into an inky blackness of churning limbs
as they were ripped away from his head. The man's other
hand held Bolan's gun arm in a viselike grip as he drove him
backward.

The Executioner was no stranger to fighting in darkness.
He rammed his gun hand back against the man's chest, and
it told him by touch where the rest of his opponent's body
would be. Bolan struck out, twisting his body and driving
the heel of his left hand into his opponent's face with all of
his two-hundred-plus pounds behind it. The man's head
snapped backward brutally, and Bolan felt the lenses and
filaments of the assassin's night-vision gear snap and crush
under the blow.

The soldier ripped his gun hand free and flicked the Beretta's fire selector to full auto as the man flailed away and
broke contact. He squeezed the trigger, tracking his opponent's path with the remaining nine rounds in the gun. For
a split second the strobing muzzle blast of the Beretta lit the
room, and Bolan knew he had missed. His opponent had
maintained his composure enough to drop and roll away
into the darkness. Bolan shook his head to clear it. Flash
spots danced in front of the Executioner's eyes as his pistol
fell silent and the room veiled in darkness again. Through
ringing ears he heard the rasp of a knife as it left its sheath.

There was no time to reload. His .44 Magnum Desert
Eagle was holstered on his hip, but in the total darkness its
firepower was an uncertain edge. Bolan dropped the empty
Beretta pistol, and his fighting knife whispered slightly as it
left its sheath. He took three rapid steps back to his right
while the Beretta clattered to the floor in front of him, then
he froze. The silence was total. Bolan's senses probed the
blackness for any clue, but they told him nothing. Despite
their skirmish, the man was controlling his breathing as well
as Bolan was. He was obviously very well trained. Now it

would be naked blades in the dark, and any move would be a gamble, but Bolan had given himself a slight edge. His opponent had to come to kill him, and he hadn't broken and run. He would almost certainly make a move on Bolan, given his obvious skill. But the Executioner had a card to play. He had emptied his gun, and the Beretta had left fifteen empty 9 mm shells littering the floor. The automatic pistol ejected empties to the right, and he had moved behind them under the covering noise of his pistol falling to the ground.

The trap was laid. The Executioner waited.

Without warning the tinkle and scrape of a brass shell casing being crushed underfoot sounded directly in front him and Bolan lunged. The fighting knife whipped forward and up from waist level and rammed into sudden resistance. The knife's chisel point punched through thick fabric, then skidded off a hard, smooth surface. Bolan continued his lunge. The fingers of his left hand felt the fabric of the assassin's coveralls, which he seized to maintain contact. He felt the shock as his opponent's knife slammed into his side. The blade drove, twisting through his armor until the point snagged on the densely woven Kevlar fibers and stopped.

A knee slammed up against Bolan's thigh and barely missed his groin. He took the opportunity to unbalance his opponent and drove forward, hooking the assassin's leg and toppling him backward. The man grunted as he hit the floor with Bolan's full weight on top of him. The grunt and the man's body position told the soldier all he needed to know. The heel of his left hand clapped his adversary's chin up and back, and the point of the fighting knife drove home. Warmth flooded over Bolan's hands, and the body beneath him stiffened convulsively, then relaxed into a final sag.

The Executioner rose into a crouch and listened intently. One man had come in for the kill, but there had to be a backup, or at least an observer. The assassin's gun had been silenced, but the staccato trip-hammer action of the Beretta would wake the dead. Bolan felt for the wire on his shoulder. His earpiece had come out during the fight, but it still dangled from his web gear. He replaced the plug and pressed the test button. The receiver chirped that it was still functioning. He didn't know where his night vision goggles were, but hard won battle instincts told him exactly where he had dropped the Beretta. The clack of the bolt slamming forward on a fresh magazine sounded deafening in the silent darkness, but its clamor was coldly reassuring. Bolan sank back into a crouch as the earpiece suddenly peeped.

Someone had just tried the front door.

The Executioner swiftly moved through the house, guided through the dark by memory and sense of direction. He stopped beside the front door and pressed himself against the relative cool of the adobe wall. Bolan controlled his breath and listened. Someone outside had taken a step outside the door, and for a moment silence reigned.

Then someone took a deep breath.

The front door smashed open under a booted foot. The front entry of the house lit up as a powerful light blazed into life. A large, shiny revolver glittered as it preceded its owner into the doorway.

"All right! Freeze!"

Bolan rapped the Beretta across the gunman's wrist, eliciting a shriek of pain and indignation. As the gun clattered to the floor, he seized the gunman's wrist with his free hand and yanked him into the house in a sprawl. The flashlight fell and spun on the stone floor. It stopped under Bolan's foot and pointed at the intruder.

A woman crouched on the floor, holding her wrist and squinting against the harsh light in her face. "You're under arrest!" she yelled defiantly.

Bolan held her at gunpoint and ran a quick survey. She appeared to be in her late twenties. She wore a khaki shirt and dark pants with a stripe down the sides. A standard Sam Browne belt with an empty holster circled her waist, and a walkie-talkie and a nightstick sat in the belt sheaths. On her right breast she wore a silver star with a small metal nameplate underneath. A brown trooper's Stetson lay on the floor beside her.

Bolan calculated. The uniform and equipment didn't prove anything, but her clumsy entry separated her from his assassin by a mile. Bolan spoke to her quietly.

"Stay in a crouch. Keep your hands away from the radio and the club. Move to your right, out of line with the doorway."

The woman glared. "Who the—"

Bolan cut her off with a voice like stone. "Do it. Now."

The trooper glanced nervously into the muzzle of the Beretta, then gingerly crab-walked deeper into the interior of the house. She sank back down and watched him warily. Bolan bent and flicked off the flashlight. Darkness fell again, but his eyes adjusted quickly as starlight filtered into the house through the broken doorway.

The woman was little more than a low shadow on the floor, but Bolan could easily see her if she moved. Her voice spoke in a husky whisper in the gloom.

"Who are you?"

Bolan modified his tone. "I need you to be quiet for a moment."

He strained his senses, probing the environment outside of the house, and tensed as he heard a dim but familiar metallic noise. It was the distinctive sound of an AK-type assault rifle's safety coming off.

The woman started as shots rang out. The rifle fired twice, and Bolan heard the loud bang and bleeding hiss of his Bronco's tires bursting and deflating. Moments later a motorcycle's engine roared into life. The engine gunned, and the sound rapidly drew away in the distance. Bolan started to move when the distant engine sound paused and idled. Two more shots rang out, then the engine noise spurred again and faded away into the night.

"Where did you leave your car?" Bolan asked.

The shoulders of the shadow on the floor slumped visibly. "About half a mile down the road, in the arroyo."

"I suspect you're going to be having car trouble."

The woman snorted.

"You were tailing me."

The woman sounded startled. "You knew?"

"I had two tails today. Who are you?"

"I'm the Crucible chief of police. Who are you?"

Bolan's voice hardened. "Bob Beckett was murdered. There is no chief of Crucible."

The woman's voice hardened, as well. "Well I'm the new one, friend."

"What's your name?"

"Larquette, and you had better start answering some of my questions or you're going to be in a hell of a lot of trouble."

Bolan paused at the name. His mind swiftly went through the scant briefing Brognola had been able to give him. He looked more closely at the woman. "Patricia Lynn Larquette. You're Beckett's daughter. You kept your married name when your husband died."

The woman stood up as her anger and loss overcame her caution. "Just who are you?"

She wouldn't like the answer, so the Executioner decided to sidestep the question.

"I believe Hal Brognola was a friend of your father."

The woman's face was dimly illuminated where she stood and he could see her looking at him quizzically.

"Uh...now I remember. My dad used to speak of a friend in Washington. Could it...?"

"The same. Now I need some answers. When did you become chief of police?"

Larquette's voice dropped in embarrassment. "Two days ago. The citizens' committee elected me. Can we turn on a light?"

Bolan moved to the standing lamp and the room lit up. He surveyed Larquette as she blinked in the sudden light. She was short, with broad shoulders for a woman, and a narrow waist. He noted she was well tanned and athletic looking, with long dark hair done in a low-maintenance French braid in the back. Her uniform had obviously been hastily tailored down to fit her, but she filled it out surprisingly well. She appraised Bolan just as frankly, taking in his blacksuit, body armor and Beretta with a raised eyebrow.

"So, you work for the Justice Department?"

"I work with Hal. He heard about your father's death and asked me to come down here to see if there was anything I could do to help."

She peered at him speculatively. "He sent you?"

"Yes."

"Did he—" Her eyes flew wide as she suddenly took in the dead man lying in the middle of the living room. She paled slightly at the spreading pool of blood on the floor. "Oh, God." She bit her lip and visibly pulled the reins on her composure as she looked at the body clinically.

"Who is he?"

Bolan shrugged. "I was hoping you could tell me." Bolan scooped up her fallen revolver. The big nickel-plated Colt Python .357 Magnum looked timeworn with long use but was obviously well maintained. He spun the big pistol in his hand and presented it to her butt first. "I believe this is yours."

Larquette's face reddened as she took the gun. She snapped out the cylinder to check the load and holstered it with a satisfied nod. "It was Dad's."

Bolan shot a glance outside. "You don't seem to have any backup."

Her lips tightened angrily. "Oh, I have a deputy. Good old Ken Severn."

"And where is he?"

"That's a damn good question. In the past two days he seems to disappear just when I need him. He's a local boy, but some friends on the citizens' committee told me he and my father didn't get along well. He ran for chief against Dad, and he lost big time. I guess he was expecting to get the job after dad died." She shrugged. "I don't think he loves me much, either. I think my father would have fired him, and frankly so would I except that Crucible is so short-handed these days."

Bolan filed that away. "By the way, what kind of car do you have?"

"I've got a Jeep Cherokee."

"Did you have a spare tire?"

"Of course."

"Give me your keys. I'll get the spare from your truck. If mine's intact, between the two of them we might get one of our cars moving." Bolan picked up his night-vision goggles and fitted them over his face. "Don't open the door for anyone but me."

She suddenly looked around. "What am I supposed to do while you're gone?"

"You keep an eye on our friend here."

THE PHONE in the shack rang once.

"Report."

"Failure, Commander."

"The man is still alive?"

"Yes."

"How is this possible?"

"I heard automatic fire within the house, however, Yuri's weapon was silenced. I believe Yuri is dead."

The commander's voice turned to ice. "You did not finish the job?"

The caller swallowed hard. "There was a complication, Commander. The woman arrived on the scene. She was armed, and in uniform. I had no authorization to kill her, and to have done so would have betrayed my position to the primary target. Neither emerged. I believed they were laying in wait for further attack. I had orders to maintain radio silence and the situation had deteriorated. I disabled their vehicles and broke contact."

There was a long pause. "Very well. It is done. It seems the woman really has assumed her father's office, as reported. I believe it is most likely she and this man will go to the jail. Put an observer on the jail now, then assemble a full strike team. I will meet you within the hour and take command personally. We must end this quickly."

The caller almost sighed with relief. There would be no reprisal for this failure.

2

"Do you recognize him?"

Larquette gave the corpse on the table a hasty look as Bolan dropped a heavy nylon gear bag by her desk. Its head was tilted back and the wound in its throat gaped horribly. She wrinkled her nose and peered at it more closely. "I don't know. Maybe. There are a lot of new men out at the mine. But you don't hardly see them in town. I can't go into the mining camp itself without a warrant, and the county seat won't issue me one."

Bolan ran it over in his mind. What little he knew about Crucible would barely fill a travel pamphlet. The little Arizona border town had been dependent on cattle and cotton until copper was discovered just after World War II. For two decades Crucible had been a boomtown, until the mines had coppered out. The isolated little town had slowly shrunk back to its agricultural roots, while some hunting and spectacular rock formations in the nearby desert added a trickle of tourism to the economy.

"Tell me what you know about the mines."

Larquette frowned tiredly and rubbed her temples. It had taken them over an hour to cannibalize tires from their two vehicles and transport the corpse back to the jail. It was nearly dawn. "Well...they're open. Red Star Mining bought out the land rights about a year ago."

A ghost of a smile passed over the Executioner's face. "Red Star Mining?"

Larquette blinked at him. "Yeah, Red Star. So?"

"Come over here." Bolan went over to the folding table Larquette was using for evidence and pointed at the dead man's pistol. "Do you know what that is?"

"I don't know, a gun?" she said sarcastically.

"It's a Russian made PSM automatic, fitted with a silencer."

"So?"

Bolan locked her eyes with his. "So let's go over a few things. Why did you become chief of police?"

Larquette stared at him. "Because my father was killed."

"How was your father killed?"

Larquette's lip trembled slightly. "He was killed...by the roadside."

"How?" Bolan pressed.

"He was shot. Eight times through the chest, with a .22-caliber pistol."

"He'd taken the job as chief of police, but before that he had been a U.S. Marshal for two decades. Didn't he wear body armor out on patrol?"

"He always wore his vest."

Bolan folded his arms. "Then how could this have happened?"

"The coroner reported it as a catastrophic failure of the armor, and that—" her voice almost broke "—he wasn't wearing it properly."

"Does that sound like your father?"

Larquette looked up, and her face twisted into a mask of anger. "No! He always checked his guns, he always wore a seat belt and he sure as hell knew how to put his vest on in the morning! That coroner is full of it!"

Bolan nodded. "It doesn't sound like the man Hal Brognola described as the best cop he ever knew. You're right. The coroner is full of it."

She shook her head. "But how could it have happened?"

He pointed at the pistol lying by the corpse. "That is a Russian PSM pistol. It shoots a .22 caliber, steel-sleeved, steel-core projectile at just under the speed of sound. The pistol was designed with one function in mind. To penetrate soft body armor. It's an assassination weapon." Bolan gestured at the corpse. "Now look at this man's vest. It took four 3-round bursts of high-velocity 9 mm ammunition, and not one shot penetrated."

Bolan leaned over and thumped the corpse's chest with his knuckles. "It's core is titanium plate, Russian manufacture. Look at his goggles." The Executioner hooked the backstrap with his finger and held the device up to the light. Larquette could see strange letters and numbers engraved in the side of the shattered lens towers.

The Executioner watched as she tried to read it, then stated, "It says made in Moscow."

Larquette stared at him incredulously. "You're saying the Russians have invaded Crucible?"

Bolan folded his arms across his chest and thought about how to answer. After a moment he shrugged. "Yes."

"How? Why?"

The Executioner frowned. "I don't know. But I suspect it has something to do with the mines."

Larquette shook her head in bewilderment. "I think I should call someone."

"You might, but think about this. Your father was killed, and the case was filed away as a random killing. You wanted a warrant to go out to the mines, and you were denied. You should probably assume that the county coroner, the county sheriff and the county circuit judge have all been bought off or gotten to. This would undoubtedly mean corruption at a very high level."

Larquette brightened suddenly. "Anne Tyler!"

Bolan cocked an eyebrow.

The chief sat at her desk and grabbed the phone. "The Arizona attorney general! I met her at a Women in Law conference in Phoenix last year. She gave me her card." She began to flip through a card file on the desk.

Bolan's face tightened. He had to admit it was a good ace she had pulled out of her sleeve, but his presence here wouldn't stand up to federal inquiry. "I don't think that would be a good idea just yet."

Larquette stared at him quizzically as she punched numbers into the phone. "I don't see why not." She suddenly looked at the phone and pressed the receiver several times.

Bolan's eyes narrowed. "What is it?"

She shrugged her shoulders. "It's dead."

"Try the radio."

Larquette swiveled her chair and keyed the transmitter button. She flinched and jerked away as a blast of high-pitched static shrieked through the speaker.

"Do you have a rifle?" Bolan asked.

She glanced at him distractedly as she flicked dials on the radio. "Yes, of course."

"Get it."

The lights cut out with a popping of fuses.

After several long seconds a low whine hummed through the walls, and the emergency lights popped into dim life as the jail's generator kicked in. Larquette glanced about in confusion. "What the hell is going on?"

Bolan dropped low and began to unzip his gear bag.

"We're about to be attacked."

ACROSS THE STREET the side door of a brown van slid open soundlessly on well-oiled tracks. Inside, men in dark blue coveralls checked their weapons a final time. Each man carried a large, heavy automatic pistol with wire shoulder stock attached to the butt and the long black tube of a silencer screwed onto the threaded muzzle. The communications man spoke in a soft whisper from his stack of electronic gear behind the driver's seat.

"Success, Commander. Power to jail is down. Phones to jail are down, police-band radio has been overcome across all frequencies."

The commander nodded in satisfaction. "Team one, the front, as planned. Team two, the rear. He slapped the shoulder of a man armed with a long, scope-sighted rifle. You are our insurance, Comrade, deploy now."

The man slid from the van and disappeared into the night.

The commander observed the dim glow of the second hand on his watch. "I want a simultaneous breach of the jail in two minutes from go. Synchronize now."

Ten men watched the second hands crawl interminably across the dials of their watches.

The commander suddenly sliced his hand down. "Go!"

Dark figures moved swiftly through the predawn, like the silent shadows of wolves on the scent.

LARQUETTE LOOKED at him incredulously. "Attacked?"

Bolan nodded as he chambered a round in the M-16 A-4 carbine, then opened the breech of the 40 mm grenade launcher mounted underneath the barrel. He scanned his grenade belt, passing over the high-explosive, fragmentation and smoke rounds, and slid in a 40 mm projectile with a cylindrical, crimped nose. He racked the grenade launcher into battery and flicked the carbine's selector to full-auto.

"Yes. Attacked. We don't have much time. Are there any other entrances besides the front door?"

Larquette seemed almost in a daze. "Um, yes. The back. But it's steel, and it's always locked."

Bolan checked the .44 Magnum Desert Eagle pistol and slung the grenade bandolier over his shoulder. He glanced at Larquette. She was looking about herself wild-eyed. He knew she had backbone. He had seen it when she had entered the bungalow and tried to arrest him. But in combat, training was the key. She had obviously never been in a firefight. Now she was freezing up. Like any green soldier, she needed direction.

The Executioner scanned the room quickly, then barked a command. "Chief Larquette! Get your rifle and get between the two cabinets by the rear hall. Shoot anything that isn't me."

She stared at him.

"Move!"

Larquette snapped out of her daze. She pulled a lever action rifle from a rack off the wall and chambered a round. With a sudden afterthought, she snatched up an extra box of shells and then positioned herself in a crouch between the filing cabinets.

Bolan looked down the hall toward the back door. The rear hall was little more than a narrow corridor with a door to a bathroom and a closet halfway down. It would make a perfect fire lane. He positioned himself by the doorjamb and jerked his head at Larquette.

"Cover the front."

The Executioner pulled a stun grenade from his bandolier and pulled the pin. His other hand held the carbine and grenade launcher ready across his knee. He mentally cal-

culated. It had been almost a minute since the power had
been cut off. If there was going to be an attack, it would
have to come soon.

Twin hissing cracks split the air. Bolan recognized the
sound of the cutting charges even as a heavy booted foot
kicked the steel security door off of its shattered hinges. He
heard Larquette's rifle firing toward the front door as
heavily armed men swarmed into the rear hall.

The Executioner snugged the carbine against his shoulder and squeezed the M-203's trigger.

Pale flame erupted from the 40 mm muzzle of the grenade launcher, and the lightweight weapon recoiled savagely. The narrow hallway became a killing zone as the
M-203 filled the corridor with buckshot. The defensive munition was literally a 40 mm shotgun shell. The lead man
twisted and fell before the lethal point-blank swarm of lead.

Bolan released the arming lever of the stun grenade in his
left hand and lobbed it into the hall. He jerked back around
the doorjamb and shut his eyes as the hallway erupted in a
storm of sound and light. The rear hall channeled the concussion wave into the main jail in a hurricane of force and
blinding brightness. Windows blew out and papers flew
everywhere.

The soldier opened his eyes and whirled on the front door.
A man in dark coveralls filled the doorway, shaking his head
to clear it from the unexpected explosion. He cradled a silenced machine pistol in both hands.

It was incriminating enough for Bolan. He put a short
burst from his carbine into the man's chest. The attacker
staggered, fumbling to bring his weapon into line. Larquette's rifle boomed three times in rapid succession. With
the third shot his head snapped back, and he fell backward
through the door and out onto the pavement. Bolan moved
forward, sliding a fragmentation grenade into the M-203's
breech. He caught Larquette's eye as she shoved fresh shells
into her rifle.

"Switch. Cover the back."

He approached the shattered front door in a crouch and
saw the fallen man's boots disappear as he was dragged out
of view. Bolan hurled himself past the open door and

glimpsed the street for a split second before he rolled to safety behind the other doorjamb. He briefly saw a brown van across the street, moving figures, and the muzzle flash of the sniper on the opposite roof as the man reached out to kill him. Bolan crushed himself against the wall as bullets spanged off the linoleum floor of the doorway and ricocheted into the jail. He flipped up the ladder sight of the grenade launcher and popped up in one of the shattered windows. Bolan heard the supersonic crack of a rifle bullet as it passed near his head as he aimed at the muzzle-flash on the roof across the street.

The M-203 boomed and Bolan dropped beneath the sill. A moment later the 40 mm fragmentation grenade detonated.

The sniper fire fell silent, and for a moment nothing moved.

Larquette hissed at Bolan from across the room. "What are they doing?"

Bolan slipped a fresh magazine into the M-16 and racked a high-explosive grenade into the launcher. "Regrouping. We've given them more than they'd been bargaining on. How many are down in the hall?"

Larquette shrugged as she peaked around. "None. They're all gone."

The Executioner's eyes slitted. He didn't like it. There was no way his opponents were hit men or local drug muscle. They had cut off all communications and executed a perfectly timed two-headed attack. When they had been met with automatic weapons and grenades they had fallen back in good order and carried off their wounded.

Bolan's face tightened. There was no doubt in his mind. They were being attacked by professional soldiers.

He calculated the odds. His opponents were professional soldiers, and they had met unexpected resistance. They would do one of three things: break contact, lay in ambush or regroup and attack in force. The odds kept coming up ugly. They were in a small town in the United States. The enemy couldn't sit around while a growing army of witnesses watched a siege. Nor could they allow the chief of police to survive and report what had happened to the FBI. They would have to finish it. Immediately.

The jail erupted into an eerily silent war zone as the enemy opened fire. Bolan could barely hear the rapid metallic clicking as a dozen silenced weapons fired on full-auto. The silent bullets tore through the doorway and the shattered windows, smashing furniture as if by magic. The only real sound was the spattering they made as they ricocheted off the walls. Green tracers streaked through the night like silent swarms of angry wasps as the whispering firestorm went on unceasingly. The Executioner recognized the fusillade for what it was—covering fire.

He gritted his teeth and rolled prone into the doorway. Green tracers streamed through the door over his head. The enemy was expertly laying down covering fire for a man charging the jail. The runner held a silenced machine pistol in one hand, and in the other he carried a large canvas satchel. As he ran, he reached over with his gun hand and pulled a metal ring on the package. A fuse hissed into life. The man's head jerked up in surprise as Bolan suddenly rolled into view in front of him.

For a moment the soldier was protected from the covering fire by the body of the man it was trying to protect. Bolan could see the bulge of armor under the man's coveralls, so he aimed low and drilled the entire magazine into him on full-auto.

The man staggered in midstep as the hail of bullets hit and walked up his chest in a ragged line. With a grunt he stumbled and fell forward onto the demolition charge he carried. Bolan squinted his eyes as the street lit up in a ball of orange fire. Storefronts along Crucible's main street blew out in showers of broken glass as the blast wave hit. He ducked his head and grimaced as the blast and heat washed over him. There had to have been at least fifteen pounds of high explosive in the charge. He rolled back into cover as avenging fire raked the front of the jail. He knew he had bought only a few seconds. The enemy would storm the jail now, and if they had any more explosives, the jail would be a death trap.

A voice across the street roared angrily in the unmistakable sound of command.

"Ataku! Ataku!"

The Executioner's gaze narrowed with recognition. He had heard those same words shouted from Africa to Afghanistan. All too often he had been the subject of those words. The language was Russian, the words clear and easy to understand on the battlefield.

Attack! Attack!

Bolan moved. They had to get out now.

He jerked his head at Larquette. "Follow me."

She didn't need any urging.

Bolan slung the carbine and drew two grenades from his belt as he moved in a crouch to the rear hall. He could hear the thud of boots on the street outside. Tracers streaked through the windows. Larquette stared at the grenades in Bolan's hands.

"Wait!"

With sudden determination she smashed the remaining glass from a standing cabinet with the butt of her rifle. She reached in and grabbed four dull blue metal cylinders from the shelf. In the dim glow of the surviving emergency lights, Bolan could read the block lettering on their sides: CS TEAR GAS

Bolan jerked his head toward the jail. "Two of them, in the middle of the room. Now." Larquette pulled the pins and rolled two of the grenades back into the jail. She picked up her rifle and jammed the two remaining grenades into her belt as she followed Bolan down the narrow, blood-spattered hall to the shattered security door. Behind them the gas grenades detonated with a popping hiss.

The Executioner pulled the pins on the grenades in his hands. "Stay behind me. Shoot anything that moves." He flattened himself against the wall and released the cotter pin on the first grenade. "Close your eyes."

Bolan squeezed his eyes shut and tossed the grenade out the back door.

Out in the open air, the earsplitting sound and concussive wave of the stun grenade would do little, but the incandescent dazzle of its burning magnesium flash would destroy the enemy's night vision for vital seconds. He pulled the pin on the frag grenade and tossed the bomb out the door. There was a sharp crack and a scream of pain. Bolan jerked his head at Larquette as he moved.

"Come on!"

The Executioner came out the door firing on full-auto. He twisted around and saw two men supporting a third who sagged between them. One of the men brought up his machine pistol and fired a whispering burst. Bolan threw himself against the wall and returned fire as the enemy tracers flew past.

The men ducked around the corner of the jail, all three covering themselves with long bursts as they sagged behind cover and Bolan and Larquette dived to the ground. A voice rang out in Russian from the street in front of the jail.

"Break contact! Now!"

Bolan slung the spent carbine and drew the Desert Eagle. It was time he and Larquette broke contact, as well. He scanned the surroundings behind the jail. There was a single row of houses and some sheds, then Crucible faded into open desert. He shot a glance at Larquette. Blood stained her hands and shoulder, but she didn't seem to have noticed yet.

He peered out into the desert. Dawn was just beginning to break, and the bright stars were slowly beginning to dwindle. He could see the purple humps of rock formations out in the gloom. He grabbed Larquette's hand. "Come on."

They passed a house and Bolan could hear the muffled sound of a woman screaming hysterically. He couldn't blame her. It had to have sounded like World War III had just started. Dogs began to bark and howl in a widespread chorus of indignation. Bolan grabbed a watering can from the screaming woman's porch, and it sloshed satisfactorily when he shook it. The pair slipped past the last houses and moved into the deeper shadows outside of town.

The Executioner had been right.

It seemed the Russians really had invaded Crucible.

3

The woman's voice rang with anger over the telephone. "How has this happened?"

The commander took a deep breath. The bitter fact of the matter was simple. He had failed. Throughout his military career, it had been drummed into him that failure was unacceptable. However, more than two decades of war had taught him that battle was an uncertain thing. Now he needed answers as much as his superior. "We encountered unexpected resistance."

The woman's voice sounded incredulous. "You assaulted the jail without authorization! Are you mad?"

The commander bit back an angry retort. "Beckett's daughter is now Crucible's chief of police. The man who was asking questions out at the mines was with her."

"This is the same man that you failed to kill earlier in the evening?"

The word tasted like bile in his mouth. "Yes."

"So you and your men could not kill one man and an inexperienced woman?"

"He had automatic weapons and explosives, grenade launchers, gas. He knew tactics and was in a well-fortified position. How was I to know this? My tactics were perfect." His tone lowered into accusation. "You are the one who is supposed to keep federal agents out of Crucible. If interference is to come from the outside, you are supposed to keep me informed. Now I have men dead because you do not even know that United States Special Forces troops have infiltrated Crucible!"

"What? You are being ridiculous, Major. Do not try to cover your incompetence with lies. Do not test my patience further, or you will regret it."

The commander's anger boiled over. "I am Major Pietor Ramzin! I am a Hero of the Soviet Union, and I have the medal to prove it! I have fought United States Special Forces troops in Afghanistan, Central America and Africa. This man is no Yankee policeman or some undercover cop. I tell you he is a professional soldier. You are the one with your vaunted status and connections. You tell me what this man is doing in Crucible."

For a moment there was silence on the line. The woman calculated. She didn't like Ramzin, but she knew he was extremely competent. One did not reach the rank of major in Spetsnaz by being a fool, and the honor of Hero of the Soviet Union was earned only in desperate battle. That Ramzin and a squad of his hand-picked men had been defeated by one man and a woman was a disturbing anomaly. She also knew that Ramzin was a dangerous man, and she needed him. She could afford to push him only so far.

"Very well, Major Ramzin. I accept your report as given. What do you suggest?"

Ramzin allowed himself to be mollified. "Very well. Let us dispense with accusations for the present. Somehow a fox has entered the henhouse. I propose we do not let him out. My men are already at work. The Crucible phone exchange will have an immediate failure that shall last for several days. Radio frequencies shall continue to be jammed. The man and woman fled into the desert. I believe we should make use of our friend to have the roads in and out of Crucible closed. We will blame the attack on Mexican drug gangs. That will at least temporarily explain the road closure. Within seventy-two hours I will hunt down this man and the woman, Larquette, and kill them. In the meantime, I believe you must do two things. Exert any necessary influence to keep federal agencies out of Crucible during this time frame, and find out who has sent this man."

"Yes, Major, we are in agreement. Now, our partner's next shipment will be ready in two days. Will this be a problem?"

Ramzin considered. "No. The man and Larquette will be running from my men. I will make this Captain Baibakov's responsibility. He is very good at these sorts of things. He hunted a lot in Afghanistan."

He waited in amusement as there was no response. Ramzin knew the Witch didn't like him very much, but Baibakov actually frightened her. He enjoyed her revulsion a moment more and then continued.

"As I see it, even if the man and woman are not dead in forty-eight hours, they will be too busy running for their lives to interfere. I will maintain the schedule as planned."

She cleared her throat. "That is good, but you must do one other thing."

"Oh?"

"If at all possible, extract whatever information you can from the man and Larquette before you kill them. The methods I leave to you and Baibakov's discretion, as long as no bodies are found."

An unpleasant smile crossed Ramzin's face. "Certainly, Comrade. I am sure that Captain Baibakov is up to the task."

BOLAN WATCHED the sun rise over the Arizona desert. It was nothing short of spectacular. The purple shadows of rock and mountain took on a rosy glow and then caught in golden fire as the sun rose up over the horizon. The sky was cloudless, giving up the purple of dawn for a few moments of orange fire before finally crystallizing into the brilliant azure blue of day.

Larquette managed a tired smile. "Beautiful, isn't it?"

Bolan nodded his agreement. He allowed himself another drink from the water can. The water was tepid and tasted of rust, but it was wet. He handed the can over, and Larquette looked at him. "How much more should I—"

Bolan cut her off with a smile. "You've lost blood. Drink."

She looked at him guiltily for a moment and then began to drink with gusto. Bolan smiled. For a lawyer who had left her policing days far behind, she was holding up well. Bob

Beckett hadn't raised a shrinking violet. She wiped her lips and handed the can back to him.

"So what now?"

The Executioner looked her up and down appraisingly. "How do you feel?"

She snorted. A bullet had grazed the fleshy part of her shoulder, and she had cut both of her hands on broken glass. "Well, tired, bloody, shaky..." She grinned at him and touched her shoulder gingerly. "And shot. That's a new one. But I can walk out of here, if that's what you mean."

"I figure it will take two hours to skirt town and hike out to the bungalow."

Larquette frowned. "We're not going back to the station?"

Bolan shook his head. "Not now. They'll be watching it, and I suspect the body and the evidence has conveniently disappeared by now. I have equipment that I need back in my truck."

"So where are we going to go?"

"Where they don't expect us."

Larquette shrugged. "And where is that?"

"Among them."

Her jaw dropped. "You mean actually go to the mining camp?"

"Why not. I want a closer look. I assume you do, as well."

Larquette mulled it over and then picked up her rifle. "Lead on."

THE EXECUTIONER LOOKED across the desert, and he didn't like what he saw. The noon sun beat down on him in near-vertical brutality as he lay on the lip of the mesa. He ignored the shimmering heat and adjusted the focus of the range-finding binoculars as he swept the Red Star Mining camp again. From the road it looked like any other fenced industrial complex. From up on the mesa, it took on a disturbingly familiar face.

The electrified perimeter fence was topped with razor wire and formed an irregular six-pointed star that conformed to the terrain. Brush, cactus and any boulders large enough to conceal a man had been removed within a hundred-yard radius of the fence, creating a featureless killing zone. To the untrained eye the arrangement of sheds, lean-tos and ditches would have seemed random, but Bolan recognized them for what they were. They were strong points, strategically placed to form interlocking fields of fire in all directions of possible attack. He would bet anything that the sheds were reinforced on the inside with concrete and sandbags. In the center of the camp was a helicopter pad and a number of large corrugated iron warehouses. Large dogs rested in a shaded kennel, and an observation tower loomed in the mining camp's center.

There was no doubt in Bolan's mind. What he saw below him in the desert of Arizona could be only one thing—a firebase.

The question was, what was it defending?

Bolan swung the binoculars across the camp and out to the hillside. A road led out from the camp to the main mine entrance. Earth-moving machines, bulldozers and mining equipment churned up the red dust of the desert in huge shimmering clouds.

Something was going on. Red Star Mining was more than just a front. Work was being done. It looked like some kind of mining, but what was being mined? What was going on under the red earth of the Arizona border?

He needed more information before he went on a close-range reconnaissance. Larquette lay below the mesa. She had gamely said she would climb, but fatigue and blood loss had left her exhausted. Once he had forced her to sit in the shade she had been asleep in seconds.

Bolan rose and moved to the other side of the mesa. It was time to find out all he could about Red Star Mining.

Then tonight he would pay them a visit.

"WE REALLY NEED a car."

Bolan looked at Larquette critically as they trudged through the desert. Her face was red and covered with dust, and her shoulder was oozing blood through the dressing. The water can had been emptied hours earlier, and he could tell she was on her last legs. Only will and a sense of humor were keeping her going.

"You're the chief of police. Requisition one."

"I should have thought of that."

A small spring went into her step as the idea buoyed her. Bolan scanned the horizon. "Only about a half mile back to the bungalow. Think you'll make it?"

She ran her tongue across cracked lips. "I'll make it."

The Executioner suddenly pulled up short. Larquette nearly stumbled into him. "What?"

Bolan pointed at a footprint in the red dirt. He squatted on his heels and examined it. The pattern was distinctly different from his own, it was made by a foot several sizes larger. The impression dwarfed Larquettes's small feet, and went startlingly deep into the gritty soil, as well. The man who had made it would have to be a physical giant.

The surrounding desert was still as the Executioner scanned it. His instincts ranged over the terrain together with his senses, searching for any discernible clue. Larquette spoke in a hushed whisper.

"There's something wrong. I can feel it."

The Executioner could feel it, too, as it crawled up and down his spine. He knew it lay waiting out there in the rocks.

An ambush.

He sat motionless. The desert breeze slowly blew over him from the east, raising small dust devils in the flats as he waited. Suddenly his nostrils flared.

It was there. Almost indistinguishable, but still it lingered for a moment in the heated air.

Tobacco smoke.

The Executioner flipped up the ladder sight of the grenade launcher and fired.

4

Captain Igor Baibakov sat and waited. He sat on his heels, his huge frame impossibly folded into the shade and cover of a small overhang of rock. The heat, dust and discomfort didn't bother him. He could maintain the position for hours if necessary. Hunting was his passion, and nine-tenths of the hunt was waiting. His prey was out there, and he knew it. He could feel it in his massive bones. His AK-74 rifle, with its 30 mm grenade launcher clipped under its barrel and low-power scope sight, rested lightly across his knees. It was his favorite weapon for hunting men, and it had been modified to his specifications.

His stratagem for hunting men was simple: encircle the prey, drive it before you with suppressive fire, corner it, then blast it to pieces with grenades. Anything that lived through being brought down, well . . .

Baibakov's face split into a mirthless grin as his knuckles cracked around the stock of the rifle. If the prey still lived, then he used his hands.

It had been remarkably effective in Afghanistan. So effective that he had been decorated many times during that conflict. In the sand and rock of that distant land Baibakov had consistently been able to outwit his native opponents. The rebels had called him the Red Demon, and used stories of his atrocities to frighten their children into being good.

Baibakov scanned the desert. It was good to be hunting again in clean air, rather than digging beneath the cramped earth like a mole. It was good to be hunting for Major Ramzin. He was an excellent commander. He cared only for results, and Baibakov would move heaven and earth to deliver them to him.

He scratched the blond stubble on his chin. It was an intriguing quarry. One man and a woman. The man was an unknown, the woman an inexperienced police officer. Yet they had escaped the assault on the jail. Ramzin said he believed the man was military. But if so, why would he be operating by himself within his own country?

Baibakov grinned. It didn't matter. He had brought down American commandos before on several continents. He would bring down this one, and then the man would beg to divulge all he knew under the knife. It would—

What the devil! Baibakov's eyebrows shot up in disbelief as he smelled the air. He quickly scanned the half circle of firing positions he had set and a snarl split his face. It was their American ally. The man sat with his back to Baibakov in his ridiculous khaki uniform, oblivious to the simplest of ambush tactics, smoking a cigarette! Baibakov's teeth ground against each other in rage. He yearned to kill the man, to break him in his hands like kindling. But that would have to wait. Baibakov scanned his men's positions angrily. Markov was closest.

Baibakov picked up a small rock and winged it into the corporal's side. Markov flinched and looked back nervously at his captain. Baibakov pointed at the American and brought his fingers to his lips in a smoking gesture, then suddenly clenched his hand into a fist with a silent snarl.

Markov glanced at the American and was utterly appalled. He nodded quickly and slung his assault rifle over his shoulder as he began slithering silently through the dust toward the oblivious American. Markov slunk up behind him and with a lunge grabbed the back of the man's head and rammed it brutally into sand, grinding out the offending cigarette and keeping the idiot from shrieking at the same time. He held the thrashing American's face in the dirt for several long moments with one hand, and with the other shot Baibakov a smart salute.

Baibakov snorted silently and returned the salute. Markov was a good man.

Now, if only—

A hollow thump split the stillness close by to the west. Baibakov roared, "*Grenatya! Grenatya!*"

The grenade exploded with a crack, and shrapnel flew through the air and shrieked off of the surrounding rocks. His men instinctively opened up with their rifles, firing for effect into the general direction of the enemy sound. Through ringing ears, Baibakov heard a second thump, then a moment later a third. He flipped up the ladder sight of his own grenade launcher and estimated the distance. He squeezed off the fragmentation round and stayed in cover, reloading his launcher and waiting for the incoming enemy grenades to hit. There was a sharp second explosion, followed immediately by a third. Baibakov instantly broke cover and began the charge. They would overwhelm the enemy with superior numbers and firepower now, before the situation could deteriorate.

Baibakov's voice boomed over the desert like thunder as he waved his men to follow him.

"Attaku!"

BOLAN FIRED the third grenade and grabbed Larquette's hand. "Move!"

Return fire raked the surrounding rock formations as the enemy performed reconnaissance by fire. Bolan heard the thump of a grenade launcher and shoved Larquette to the ground among a clump of rocks. Shrapnel whizzed by overhead and spattered against their cover. He yanked her to her feet as tracers drew smoking lines through the air around them. They heard the thump of a grenade launcher, and another one from a different position joined it a second later.

They dived behind a large outcropping as the two grenades landed against the rock with shattering impact.

The enemy was getting close.

Larquette racked the lever of her rifle. Bolan grabbed the muzzle and swung it back down. "Not yet. It'll tell them exactly where we are." He listened for a moment. The enemy was close enough that he could hear them moving out in the rocks.

"The tear gas. There should be two grenades left."

Larquette reached into her fanny pack and pulled the two metal cylinders free. Bolan took them and pulled the pins.

In the open, the gas wouldn't stop trained soldiers for long, but it would slow them, and men choking on gas had notoriously bad aim. If they had gas masks, they would waste vital seconds pulling them out and putting them on.

Bolan hurled the first grenade out over the outcropping and sent the second one to the left of it a moment later. He heard the pop and hiss of detonation and then startled shouts of anger. He tossed a frag grenade between the two blossoming gas clouds to keep the enemy's heads down.

"Move!"

They broke cover and ran over the sand.

Larquette gasped. "Where?"

Bolan looked around as they ran. He dropped a gray smoke grenade behind them, giving the enemy a false gas cloud to skirt. A flash of reflected light caught his eye in the distance.

"The road."

He caught the reflection again. It was moving in from town, down the agricultural road that led to the bungalow. They had to intercept it before it got past them and ran into the Russians. He grabbed Larquette's hand and urged her to greater speed. They hit a flat section of ground and broke into a dead run.

Bolan could see the vehicle now, a dusty blue pickup, tooling down the road at a good clip. He judged the speed and the distance and instantly knew.

They weren't going to make it.

He released Larquette's hand. "Keep running!"

She faltered and turned with a gasp. "But—"

"The road! Move! I'll stop the truck. You grab it!"

Her face set in grim determination, she sprinted for the road fifty yards away. Bolan crouched and broke open the breech of the M-203 grenade launcher. He slipped a grenade into the chamber and slammed the weapon into battery. He hastily adjusted the sight and tracked the moving truck. He adjusted his aim to lead the vehicle and fired.

He was up and running as the grenade looped through the air. The truck's brakes screeched, and the locking tires boiled up the desert dust as the white phosphorous grenade detonated thirty yards ahead of it. There was a burst of

white light and fire, and burning streamers of white phosphorous arced through the air over the desert like the Fourth
of July.

The Executioner sprinted for the road. He saw Larquette
by the side of the truck, brandishing her badge in one hand
and her rifle with the other. He shunted to the side as a
stream of bullets raked the sand to his right. He bellowed
over the sound of incoming fire.

"Turn it around! Toward town!"

Larquette yelled at the driver as she swung into the cab,
and the truck churned up dust as it squealed into reverse.
Bolan charged on to the dirt road and leaped onto the old
Ford's running board. "Step on it!"

He grabbed the doorframe and swung himself back into
the truck bed as the vehicle surged and fishtailed forward.
Bullets struck the cab and bed, and tracers stitched the
road's surface, reaching for the truck's tires. Bolan brought
the carbine to his shoulder and fired burst after burst. He
could see the enemy now as they came out into the flat.
Heavily armed men in body armor and gas masks fell prone
to aim accurate fire at the moving vehicle. He dropped the
empty carbine and pulled his last smoke grenade and another white phosphorous. As he tossed the grenades, he saw
a figure move out onto the road.

The man was a giant.

Through the boiling dust it was hard to get perspective,
but the man dwarfed the other soldiers around him. Bolan
brought up the carbine, rapidly slipping in a fresh magazine as the giant brought his own rifle to his shoulder and
took aim through a telescopic sight. Ribbons of burning
phosphorus shrieked into the air, and thick white smoke
bloomed between the two men as the grenades detonated
and mixed with the clouds of red dust churned up by the
truck's tires. A bullet shrieked off of the lip of the truck bed
in a shower of sparks, but the vehicle was already obscured
and quickly accelerating out of range. Bolan slipped a frag
into the grenade launcher, then leaned back against the
truck's cab.

They had been lucky.

BAIBAKOV STOOD in the middle of the road, enraged. He lowered his rifle and stripped the gas mask from his head. Its lenses cracked and snapped in his hand, and he hurled the ruined mask to the ground.

His quarry had escaped.

He let the rage roll through him, yearning to kill something with his bare hands until he sensed someone waiting behind him. He whirled and found Corporal Lukov staring at him nervously at attention. The corporal knew well that Baibakov didn't take failure lightly. Baibakov stared at him with eyes like tombstones until Lukov shuddered and looked away.

The captain took a long, slow breath. "Casualties?"

Lukov sighed with relief. Baibakov wasn't going to kill him. "Three wounded, and one dead, Captain."

"Who?"

Lukov frowned. "Corporal Markov. He shielded the American when the grenades hit. His armor stopped most of the fragments, but he received shrapnel in his throat. The American is shaken, but remains unharmed."

Baibakov's eyes closed as he began to see red. His men were loyal and capable. The American was an idiot and a coward, but he was also a valuable intelligence resource. He had killed Beckett when he had been told, though the appearance of this American commando seemed to show that he had bungled it somehow. Markov had defended the idiot as a needed asset. Now he had another man dead due to bungling. Baibakov's pulse pounded in his temples. First the Witch hadn't done her job and failed to ascertain the nature of their enemy, ruining the first assassination attempt and the assault on the jail, as well. Now Markov was dead, defending the fool who had betrayed their position and destroyed the ambush.

Worse still, he would have to explain this failure to Major Ramzin.

But first he would have to minimize the damage. Baibakov opened his eyes and spoke in a low voice.

"Corporal Lukov, gather the men and prepare them to move. Contact base. Tell them the quarry is in a light blue truck headed toward town. Alert the roadblocks for possible intercept. Tell base I want the helicopter in the air in ten minutes. Then..." Baibakov shook his head. This wasn't going to be an enjoyable experience. "Then get me Commander Ramzin."

Lukov saluted sharply. "Yes, sir."

Baibakov watched as Lukov ran to carry out his orders, then turned to regard the cloud of smoke and burning phosphorus as it dissipated in the hot desert wind. The American was very good, and he was lucky. A formidable combination in the hunt, but it wouldn't be enough to save him. The playing field was set, and he had only so far he could run. Baibakov's eyes slitted. He would bring this American down, and he would extract every last shred of information out of him.

The captain smiled horribly. Then he would twist off this Yankee's head with his hands.

TOM DONOVAN GRIPPED the wheel shakily as he sped down the road toward town. "Lord, Almighty, Patti, I would have stopped!"

Larquette shrugged. "I'm sorry, Tom. I didn't know it was you, and I couldn't take a chance that you might have just kept on going when you saw our friends."

Donovan slowly regained some color in his face. "You didn't have to pull a gun on me." He peered past Larquette and glanced at Bolan. "And G.I. Joe here didn't have to try and blow me up, either."

Larquette grinned in embarrassment. "Oh, I'm sorry Tom, this is..." She trailed off and looked at Bolan inquiringly.

The Executioner offered his hand. "The name's Mike Belasko. Sorry if I startled you."

Donovan gaped and shook Bolan's hand with a slight tremble. "Startle me? You nearly—" He gave up. "Pleased to meet you, Mike. Tom Donovan, acting chair of the Crucible citizens' committee."

Larquette cut in. "Mike is a..." She searched for a word and smiled. "A friend. He's helping me with the current trouble we're having."

42 *Death Whisper*

"Current trouble? That looked more like World War III! Patti, we all thought you were dead after those Mexicans attacked the jail."

"Mexicans?" Bolan queried.

"Yeah, they said a Mexican gang trying to bring some drugs through Crucible decided to shoot up downtown. Damnedest thing I ever heard." Donovan shook his head. "They said you were dead, Patti."

"Yeah, well, I'm not."

He noticed her shoulder. "Patti, you've been shot!"

"Yeah, well, sort of." She whirled on Bolan. "Hey! Why the hell did you start shooting at them?"

"I needed to get them away from the bungalow. I didn't expect them to be there in platoon strength."

"We could have been killed!"

Bolan shrugged. "It was a gamble."

"Well, gee, is there anything else I should know?"

Bolan nodded. "Yeah. We're going to Mexico."

"What!"

"I don't believe they'll expect it. I figure it's a four- to six-hour hike to the border."

Larquette regarded the Executioner silently for a moment. "All right, Tom. Pull over."

He pulled over hesitantly, giving Bolan a long look. "Are you sure, Patti? I can take you into town."

Bolan slung his carbine as the truck pulled to a stop by a series of low cliffs and buttes. "They'll be watching town, and I think we'll stand a better chance heading for the border. Tom, you'll probably be questioned by someone claiming federal authority. Tell them you dropped us off just outside of town. If they start talking about aiding and abetting fugitives, tell them we took you at gunpoint."

Donovan snorted. "Well, you did." He looked at Larquette again. "You sure you'll be all right?"

She gave him a tired grin. "No, but I'm as safe running around with Mr. Belasko here as anywhere else at the moment. You'd better get going."

He nodded and put the truck into gear. "Luck!"

Bolan watched him pull away. "Is he trustworthy?"

She shrugged. "Well, Bob started the citizens' committee. He got me elected, and he's had a crush on me since high school. I think he's okay." She looked at him calculatingly. "We're not heading for Mexico, are we?"

The Executioner shook his head. "We're heading for the mines."

5

Ramzin sat in the swivel chair and cleaned and checked his 9 mm CZ-75 pistol. The Czech pistol was locked and loaded with fifteen hollowpoints in the magazine and one in the chamber. If it wasn't for its dark blue finish, the gun would have sparkled. The pistol had been given to Ramzin by his father, who had gone to great lengths to acquire the pistol on the black market in Moscow for a son who was going to the war in Afghanistan. It had saved Ramzin's life on more than one occasion. As the telephone rang, he ran a cloth over the slide to wipe off any oils from his fingertips and slid the pistol into his shoulder holster.

He picked up the receiver on the second ring.

"Report."

Ramzin was startled to hear Baibakov's voice. Usually he let his adjutant do it. "Trouble, Commander."

"Explain."

There was a lengthy pause. "The quarry has been... temporarily lost."

Ramzin himself paused, letting the moment draw out while he sensed Baibakov squirm on the other end of the line. Finally he spoke.

"This is not like you, Igor. I am very disappointed. How has this happened, and how am I to explain this to the Witch?"

There was silence as the captain let the words sink in. Ramzin knew that Baibakov wasn't a completely sane human being, but he was an incredibly lethal weapon. Under his command in Afghanistan, Baibakov had flourished. Ramzin knew the giant would die for him if it was asked, but he had to be kept in line.

"The man and the woman escaped by luck. They were picked up on the road by this Tom Donovan of the citizens' committee. I had our idiot Yankee friend speak to him. He says that they talked of heading to Mexico, and he let them off outside of town. I have men in the desert between the town and the border. I have instituted around the clock aerial reconnaissance. If they had tried for the border, I find it unbelievable that they could have slipped past." Baibakov's voice lowered an octave. "I do not believe this Tom Donovan. I do not believe that they have run for the border of Mexico."

Ramzin nodded. It was time to release the reins. "I accept your report, Captain. You have acted correctly. I accept your assessment. I do not believe our quarry is running anywhere. I believe he will soon show himself again. Have our agents in town run a sweep. Have the men along the border mobilized and brought back to base. We are going ahead with tonight's operation as scheduled. Base camp is now activating full security protocols. Meanwhile, we do not know if the chairman of the citizens' committee is lying or not, so I wish you to make sure of this personally."

"Yes, Commander."

"I do not wish him killed, Igor, but make the precariousness of his situation clear to him. When you are finished, bring him here. Report immediately after my orders have been carried out."

"Yes, sir."

Ramzin hung up the telephone and scanned the geological survey map over his desk. He didn't envy Tom Donovan. Baibakov was on the hunt, and he wouldn't be gentle. Ramzin peered at the map. A man and a woman, on foot. They had broken two ambushes and had eluded Baibakov in the desert. Incredible. Truly the man had to be a fox. He smiled slowly. This fox was brazen, as well. Perhaps he didn't know where this fox was now, but this man had a mission. Ramzin gazed at the red star of the mining-camp site marked on the map. He nodded in satisfaction. Yes, sooner or later, Ramzin suspected, he knew where this fox would show himself.

THE EXECUTIONER cut the bread diagonally with his fighting knife and neatly flipped the pieces together into a pair of sandwiches. Larquette stared at him in utter amazement.

"I can't believe you're making peanut-butter-and-jelly sandwiches while there are two Russian Green Berets outside."

Bolan peered through the bungalow's kitchen shutters at the two Russians in position down by the road. They wore camouflage and had chosen their positions well. They would be invisible to anyone approaching the bungalow from town.

"They're not Green Berets. They're Spetsnaz, Russian special purpose troops." He handed her a sandwich, and she tore into it ravenously. "But they might as well be Green Berets. They're highly trained, highly motivated elite soldiers. But we're safe from those two as long as we don't make noise and their orders don't change. They're watching the road for anyone who might come by. They weren't expecting us to flank them on foot and come hide right under their noses."

"So what is the Russian Spetsnaz doing here?"

Bolan frowned as he poured two glasses of milk. "I don't know. The Russians downsized their armed forces after the Soviet Union broke up. Many of their special warfare units got downsized during the reductions, as well. That left a lot of very dangerous, capable men without jobs. You can find Russian special warfare officers and men working as private mercenaries and advisers in the Third World. Some are even providing security and bodyguarding services for respectable companies overseas. But the group we've run into, they're operating on U.S. soil, and in platoon-strength units. It's . . . puzzling."

"So what are we going to do?"

"Wait until dark. Which means you get a nap."

Larquette narrowed her eyes. "How about a bath?"

Bolan cleaned the fighting knife's blade on the kitchen towel and slid it into its sheath. He gave her a rueful smile. "I'm sorry, Patti, but if the Russians suddenly come bursting in unannounced, you're not going to be much good to me if you're sitting in a tub of water.''

"I get your point."

He turned to the window again and checked on the Russian sentries. "Tell me what you can about Red Star Mining."

She concentrated as she finished her milk. "Well, they came into the county about a year and a half ago and bought out the rights to the old copper mines south of town. Then they started buying up all the land around it that wasn't federal. They paid big money for it, too. Not a whole lot of haggling, just a lot of big checks. Some people didn't want to sell, and the word is some of them got muscled into it. Red Star also pumped money into civic projects and gave money to the school. They made a lot of friends in town and bought a lot of influence. They also started moving a lot of dirt. According to Dad, you could hear them blasting around the clock.''

"So there wasn't any real trouble locally?"

Her frown deepened. "Well, not initially. At least nothing you could put your finger on. Some people up and left without any explanations. Most of the local prospectors disappeared. Red Star fenced off all of the land they bought, which irritated the hunting and camping folks. But the real weird thing was that they didn't hire any labor locally. That made a lot of people mad. Folks in town were expecting substantial job opportunities to open up, but Red Star brought in all of its own labor. What's weirder, the miners hardly ever come into town. The local merchants were expecting a boom, as well. I mean, some of the businesses have gotten big orders, like for food, clothes, blankets, tools and such, but the bars, the restaurants, the hotels, hell, even the cathouse by the county line, they just haven't seen any business out of Red Star. Most people think they're just doing their rest and recreation across the border to save money. But it's plain weird. You just don't see any Red Star employees. Just the local representatives, who do their business for them.''

"But you're sure the mining site is active?"

Larquette shrugged. "They're moving one whole hell of a lot of dirt and rock." She looked at him narrowly. "Why don't you tell me how you got yourself on their good side the other night?"

"I showed up at the gate in a suit and started talking about being a land assessor, asking to inspect the facility. They didn't like that at all. They told me I'd have to come back the next day while they checked with the management. I told them I'd be back the next day with a court order. They got very frosty when I said that. When I left I noticed a helicopter in the air as I drove away. When I got into town, I picked up a tail, and that's when I picked up you on my trail, as well."

She rolled her eyes. "Okay, so I'm not James Bond yet. But you were another stranger in town, and I thought if I followed you I might get a lead." She grinned. "And, boy, I was right."

"How did your father figure into things?"

Her lips pursed. "Dad was born in Crucible. He came back here to retire. He didn't like Red Star, or the way they threw their money around. A lot of other people didn't like it, either. Ken Severn was the old chief, and a lot of people thought that Red Star owned him, too. When the post came up for election last year, Dad won hands down. Then Dad started poking around, and he formed the Crucible citizens' committee." She stared at the wall for a moment.

"But this is just what I've heard. I mean, I hadn't talked to Dad in a while. He and my husband didn't get along that well. Dad really didn't like lawyers much. He didn't like the fact that I left the FBI and went off and became one, much less married a defense attorney. When my husband died, Dad and I, well, we just didn't really communicate much, and now he's..."

Her voice trailed off and she turned away, too proud to let Bolan see her cry.

"Can you tell me about anything that your father may have found, or suspected?"

She pushed at her face with the heel of her hand and let out a broken laugh. "Well, I don't think Daddy suspected a Russian invasion, if that's what you mean. He thought it had more to do with crooked land dealings. There's a lot of that here in the Southwest. There's a lot of it everywhere.''

She rubbed her eyes tiredly. ''So what now?''

Bolan nodded toward the couch. You get some sleep. We've got a long hike after it gets dark.''

''Okay, but what about you?''

Bolan pulled a chair up to the kitchen window and sat down. ''I'm going to keep an eye on our friends.''

TOM DONOVAN WANTED to scream, but a massive hand covered his mouth and clamped his nostrils shut. A thumb as hard as a chisel ground inexorably into the inner joint of his elbow. His whole body locked rigid, then sagged as his elbow was suddenly released. His face was brutally shoved back down onto the coffee table. The tabletop had a wet, greasy sheen from the sweat that was bursting out all over his body. His arm was on fire from his shoulder to his elbow. Below his elbow he couldn't feel anything. If it wasn't for the fact that he could feel his hand and forearm flopping against his side, he would have believed they had been twisted off completely. Fingers cruelly twisted into his hair and yanked his head up to face the muzzles of two automatic rifles. Even if there hadn't been two men with machine guns, Donovan knew he would still be utterly helpless. The giant's strength was inhuman. He could barely comprehend how physically powerful the man was. The man could kill him in an instant, and there was nothing he could do to stop him. The giant's voice grated in broken English.

''Tell me, again!''

''I already—''

He was cut off as his face was rammed into the table hard enough to make him see stars.

''Again!''

''I hit the brakes when the grenade went off. Patti got in my truck.''

''Patti, the chief of police, yes?''

''Yes, Patti Larquette, the chief of police. Then the man got in, and everyone started shooting. I stepped on it.''

''Then?''

"I dropped them off outside of town. They said they were headed for Mexico."

Without warning, the hand clamped over his face again, and Donovan's elbow became the howling center of his universe. After an eternity, the pain stopped. The giant shoved him down against the table again. "I do not believe you."

Donovan gasped. "I've told you everything. I swear to God I've told you everything."

The giant leaned very close to Donovan's ear.

"Listen to me. Listen to me with great care. I am going to give you an opportunity to live. Cooperate fully. If you do not, you will die. Your sister and her family live two and a half kilometers from your home, yes? Your mother six kilometers outside of town, yes? You have relations with the woman who works at the newspaper, yes? If you do not cooperate fully, these women will be raped and killed in front of you, before you yourself are killed. Your own death, it will require a great deal of time. You understand, yes? Cooperate, and you will live. Cooperate, and you will be given an opportunity to work with us, using your influence on the citizens' committee. You will be given an opportunity to make great profit from this experience. Do not—"

The world exploded in agony once again. The blinding pain continued on and on until Tom Donovan could feel almost blissful blackness close in around the edges of his senses as he approached unconsciousness from the choking. His lungs heaved in a shuddering breath as he was hurled down again.

The giant loomed over him implacably. "Decide. Now."

Donovan tried to think of anything to stall, to delay, but his mind was as numb as his arm. "Listen—"

He felt his arm yanked back up behind his back, and the rasp of a knife leaving its sheath. "Decide!"

Willpower failed, and Donovan found he would say or do anything to make the pain stop. The words came out of his mouth as if someone else was speaking for him. "I'll cooperate... I'll do anything you say."

"This is good."

He fell in a heap as he was thrown onto the sofa. The giant yanked him up by his shirtfront into a sitting position and held his gaze with eyes as flat and gray as tombstones. "Where did you let them out?"

Donovan took a ragged breath, his insides shriveling at his betrayal. "Barely a mile or two past where I picked them up."

The fist tightened in his shirt. "One mile or two?"

He flinched as the huge man held up the knife. Its blade was a flat black except for the edge, which glinted silver in the light. "One, two, I don't know. We were still in the rocks before you hit the flats outside of town."

The giant turned his gaze to one of his men, and they spoke rapidly in Russian for several moments. The giant returned his attention. "You would say, twenty to twenty-two kilometers from town?"

Donovan shook his spinning head. "I don't know kilometers...I—"

The giant shook him into silence, and he flinched as the behemoth looked through him, apparently lost in thought. The giant's stone-colored eyes suddenly narrowed.

"How many minutes?"

"What?"

"How many minutes from the town? Answer!"

The answer was suddenly terribly clear in Donovan's mind. He knew the exact spot. The Kiowa Buttes. He had driven past them thousands of times. His shoulders sagged. "The Kiowa Buttes. They're about fifteen minutes outside of town." He felt sick as the words came out. "I can take you there."

Baibakov nodded and released him. The giant sheathed his knife and calculated. They had left the truck only minutes from the ambush site. The woman was wounded. Mexico would hardly be an option by foot. He consulted his map. There were several smaller roads that exited the town and scattered ranches along them. Any of them could act as a refuge. The ranchers had no love for Red Star Mining. Or perhaps the man had a hidden lair in the cliffs. Either way there would be a trail.

The giant hunter grinned savagely.

This time there would be no escape.

"Lukov, get me base camp, immediately."

Baibakov drummed his massive fingers on the coffee table while Lukov patched into the secure line.

Lukov handed him the receiver. "You are on line, Captain."

Baibakov spoke rapidly to the base camp communications operator. "This is Captain Baibakov. Mobilize a strike team to converge on these coordinates." He quickly read off the numbers from the map's survey grid.

He handed the receiver back to Lukov and jerked his head at Donovan. "Bring him."

The giant grinned as he felt his adrenaline start to flow.

The hunt was on.

6

Bolan rose swiftly from the chair, his eyes narrowing in the gloom.

The Russians were moving. One man stood, held his canteen upside down and shook it. The second Russian nodded and gave a short series of hand signals before returning to watching the road. The first Russian began walking toward the bungalow.

The Executioner moved rapidly through the house. Larquette lay sleeping on the couch, and he shook her foot to wake her. She snapped awake with a start, reaching for her pistol. She shook her head to clear it as she looked up at him.

"What's happening?"

"One of the Russians is coming. Get your rifle."

Larquette grabbed her Winchester. "What do you want me to do?"

"Get in the kitchen. If something goes wrong, get out. If you see anyone besides me, shoot him."

Bolan headed to the broken front door. He could hear boots crunching on the gravel drive even as he positioned himself beside the doorjamb. His knuckles whitened as his right hand curled into a fist.

The Russian was large and moved with the easy, confident power of an elite soldier. However, he obviously believed the bungalow was abandoned, and he walked nonchalantly through the door, whistling tunelessly to himself.

The Executioner struck, his fist uncoiling with all the power of his body, hitting the Russian just above his right kidney as he passed. The man spasmed, then locked in agony, his canteen falling from his nerveless fingers. Before he could fall Bolan snapped the knife edge of his hand into the base of the soldier's skull.

The Russian dropped as if he'd been shot.

The Executioner grabbed the fallen man by his shoulders and dragged him into the kitchen. Larquette stared and whispered hoarsely, "Is he dead?"

"No. But he'll probably wish he was when he wakes up."

"What do we do now?"

"Find me some rope or an electric cord, anything to tie him up with. Find something for a gag, as well."

Larquette rummaged through the kitchen drawers. "How about these?"

She handed him an extension cord and a roll of packing tape. Bolan nodded and swiftly bound the man's wrists and ankles. The Russian moaned as the Executioner took the remaining length of cord and joined the bindings tightly behind his back. His eyes opened as a piece of packing tape sealed his mouth shut. The Russian glared in pained indignation.

Larquette crouched beside Bolan with her rifle across her knees. "What now?"

Bolan rose and looked outside. The light was fading quickly, and he could barely make out the second Russian still in his position. In a few minutes it would be too dark to see much of anything. "We're going to have to deal with his friend, and do it quickly."

The Executioner took a kitchen towel from the oven handle and wadded it into his fist. He loosely covered his mouth, then spoke out the window in slightly muffled Russian.

"Hey, come look! We must report this!"

The bound Russian's eyes widened, and he began to thrash savagely on the floor. Larquette put the muzzle of the Winchester against his forehead. The hammer's click seemed very loud as she cocked the rifle. The man ceased his struggles and stared up at her.

The other Russian rose from his position and called back. "What is it that you have found?"

The Executioner didn't reply, but turned on the kitchen light and began loudly opening the kitchen drawers and making obvious noises of rummaging. Larquette pressed the muzzle of her rifle hard into the bound Russian's temple for silence.

The second sentry gazed down the road for a moment, then slung his rifle and walked toward the house.

"Keep him quiet." Bolan drew the Desert Eagle and moved back into the darkened interior of the house. The second Russian entered the house as innocently as the first and crumpled as the slide of the heavy automatic cracked against his temple. Bolan dragged the second Russian into the kitchen, and Larquette watched as he bound and gagged him, too.

"Boy, we're starting quite a collection."

The Executioner peered up at the kitchen clock. "It's past eight. I don't know what their schedule to report in is. We're going to have to get out of here, fast."

Bolan reached into a satchel hanging from the Russian's shoulder and brought out his night-vision gear. He handed the goggles to Larquette. "Take these."

She slung the goggles around her neck, and Bolan grabbed her hand. "Come on."

"Where are we going?"

"My truck."

She frowned as they went outside. "But I thought it was out of commission."

"It is."

Bolan unlocked the Bronco's rear gate. The interior showed obvious signs of having been searched. He holstered the big .44 pistol and began to twist the interior luggage cleats. There was a muffled click as he twisted each of the four cleats upside down. He slid his fingers under the rear doorjamb and lifted. The floor of the truck came up, revealing a shallow storage area. He propped open the floor and began to pull out equipment.

"Here, take these."

He handed her a two-quart canteen and a large fanny pack of supplies. Larquette watched as he began festooning himself with weapons and gear. He slung two canteens across his shoulders and took a scoped Weatherby rifle from its case. Bolan flicked on the power to the day-night optical sight and nodded as the distant rock formations zoomed into sharp gray-green focus. He powered down the sight and slung the rifle. Finally he took out a spare pair of night-vision goggles and seated them on his forehead. He secured his carbine and grenade launcher in the hidden compartment and closed up the truck. It appeared exactly as it had before.

He looked at Larquette. "Ready to move?"

She pushed the goggles onto her forehead in imitation of Bolan. "How do these work?"

Bolan gently pulled the goggles over her eyes and adjusted the straps. He guided her fingers to the switch. "Here."

"Oh!"

Larquette looked all around, examining the sky and the surrounding terrain in wonder. "I can see everything, but it's so... weird." She peered up at Bolan, the goggles and mask making her look like an inquisitive bug. "Shouldn't everything be red?"

Bolan shook his head. "No, that's infrared. Those devices sense heat. These work by light amplification. They're taking the ambient starlight and magnifying it fifty to a hundred times."

She looked around again. "It's a little disorienting."

"You lose some peripheral vision, and the monotone color can throw you off a bit at first, but you get used to it." He reached over and flicked off her goggles. "We'd better not waste the batteries until we need them. Until we hit the cliffs, we can navigate by starlight."

She pushed the goggles back on her head and blinked as her eyes adjusted to the dark again. "So, it's off to the mines."

BAIBAKOV KNELT in the sand. In the glare of the flashlight, he could see the unmistakable mark of a footprint. The print was small, and he recognized the pattern as the woman's. He nodded to himself. The man was very good. Nearly a ghost. He knew how to move from hard spot to hard spot, utilizing rock and avoiding loose dirt and sand. The pattern showed the woman trying to shadow his footsteps, walking where he walked. But she had made mistakes, leaving small traces for him to find. She had obviously been weary—her marks were uneven, and there were impressions in the ground as if she was leaning on her rifle through steep inclines. She had stepped on the dry desert grasses and broken them along the trail.

Baibakov grinned. Exhausted as she was, she was ghosting her partner. The giant scratched his shovellike jaw. It was strange. They were heading southeast, which would make for an arduous trip to Mexico. The town was north. Out past the flats, there were few ranches, and they were isolated. Tactically they would be death traps. As the terrain got harder, the woman would become exhausted quickly. They would have to rest. The woman was wounded and tired, and the man himself had been running and fighting for some time. They wouldn't have the strength or time to lay false trails. If he had a lair in the mountains, he doubted the woman could make the climb. The man wouldn't be able to carry her.

They would go to ground.

But where? Baibakov considered his prey and his grin grew. The man was a predator himself. Baibakov was hunting a hunter. The man wouldn't run himself ragged as the pack ran him down. Nor would he crawl into a hole and shiver there, hoping not to be found. He would shadow his hunters, keeping them in sight, choosing his own moment to strike.

The woman was the key. She would be done in. Donovan said she was wounded, and they had found significant amounts of blood trailing from the back of the jail. She would have to rest. The question was where.

Baibakov shot to his feet. Mexico, town, the outlying ranches and the desert itself weren't viable options. They would hide where no one would look, a place that had already been searched.

They would hide in plain sight.

"Lukov! Get the radio, now!"

The giant put his hands on his hips as Lukov patched in the secure frequency.

The prey had doubled back and undoubtedly rested themselves. His men at the bungalow would be on a low state of alertness. They would be watching the road to see if anyone came looking for the man at the bungalow. They could easily have been flanked.

The prey was right under their very noses.

Lukov handed him the handset.

"This is Captain Baibakov. Have all search teams converge on the bungalow. Advise observation team on-site that quarry may be inside. Do not engage, repeat, do not engage. Observe house, fire only if quarry attempts to break away. I will arrive and take command within ten minutes." Baibakov handed back the transmitter, and his voice roared through the buttes to his men.

"Return to the trucks! Now! Night-vision protocols, prepare for assault!"

Baibakov and his men raced through the dark across the broken ground. The giant grinned as they approached the road and the panel trucks, and the blood sang in his veins.

The noose was tightening.

THE WITCH WAS TERSE over the secure telephone.

"What is happening?"

Ramzin reclined in his chair. "Baibakov is running them down." He looked up at the clock, then at the survey map. "The assault should begin in minutes."

The woman was somewhat mollified. "Good. Make sure the madman does not slaughter them both before we have a chance to interrogate them."

Ramzin's lips tightened. "That will be difficult. The man is obviously a trained soldier, and the woman appears to know which end of a rifle is which. Baibakov knows his duty well, and all attempts will be made to bring them in alive. However, if it comes to a shoot-out, I consider the quarry expendable. My men are not."

"Your men will do as they are told."

Ramzin's voice was stone. "Exactly so. They will obey my orders without question."

The Witch was silent for a moment. The underlying threat in Ramzin's remark was obvious. She reined in her temper. Now was not the time for a power struggle within the organization. She needed to impress Ramzin. She modified her tone.

"The woman is unimportant. I have already begun arrangements to explain her demise."

Ramzin's interest was piqued against his will. "How so?"

The Witch laughed. "Did you not know? She is a wanted fugitive. Evidence will show that she was the one who murdered her father. She took her father's job to smuggle drugs. She herself orchestrated the attack on the jail to steal confiscated money and drugs being stored there. Truly she is an evil woman."

She continued. "But I want the man, Major. He is an anomaly that must be explained. I have considered your idea that he is an American Special Forces soldier, but if he is, why has nothing else happened? Why do not American Army helicopters fill the skies of Crucible? Why have they not reacted? Even if he has not been able to report, as you suspect, he is on American soil. Surely his failure to report would spark action, but I have heard nothing through my channels. There is only this inexplicable man, eluding us in the desert. How can this be explained?"

Ramzin was silent. These things had weighed heavily on his mind, as well. He, too, wished to get his hands on this man and carve his mysteries out of him with a knife. "I do not know. I cannot explain these things."

"I have given these matters thought. I do not believe this man is a soldier."

Ramzin scoffed. "Ridiculous. His tactics, his weapons, he is well schooled in escape and evasion. Clearly he is a Green Beret, or perhaps a Navy SEAL."

"Tell me, Ramzin, are you currently serving as a Spetsnaz major in the Russian army?"

"No! You know I—" He cut himself short as he saw the point. "You believe this man is a mercenary?"

"Our problem, Major, has been our perspective. We have been so afraid of being discovered by the American government, the FBI, the CIA, that we have not entertained other possibilities. It is my belief that one of two things is possible. One, our friend is working for a rival concern. Second, perhaps he does work for a branch of the U.S. government, but one that has its own agenda and cannot legally afford to be exposed in a real investigation if an incident occurs.''

Ramzin scratched his chin in thought. "I believe the former to be the most likely. I think perhaps I do not trust our Mexican friends."

"I never have. However, they are necessary. But I will not tolerate being double-crossed. I need the man. I need him alive to answer questions. I authorize you to go to any extreme. Kill the woman, and do anything you wish to the man, as long as he is begging to tell us all he knows when you are finished with him."

Ramzin took a deep breath. "Very well. I will use any extreme necessary to ensure the success of the mission. I will report immediately after the assault. Ramzin out."

He switched the code on the transmitter. "Captain Baibakov, this is Major Ramzin. The helicopter is already on its way. Listen carefully. This is what I want you to do."

7

Baibakov's hand sliced downward.

"Fire!"

Four grenade launchers boomed simultaneously. Windows on all four sides of the adobe bungalow shattered as the projectiles arced into the interior with deadly accuracy. A second later the bombs detonated within the house in a series of soft, muffled pops.

Baibakov exploded into a full sprint, roaring through his mask. "Move!"

The captain and a five-man squad raced the forty yards to the bungalow. Their masks and bulky environmental containment suits slowed them, but not one man among them resented the encumbrance as they stormed the bungalow.

The remains of the broken front door fell from its hinges beneath Baibakov's massive boot. He swept the room's interior with the muzzle of his AK-74, then flicked on the light switch. In the middle of the floor a metal cylinder the size of a soda can spun and hissed in lazy circles. From vents in the top of the grenade, Baibakov could just see the nearly transparent vapors hissing out and dispersing in a shimmer throughout the room.

The giant felt himself shudder. He considered himself a brave man. His men considered him inhuman. Stories of his personal power and the atrocities he had committed needed no embellishment. But Baibakov had seen firsthand how nerve gas killed men in Afghanistan, and even he was afraid of it. His men stormed into the house behind him, and his voice was a muffled snarl behind the protective filters in his mask.

"Search and sweep! Quickly! Moments count!"

His men quickly swept through the bungalow room by room. Lukov shouted from the kitchen. "Captain! Come quickly!"

Baibakov covered the distance in four strides, and what he saw made his blood run cold.

Two of his men, Larionov and Marius, lay bound and gagged on the floor, shuddering and twisting. Their eyes rolled in their heads, saliva drooled from under the tape that gagged them. Clear fluids ran from their noses and ears as their entire nervous systems went into revolt. Baibakov grabbed the team medic by the shoulder and nearly hurled him into the kitchen.

"Atropine, Senior Sergeant! Now!"

The medic knelt beside the convulsing men and clumsily broke open a sterile medical pack with gloved fingers. He produced two small syringes and quickly prepped them. He waved frantically at Baibakov and Lukov. "Hold them fast! I do not want the needles breaking in them!"

Baibakov and Lukov each grabbed a man's leg and forced the folding, shuddering limb straight. The medic swiftly pierced each victim's clothing and injected the atropine directly into the femoral arteries in their thighs. "Good. Get them out of here quickly."

The other two men of the squad ran into the kitchen. "The house is empty, Captain! No sign of the fugitives."

The giant rose as the stricken soldiers were rushed into the open air. Then he gazed around him.

There were crumbs on the cutting board in the kitchen. On entry he had seen a blanket rumpled on the couch. His quarry had been here, of that he had no doubt. They had spent hours resting themselves, hiding in plain sight while he had fruitlessly searched the desert. The man had defeated two of his soldiers and slipped out of his hands again.

Baibakov strode outside and felt his anger pulsing in his temples.

He had gassed his own men. It galled him, but he decided the action was acceptable. The quarry had to be taken alive. In a firefight, they might have been killed. If he had used tear gas, they might have been able to fight on, or they might even have had masks. Only full chemical-biological warfare suits could protect them against nerve gas, and even this fox wouldn't have those in his bag of tricks. Ramzin's tactics were brilliant, as always.

The thick plastic gloves of his suit creaked as Baibakov clenched his fists. Still, he had failed again. The prey had remained one step ahead of him, and now he would have to waste vital time as his men decontaminated themselves and unsuited. He stood in the desert breeze and trembled with rage. He yearned for the kill. If he couldn't kill the man, he would hurt him. With his own hands he would break the man's body and will, and after he had reduced the man to a crippled, whimpering freak, he would kill the woman before his eyes.

Baibakov stared out into the desert night without seeing, playing the scenario over in his mind, visualizing it in greater and greater detail until his anger passed. His vision suddenly became lucid, and he scanned the desert terrain with renewed interest. His quarry was rested and had a head start of at least several hours.

The question was, where would the prey go now?

BOLAN TOOK Larquette's hand and helped her up on top of the boulder. They were in broken country, steadily rising into the mountains. The nap had done her good, but they had been marching for hours, and she was flagging as they climbed higher. She stood shakily on the rock and looked upward with a sigh. Bolan followed her gaze. In the flat, monochromatic view of the night-vision goggles the world was an unending pile of giant gray-green rocks that climbed relentlessly into the sky.

"Beautiful country you have out here," he said.

A ghost of a smile moved across her face. "How much farther?"

Bolan looked upward again. "If we can get over that, we'll be looking down on it. The rest of it should be downhill from there. Take your goggles off and have some water."

The flat, monotone world suddenly became inky darkness and brilliant stars above. Standing on the rock with the heavy goggles off their faces, they could feel the desert breeze play over them. Larquette sighed. "God, that feels good."

Bolan handed her the canteen. "Here."

She gulped at the water, finally lowering the canteen with a gasp. Her hand shook as she handed it back, and her rifle clattered on top of the rock. Bolan caught her arm as her knees buckled.

Larquette held his arm and steadied herself as he lowered her into a sitting position. "You all right?"

She grinned up at him sheepishly. "I'm sorry. I'm not much of a trooper, am I?"

Bolan squeezed her shoulder. "You impress the hell out of me."

She turned her head away and looked down into the dark. "That's nice of you to say, but I know I'm holding you back." Bolan felt her shoulder tremble. "I'm probably going to get us both killed."

He gently took her chin and looked into her eyes. "Listen, I couldn't have made it this far without you. You know the town, you know the people, you know the country. It's simple. I need you, you need me. We stick together, and we'll win. Right?"

Larquette took a deep breath and nodded. "Right. Thanks."

"How do you feel?"

"Like I'm going to throw up and start crying, but I'll get over it."

"Good. You're going to make Eagle Scout yet. There's a chocolate bar and some trail mix in your fanny pack. I want you to eat them and have some more water. We'll rest here a little while longer, then we're going to make a big push."

She unzipped the pack and started rummaging through it. "You should have told me sooner that there was chocolate involved. It..." She trailed off as the Executioner rose to his feet and lifted his gaze to the sky.

"What is it?"

He tilted his head slightly. "Listen."

A low, pulsing noise began to build slowly, rising into a rhythmic thumping in the air. Bolan pulled down his night-vision goggles and examined the edge of the boulder. Beneath it, another rock formed a ledge five feet below them. He grabbed Larquette's arm and lifted her to her feet.

"Down there's a ledge. Get onto it and stay down." He lowered her until her feet touched, then scooped up her rifle. The Executioner slipped behind the boulder as the helicopter suddenly burst into sight and roared overhead. He peered at it from his concealed position.

It was a small commercial transport, flying low and fast. Bolan recognized it as a BellJet Ranger as it swept over them and rose rapidly to cross the spine of the rocks before descending again out of sight.

"Are they looking for us?" Larquette whispered in Bolan's ear.

He shook his head. "No, they were transporting someone, or something, and they were in a hurry."

"But they will be, soon enough."

BAIBAKOV STRIPPED OFF the leggings of the chemical suit over his boots. Barsukov, the medic, ran the chemical alarm over him as he kicked the crumpled suit away in disgust. "The nerve agent is dispersed, Captain. No sign of lingering contamination."

"Have the rest of the men unsuit. I want them ready to move in ten minutes."

Barsukov saluted. "Yes, sir."

It would probably be more than an hour before the house could be safely searched for clues, but he believed what he had seen told him enough already. The prey had entered the desert on foot. They had undoubtedly reached the rocks already, and now tracking them would be very difficult. His thoughts were interrupted as Lukov came running with the radio.

"Captain, it is Major Ramzin!"

Baibakov grimly took the handset. "Yes, Major."

"Captain, have you found any sign of the quarry?"

"No, sir. My men and I have just finished decontamination procedures. I will begin circling the house to pick up the quarry's trail."

"No, return to base, immediately."

Baibakov was stunned. "But, Major, I..."

"Do you question my orders, Captain Baibakov?"

He instinctively snapped to attention. "No, Major."

"Good. Listen to me. I do not know where this man and woman are right now, and I do not care. I do not want you and your men exhausting yourselves in the rocks and desert. We will let the quarry do this. The man is on a mission. He will come to us, and when he does, I want you to be ready for him."

"Exactly so, Major. May I inquire about my men?"

"Certainly. Marius wishes he was dead, and will undoubtedly continue to do so for several hours. However, he should be fit for light duty tomorrow."

"And Larionov?"

Ramzin's voice lowered over the handset. "Evidence indicates that Marius and Larionov were defeated in hand to hand combat. Larionov's kidney was torn in the struggle. The nerve gas and the resulting convulsions were extremely detrimental to his condition. I am having him flown to Mexico, despite the Witch's objections."

"Thank you, Major."

"We take care of our own, Captain Baibakov."

"Exactly so."

"Bring your men in, Captain. They need to eat and rest. I commend your efforts. You have prevented the man from contacting the outside, and we have driven him into the desert. When he shows himself, you will be there waiting for him."

Baibakov nodded. Watching the baited trap wasn't his preferred mode of hunting, but he had done it many times. If it was required, he would do it now, with pleasure.

"Indeed, Major, I will be waiting for him."

8

"There it is. You made it."

"Thank God." Larquette sagged as Bolan pulled her up to the peak and slumped onto a rock. She stripped off her night-vision goggles and looked down into the valley with an exhausted frown. "It looks like Christmas."

From their vantage up on the peak, the valley spread out beneath them in an ocean of darkness beneath the stars. To the east they could see the lights of Crucible as they glowed in the distance. Nestled against the hills directly below them, the mining camp shone like a gaudy six-pointed star. The center of the star was brightly lit with floodlights, and they could see the activity of men and machines. A helicopter sat on the pad in the center of the complex with its rotors turning. Out toward the fence were dimmer, irregularly spaced orange perimeter lights forming the points of the star, and smaller moving lights patrolled the edges. Bolan didn't doubt that when the alarm went off the whole complex and everything around it for several hundred yards would light up like the sun.

"It's not Christmas. It's a firebase. With a mining camp inside it."

She looked up at him tiredly. "A what?"

"A firebase. Look at how it's set up. It's star shaped. Each arm of the star can receive supporting fire from at least two others. Anything inside the points of the star is in a cross fire. The whole structure is a series of interlocking fire lanes, with concentric strong points until you reach the center. Everything within a two-hundred-yard radius of the fence has been cleared, and anybody caught in that perimeter would be cut to pieces. If the DEA or the FBI hit this place they would be slaughtered. It would take the Army, with infantry, air support and armored vehicles to breach this setup. Even then it would take time and a lot of lives to do it, and who knows what kind of heavy weapons they have concealed down there.''

Larquette shook her head tiredly. ''But what's the point? I mean, they're in the United States, for God's sake. They can't win. They're trapped with no place to go. The Feds would call in the Army and they'd get stomped. Why would someone go to all the trouble to build a base like that just to be trapped in a prolonged siege?''

''That's a very good question.'' Bolan stared at the complex, his face setting in grim lines. ''There has to be something we've missed, or we haven't figured on, or else...''

''Or else what?''

The Executioner folded his arms across his chest as he gazed at the fortress below. ''Or else there's something down there that they're all willing to die for.''

IGOR BAIBAKOV STOOPED LOW as he entered Ramzin's office, then rose to his full height. His head brushed the corrugated shack's ceiling as he stood at attention and snapped a smart salute. Ramzin returned the salute and waved the man to a chair. The chair creaked in protest as Baibakov sank his huge frame into an utterly relaxed sprawl. It never failed to astound Ramzin how a man so large could move with such catlike ease.

''Tell me, Captain, how go the preparations?''

''Everything is in readiness, Major. I have picked my teams. The security protocols have been altered to your specifications. The helicopter is being refitted as we speak.'' He nodded, more to confirm this to himself than to Ramzin. ''This time there will be no mistakes.''

Ramzin nodded. ''I do not doubt this. What of our friends?''

''They say everything proceeds on schedule. If they are to be believed, all will go ahead tonight as planned.''

The major folded his arms across his chest and regarded the giant. ''And what of you, Igor, what do you think?''

Baibakov's eyes slitted. "I believe your tactics are correct, Commander. He is out there in the dark. I can feel him. He is watching us. He will be watching tonight."

Ramzin nodded. He trusted the huge hunter's instincts. "Then tonight he will see something very interesting."

"Indeed," Baibakov stated, "and it will be the last thing this Yankee and the troublesome woman shall ever see."

THE EXECUTIONER AWOKE, rolling to one knee with the Beretta 93-R in his hand. The safety came off instinctively as he cocked his head and listened.

He could hear a helicopter.

Larquette knelt to one side with her hand half outstretched. She was somewhat taken aback. She hadn't even touched him. "Ah, you told me to wake you if anything happened."

Bolan nodded. "The helicopter is up."

"Yes, and there's a lot of lights on and a lot of people and vehicles moving around. Something's definitely going on."

The soldier rose to his feet and holstered the Beretta as he glanced up at the stars. He had slept for two hours. It was nearly 4:00 a.m. They had reached the base of the peak at two, and Larquette had insisted that he get some rest. Bolan stretched, taking a deep breath of the desert night air. He had long ago learned to sleep anywhere and at anytime.

He watched as the JetRanger orbited the camp, then slanted off into the darkness at high speed toward Crucible. Bolan swept his gaze back to the camp. She was right. Something was going on. Some kind of preparations were being made. "I'm going to have to get closer."

The woman put her hands on her hips. "*We* have to get closer."

Bolan looked at her and said dryly, "That might not be the smartest idea."

Larquette folded her arms across her chest. "You're forgetting who the law is around here. I have every right to be in on any investigation."

"I didn't say you didn't have the right. I said it might not be a smart idea."

"Listen, you're not leaving me alone out here. What if you go in there and get yourself killed?"

Bolan shook his head. "If I get myself killed, what do you think is going to happen to you if you're with me?"

Her shoulders squared, and she glared up at him defiantly. He could tell she was scared to be left alone and too proud to be left behind. Bolan idly considered tying her up, but if he was killed it would leave her to the mercy of the desert.

Her voice dropped slightly. "You said we were a team. I need you and you need me. If we stick together, we'll win."

Bolan nodded. "All right. Do exactly what I tell you. Move when I tell you to move. Freeze when I tell you to freeze."

BAIBAKOV SAT in the ready room and sharpened his shovel.

The entrenching tool was approximately a half meter long with a solid ash handle and a broad, flat, carbon-steel blade. One length of the matte-black blade had been sharpened to a hatchetlike utility edge, while the opposing edge had been honed to a razor sharpness. The tip of the shovel blade was a shallow triangle, and its twin edges were beveled for penetration. Soldiers had been using entrenching tools as weapons since World War I, and in the intervening years since then, the Soviet soldiers of Spetsnaz had elevated it to an art form. In a riot situation, a body blow with the flat of the shovel blade would leave a man writhing on the ground in agonizing pain or a limb paralyzed and useless. In life-or-death combat, the edge would take a man's head from his shoulders like a battle-ax. The tool was well balanced for throwing, and Baibakov could sink his into a car door at twenty paces with ease.

It was a joke within Spetsnaz that in an emergency you could even use one to dig a hole.

Baibakov grinned as he ran the whetstone around the gleaming edge of the blade. The edge was already sharp enough to shave hair off of his arm. It was a ritual that simply killed time. Now it was the waiting game. His men were ready; he had personally chosen four six-man squads, all of the best men available. All had double- and triple-checked their weapons and gear. The jeeps were fueled and ready, and waited by the rolling steel doors of the warehouse. The vehicles had been reconfigured into weapon platforms, each with a light machine gun in front of its front passenger seat. Postmounted in the rear of two of the jeeps were heavy machine guns, while the other two mounted beltfed automatic grenade launchers. The vehicles would work in pairs, striking in a pincer movement to surround the quarry and overwhelm them with firepower.

Along the far wall, men sat looking at monitors while others stared into space, listening to headphones for the slightest hint of their quarry. Ramzin stood behind them with his arms folded, a figure carved in stone.

Baibakov stared idly at his watch. It was just past 4:00 a.m., nearly time for this night's scheduled activity to begin.

The trap was set. Now where was his prey?

THE EXECUTIONER lay prone in the darkness. "Do you see them?"

Larquette peered out at the camp. "See what?"

Bolan reached over and turned up the gain on her goggles. "My equipment is a generation ahead of the Russian gear you're wearing." He adjusted her goggles to full amplification. "Look now."

Larquette's jaw dropped. "My God, what are they?"

Through the view of their night vision gear dozens of glowing white lines crisscrossed the camp's perimeter like a ghostly net of light. "They're infrared lasers, low power and very well set up."

"Are they dangerous?"

"No, they aren't. They're just very sophisticated trip wires. But if you break one of the beams, they know you're there."

"But we can see them. Anyone with these goggles could see them."

Bolan nodded. "That's true. But they'd detect any casual intruder, or anyone without the proper equipment." The Executioner's face set in tight lines. "And I suspect they're only the first line of defense. Hand me my pack, would you?"

Larquette handed him the small black pack, and Bolan pulled out a flat metal case. He opened the case and fitted a plug in his right ear. After a moment of turning a dial, he nodded.

"What is it?"

"Motion detectors. They're using sound."

"What do we do about that?"

Bolan pulled out a small fan-shaped antenna and spread it out into a dish. "There are two kinds of detection gear—active and passive. The lasers and the sound are active. They're sending out beams and signals, looking for you. You can detect them, and take countermeasures. If you see the lasers, you can simply step over. Some systems you can jam. Motion detectors, like this sound system, we can fool."

He plugged the small dish into the case and made some adjustments. A tiny generator began to send pulses of high-frequency sound into the night. Green lights on the miniature console blinked as the pulses altered to align with the sound generated by the motion sensors. The earplug chirped as the sounds matched. A grin ghosted across the Executioner's face. As usual, Gadgets Schwarz was way ahead of the competition.

Larquette hunched forward. "What's the other kind again?"

"Passive systems."

"What does that mean, exactly?"

"Passive systems don't do anything. They just sit there and wait. Like a land mine. You don't know it's there until you step on it."

Larquette drew back. "You're not saying there's a mine field out there, are you?"

"No. That would be too risky. If some kids were blown up riding around on their dirt bikes, it might be very hard for Red Star Mining to explain. What we have to worry about is something we can trip without ever knowing it's there."

"Like what kind of something?"

"A seismic something, most likely. Buried in the ground. Seismic devices don't emanate anything you can detect. They're just sensors that feel the vibrations in the ground when something passes nearby and tell the bad guys you're there."

"So what do we do?"

Bolan slung the big Weatherby rifle behind his back and put a finger to his lips.

"Move very quietly."

RAMZIN STOOD and watched the consoles of the security net. The new security suite for the base had cost a small fortune, but it was one of the few expenditures he had demanded that the Witch hadn't complained about.

She believed in security.

Ramzin took a deep breath. "Anything?" It was a rhetorical question. He already knew the answer, and Lieutenant Voroshilov knew that his commander knew, as well, but the former KGB technical specialist turned from his monitor and reported anyway.

"Nothing to report yet, Major. The infrared detection system has registered several scattered breaks. Combined with local seismic readings, these breaks have been ruled as animal in nature, though of course we are maintaining a high degree of scrutiny in these areas. However, Major, their pattern strongly suggests rabbits or deer."

Ramzin nodded. "What of the motion detectors?"

Voroshilov shrugged. "Two breaks, Major, again determined to be animal in nature. One anomalous reading in the southern quadrant, ruled a malfunction."

Ramzin unfolded his arms and peered at Voroshilov narrowly. "Define for me anomalous reading, Senior Lieutenant Voroshilov."

The officer sank several inches under Ramzin's withering gaze. "Anomalous, Major. Unexplainable. They are usually chalked up to malfunction or signal problems. It is a question of pattern, Commander. A pattern of breaks or readings would indicate that something has actually been detected. But in the anomalous reading, it is a momentary blink, and it is unrepeated. We generally experience several anomalous readings on several of the systems in a night of surveillance. I will be happy to show you the logs to confirm this, Commander. It is why we use overlapping security systems. No other systems in the southern quadrant confirmed a detection, so I ruled it to be anomalous."

Voroshilov mopped at his brow as he finished. He was suddenly sweating.

Ramzin folded his arms again and released Voroshilov from his stare. "Very well, Senior Lieutenant, I accept your report."

The man returned to his screens. Ramzin glanced over at Baibakov. The giant sat peering at the gleaming edge of his entrenching tool. Ramzin shook his head in wonder. The man could outwait a stone. He was like a rifle bullet, an inert object, sitting ready in the chamber.

Until one pulled the trigger.

Lukov turned from the radio station. "Commander, the operation has begun. Estimated time of arrival is five minutes and counting."

Ramzin nodded. "Excellent. Keep me updated."

The major stared up at the perimeter map of the base and muttered under his breath.

"Come, my friend, come and take a look. Take a very close look."

THE EXECUTIONER BROUGHT his binoculars to his eyes, and the front of the complex jumped into crystal clarity. Men stood around as the electrical gate slowly rolled back on its track. Bolan rested prone on his elbows and adjusted the focus slightly.

Larquette nudged his shoulder. "What's happening?"

He handed her the binoculars and unslung the Weatherby rifle. He flicked off the scope's lens caps and swept the camp through the powerful sight. "They're preparing for something."

She raised her hand and pointed. "Look at the big warehouse!"

Bolan tracked the scope over to the larger of the two warehouses in the complex. Its gate was sliding open, as well, and a man with a flashlight in each hand was motioning something inside to come out. The Executioner squinted as lights in the warehouse burst into life, their brightness nearly blinding in the light amplification of his scope sight. He dialed down the gain and took another look. Headlights shone brightly as a vehicle moved to the warehouse door.

It was a truck.

The semi inched forward, its truck compartment nearly as tall as the gate and filling the door. The vehicle eased out of the warehouse, and Bolan could see that it had a double trailer. By the way it rode, he could tell that the truck was loaded.

"I wonder what's in it?"

"I don't know, something they don't want people to know about."

Another truck followed the first, slowly pulling out of the warehouse and maneuvering toward the front gate. The nose of a third truck edged out the door, and the man with the flashlights waved it on.

"Whatever they've got, they sure have a lot of it."

Bolan suddenly raised his sight and scanned the warehouse as a fourth semi began pulling out. He quickly ran the sight across its dimensions. The warehouse could barely hold four double semi rigs, much less allow them to maneuver inside.

A fifth truck began to wind its way out the warehouse.

The Executioner twisted into a seated position and turned the scope to face the south. His voice became stone.

"How many miles to Mexico from here?"

Larquette shrugged, still watching the complex. "Oh, I don't know. We're pretty close. From here, I'd say six, maybe seven miles, tops."

A sixth truck exited the warehouse.

Larquette frowned behind the binoculars. "How did they fit all those..." Her voice trailed off and her jaw dropped. "My God, they've—"

"They've dug a tunnel." Bolan lowered the rifle scope. "A smuggling corridor. Big enough to run trucks through."

"What could they have in all those trucks?"

Bolan grimaced. It was a Russian operation, but they obviously had to be getting help from someone in Mexico. "They could be running guns, drugs, illegal aliens, anything that will pay. If they're a terrorist group, God only knows what they might be bringing in."

"What do we do?"

He rose to a crouch and slung his rifle, pulling his night-vision goggles back down over his eyes. "We have to get out of here. I have to call in."

"But it will take us at least a day to climb back over and hike to town!"

Bolan shook his head. "No time. We stay down and get close to the road. The vibration and noise of the trucks should cover us if we're smart about it."

He grabbed her hand as she pulled her goggles in place.

"Let's move."

9

Voroshilov shot out of his seat. "Movement, Commander! Magnetometer confirmed!"

Ramzin reached the security console in three strides. "Where?"

"Southeast quadrant! Near the road!"

The major scanned the bewildering array of monitors. "Where? Show me!"

Voroshilov pointed to a monitor. "You see, our quarry is very clever. He shadows the road, where the vibrations of the convoy's big trucks will temporarily disrupt our seismic sensors. He wishes to move as fast as possible, and he knows the noise and wind of the trucks will shield him from the motion detectors in that area, as well. But look, Commander! He cannot compensate for the magnetometers. I suspect he does not even know that they are there. The magnetometers are much more sensitive and localized. They detect metal. Like the weapons and gear our quarry must be carrying. They are almost impossible to fool."

Ramzin scowled. "How do you know your magnetic readings are not a reflection of the convoy?"

Voroshilov grinned from ear to ear. He loved to show off his toys. "An excellent question, Commander. But look. If they were reflections, they would mirror the individual trucks' speed and movement. It would be a very easy pattern to recognize. But what we have are two irregular readings, very close together, small amounts of metal, moving slowly in relation to the truck convoy."

Ramzin nodded. "I see, Senior Lieutenant. What is your assessment?"

Voroshilov stabbed the monitor with his finger. "Two individuals, Commander, in the southeast quadrant, on foot. They are shadowing the road, moving toward town."

"We have them!" Ramzin whirled. "Baibakov! Southeast quadrant, by the road! Move!"

Baibakov and his men piled into the gun jeeps, the warmed-up engines revving into life as the sliding gate opened. Ramzin turned to the communication console with a savage grin of triumph.

"Get me the helicopter, now!"

THE EXECUTIONER MOVED through the darkness.

The taillights of the truck convoy receded ahead of them in the distance. Taking this route was an ugly gamble. He would have preferred to retrace his steps over the mountain, but there was no time.

Larquette panted behind him but maintained the pace. She spoke between gulps of air. "Do you think we're clear?"

Bolan pulled to a halt. "I believe we're out of range of the base's sensors now. If we tripped anything, we'll know soon—"

He raised his eyes to the night sky.

Larquette looked about. "What is it?"

The vibrations slowly crept into the audible range as the Executioner unslung his big Weatherby rifle. "The helicopter. You'd better run. Head for the rocks. Go back the same way we came. Contact your friend Tom Donovan. See if he can smuggle you out of the county."

"I'm not going anywhere. We're a team."

The Executioner's voice became stone. "The helicopter can't track two targets. If you can reach the rocks you stand a chance."

She shook her head desperately. "But—"

Bolan took a step toward her and barked, "Move!"

Larquette flinched and with a look of betrayal broke into a sprint toward the distant spine of rocks.

Bolan flicked the lens caps off the Weatherby's scope and pressed on the power switch. He looked out into the darkness of the predawn desert. The helicopter was coming in at top speed, little more than a hundred feet above the ground. Plumes of dust whirled into the sky behind it in the wake of the rotor's down wash. Bolan grimaced. The aircraft was flying directly toward him.

It knew exactly where he was.

At a thousand yards its searchlight blazed into blinding life under the chin of the cockpit and began to sweep the desert in front of it as it roared forward. Bolan raised the .378 Weatherby rifle to his shoulder. In the day-night scope, the searchlight was as bright as the sun. He squinted and turned down the gain, then wound his arm into the rifle's sling for support and assumed a solid firing stance. The soldier took a deep breath and a careful aim. It was only a matter of seconds before it saw him.

Bolan stood unflinching as the blinding circle of the searchlight swept toward him. He could feel the vibration of the rotors and let out half of his breath, his stance rock steady.

The Executioner slowly began taking up slack on the big rifle's trigger, the marksman's mantra running through his mind—*don't pull the trigger, just squeeze ... squeeze ...*

SENIOR SERGEANT Nikolai Tsapko took the helicopter down to seventy-five feet and shouted into his microphone. "Approaching target area. Gunners ready. Remember, we take them alive. Herd them to the jeeps."

Corporals Sobolev and Borchisky swung out on their chicken straps, literally hanging out the doors over the PKM machine guns mounted into each doorframe. Sobolev shouted over the rotor noise as he swept his sights across the desert floor.

"Where are they?"

Tsapko grimaced. "There is no cover! We should be right on top of them!" He turned to the copilot who manned the searchlight. "Ozhimkov! Check the coordinates—"

Sparks exploded under the helicopter's chin as the high-powered searchlight shattered. Metal shrieked inside the cabin as a heavy bullet tore through the cockpit floor and burst through the roof. Cursing, Tsapko yanked the joystick to bank the helicopter as a second bullet shattered the front windscreen and smashed Ozhimkov back in his seat. Tsapko's eyes caught the orange muzzle-flash against the black background of the desert floor even as wind shrieked into the cockpit through the shattered windscreen. He roared into his microphone.

"Sobolev! Seven o'clock! Now!"

The PKM machine gun ripped into life, sending bursts of green tracers streaming to the ground. A third bullet smashed into the fuselage above Sobolev's head, ripping into the rotor-engine housing. He corrected his aim and fired repeated bursts at the muzzle-flash on the ground.

"Go lower! I cannot see him!"

Tsapko's gorge rose as he dropped the helicopter like a stone and hit the landing lights. Sobolev yanked his night-vision goggles over his eyes as the helicopter began its descent.

"I see him! I—"

Sobolev jerked backward and sagged into his straps with a shudder. Tsapko spun the helicopter in a dizzying 180-degree turn as another bullet smashed into the upper fuselage. The engine shuddered and began to make high-pitched grinding noises. Tsapko could smell metal grinding on metal.

"Borchisky! Ignore the orders! Kill him! Kill him now!"

A fifth bullet smashed into the cockpit by Tsapko's head.

Borchisky swung the muzzle of his machine gun. "I see him! He is running, trying to reload. Bank left!"

The corporal brought his machine gun in line and sent a burst of green tracers streaking at the running figure. The bullets geysered dirt in a line parallel with his target. "Good! Hold position!"

Tsapko hauled up on the joystick and brought the helicopter to a hover, giving Borchisky a stable firing platform.

The man stopped and whirled, bringing the rifle to his shoulder and slamming the bolt shut, but Borchisky knew the enemy was too late. He had his front sight dead on the man's chest. Borchisky pushed down on the PKM's paddle triggers.

Sparks shrieked in the helicopter cabin as bullet after bullet tore into the rear of the fuselage and flew into the cabin. Tsapko jerked, and the helicopter spun as an unseen fist smashed into his shoulder, numbing his arm and leaving him only one hand to wrestle with the shuddering helicopter. He twisted his head and saw rapid muzzle-flashes on the ground to his left, firing up at his aircraft.

"Borchisky! Ground fire! Five o'clock!"

The corporal hung in his chicken straps, sagging out of the doorway over his gun. Bullets began striking the helicopter as the first target resumed fire. Above Tsapko's head, the engine screamed as something in the drive train failed cataclysmically and the besieged aircraft began to spin out of control. Tsapko keyed his chin mike desperately.

"Mayday! Mayday! Red Star One! Going down! I am going down! Mayday!"

Tsapko yanked back on the joystick with all the strength of his one good arm as the ground rushed up to meet him.

THE EXECUTIONER PUSHED fresh shells into the Weatherby's magazine. The helicopter lay in a smoking ruin some forty yards away. Its fuselage was nearly broken in two and scored with bullet holes. Near Bolan's feet lay an eight-foot length of rotor blade that had come close to decapitating him when the aircraft had crashed. He heard the crunch of boots behind him as he pushed the last round into the rifle's chamber and closed the bolt.

"I thought I told you to run."

Larquette smiled in the predawn glimmer as he turned to face her. She topped off her Winchester's magazine with rounds out of her pocket.

"I did."

"Mmm."

Bolan closed the Weatherby's breech and flicked on the safety as he turned and brought the rifle to his shoulder. Through the scope he could see jeeps tearing out of the complex, each filled with armed men and bristling with weapons. They drove at a dangerous speed across the rough terrain. It would be only moments before they arrived.

"Feel like running again?"

"Let me guess. The rocks."

"Yeah. But this time don't stop until you get there."

Larquette looked up at him with tired defiance. "I told you, I'm sticking with you."

Bolan nodded. "I know. We're a team. I'll be right along. But first I have to discourage our friends, and your rifle just doesn't have that kind of range. So why don't you get a head start, and cover me if I have to come running in a hurry."

"All right." She turned and jogged toward the rocks. Bolan faced the complex, assumed a half-kneeling position, then sat back on his heel. He pulled the big rifle firmly into his shoulder and propped his elbow onto his knee in an easy rest. The sling creaked as he wound his free arm into it, and his whole body became a stable firing platform. In the telescopic sight, the lead jeep seemed almost about to run him over. Bolan placed the scope's cross hairs on the jeep's front grille and slowly squeezed the trigger.

The big rifle roared and kicked with brutal recoil. Bolan racked the bolt and chambered the next round as the rifle came back into line. The lead jeep fishtailed as steam erupted out of the grille. Bolan traversed the scope. The second jeep tore past the first. Above its roll bar, a giant of a man stood behind the ugly black snout of a heavy machine gun. The Executioner's eyes narrowed slightly as a long burst tore a track in the sand some yards to his right, and he squeezed the Weatherby's trigger in reply.

The jeep's tire blew out spectacularly as the .378 Magnum bullet struck, and the vehicle rolled violently as it suddenly shoveled its nose into the sand. The two following jeeps spewed clouds of dust as they screamed to a halt. Hardmen jumped out and raced to the overturned vehicle while others gave covering fire.

Bolan rose from his shooting position and ran, zigzagging as he sprinted for the rocks. Bullets whined past, but he knew he was already out of range. Only a lucky shot could hit him as he opened up his stride. Larquette's head peeked up from the foot of the rock formation, and she waved him on encouragingly.

The soldier calculated as he ran. He had bought them some time, but he had only delayed the Russians. They knew which way he and Larquette were headed, and they would hunt them mercilessly under the desert sun.

"CAPTAIN!"

Baibakov dimly heard someone yelling at him as he pushed himself up out of the sand. The coppery taste of blood filled his mouth, and his pulse thundered in his head like a drum. Colors washed across his vision as he rose to his feet, and he nearly fell. He caught himself on the wheel of the overturned jeep and shook his head to clear it.

"Captain Baibakov!"

He rose to his full height as Lukov ran up to him. He shook his head again and spat blood and sand out of his mouth. "Report, Corporal!"

Lukov stared up at Baibakov, aghast. His superior's face was a mask of blood, and his features were set in a feral snarl of rage. "Yes, sir. Red Star One has been shot down. Jeep two has been disabled and will require extensive engine repair. Jeep one's tire has burst. We will have it repaired within minutes. Suryev has sustained a broken arm. All other injuries are insignificant."

"And the quarry?"

Lukov avoided his captain's eyes. "The quarry has reached the rocks."

"Have the men right the jeep and begin repair immediately. Have a second detail go to the helicopter and check for survivors. Take all wounded and casualties back to the base. Bring me fresh replacements. Make a full report to Major Ramzin. I expect you to have returned within fifteen minutes."

Lukov snapped to attention and saluted. "Yes, sir."

Baibakov raised a bloody hand as Lukov turned to leave. "Lukov."

"Yes, sir?"

"Tell Ramzin this quarry cannot be taken alive. Tell him I am going to hunt him down in the mountains. I will need RPG-7s and explosives." Baibakov's bloody face split slowly into a horrible smile.

"And I will need sniper rifles."

10

"Report."

Ramzin ground his teeth but kept his voice even as he spoke into the phone. "Convoy has reached United States soil without incident."

The Witch's voice mocked him. "Without incident? That is not what I have been told."

Ramzin's fist clenched. *Zampolits*—even here he couldn't escape them. In the former Soviet Union he had had to contend with *Zampolits,* the Soviet military's hated political officers, Party spies who watched soldiers like hawks and reported any unauthorized activity to the Party. Now he had an informer in his command, secretly reporting to the Witch. Ramzin smiled unpleasantly. Sometimes, during the war in Afghanistan, unfortunate "accidents" had happened to the political informers in the field. This person in his midst wouldn't be part of his old command from the war. It would have to be one of the newer men brought in from Moscow. He would find this man, and perhaps an unfortunate accident would befall him, as well.

The major took a deep breath. "Convoy has departed without incident and is on schedule. If you refer to this mystery American, yes, he grows increasingly as a problem."

"And what are you going to do about this, Major?"

"I have told Baibakov to bring me his head."

The Witch flared. "I have given you your orders! I want him alive!"

Ramzin's anger broke free. "He is too dangerous. He is a trained sniper, and has shot down my helicopter and disabled two of my vehicles. My casualties are mounting." He lowered his voice. "Listen to me, and listen well. He has seen the convoy. He knows of the corridor. Our first priority must be to ensure he never lives to tell of it. He and the woman are to be killed on sight, and I have instructed Baibakov to bring me proof of it when it is done. You are the politician, I am a soldier. This matter is now a military emergency. I will not have my orders questioned. Do you understand?"

The Witch hated Ramzin—him and his pet killing machine, Baibakov. She hated the way he flaunted his military expertise and the way he increasingly flouted her authority. Even worse, she hated him because he could make her lose her composure.

Worst of all, she hated him because he was right.

The Witch steeled herself to remain calm. If it was a military situation, then so be it. Let Ramzin and his tin soldiers take care of it. It was what they were there for. She calmed herself with a pleasing thought. When it was over, and the corridor was running smoothly and the operation secure, she would have Ramzin and his pet freak killed. Then she would bring in a more tractable replacement from Moscow.

She savored the idea and spoke calmly. "Very well, Major Ramzin, I accept your assessment. This is now a military situation. I give you full autonomy to deal with it as you see fit. You will assume full responsibility in this matter. I will require you to keep me updated as to developments at all times."

Ramzin paused warily. He didn't like her tone. He would have preferred her to be spitting with rage and screaming about her authority. The words "full responsibility" hadn't escaped him, either. He knew the penalty for failure and who he would have to answer to if he did. But she had handed him a two-edged sword. With full authority his success could bring great rewards. However, if he failed . . .

If he failed, the Witch would drink vodka and dance on his grave.

The major took a deep breath. "I will keep you continuously updated as to all developments in this situation."

"See that you do."

He hung up the phone and stared at the survey map over his desk. It was up to him and his men now. He peered critically at the spine of mountains on the southwest side of the camp.

It was time for Baibakov to earn his pay.

IGOR BAIBAKOV EXAMINED the terrain. Tendrils of smoke still curled up out of the crumpled remains of the helicopter some forty yards behind him. Remarkably Tsapko had survived the crash. Borchisky, Ozhimkov and Sobolev hadn't been so lucky. The casualties were mounting.

He examined the tracks in the sand before him. He knew both footprints intimately now. The man and the woman had made no attempt to hide their trail as they had run for the high ground. Baibakov raised his eyes to the wall of rock ahead. His prey was in the rocks now, with a half hour head start. He knelt and picked up one of the spent shell casings that lay scattered about and glinted in the red dust.

The brass shell was nearly three inches long. Baibakov turned the case upside down and examined the abbreviated markings stamped on its base. They read 378 WTHRBY MAGNUM in a circle around the fired primer. His eyes narrowed as he calculated from memory. A .378 Weatherby Magnum would throw a 300-grain bullet at nearly three thousand feet per second. Delivering almost three tons of muzzle energy, it was a rifle that would stop an elephant, and in calm wind conditions it would be accurate to well over a thousand yards. In the desert terrain, it would be a devastating weapon. He shook his head. How this Yankee had managed to exchange his assault carbine for such a powerful rifle only the Devil knew.

He looked back at his men as they checked weapons and unloaded gear from the replacement jeeps. Twelve of the men carried .30-caliber semiautomatic Dragunov sniper rifles. They were tough, accurate weapons, well proved in battle, but the American's rifle would have twice their power, with longer range and better accuracy. Baibakov nodded grimly to himself. He would lose men. Of that there was no question. Still, he held all the cards.

The giant looked up as the desert sun rose slowly into the sky. It would be very hot this day, and hotter tomorrow. The Americans would already be worn and tired. They would have little or no water with them. By tomorrow the man would practically have to carry the woman, if not sooner. Baibakov examined his force. He had twelve snipers, four men with RPG-7 rocket-propelled grenade launchers, two light-machine-gun teams and over a dozen well trained men with assault weapons. He also had a demolition man, and Major Ramzin had thoughtfully provided a flamethrower without being asked.

The plan was simple. He would divide his force into sniper teams and support-weapon sections. Then he would hound the quarry as the teams leapfrogged one another from cover to cover. He would give the quarry no rest and force them to show their faces. When they did, he would drive them back with his overwhelming firepower, flank them with his superior numbers, pin them down, then slaughter them like sheep.

Then he would march into Ramzin's office and present the commander with their bloody heads.

Baibakov rose and signaled his men forward. The matter was a foregone conclusion. He had run missions like this a hundred times in Afghanistan. No quarry had ever escaped him.

None would do so now.

THE EXECUTIONER SCANNED the rugged, broken terrain of the hills, and he didn't like what he saw.

The Russians were coming.

Through the lenses of his laser-range-finding binoculars, the Russians went from distant ants crawling on rocks to real, life-size opponents. They had divided into three-man sniper teams—one man with a Dragunov rifle, one man with an assault rifle with an underslung grenade launcher and a third man with powerful binoculars and a rifle as a spotter. Bolan had counted at least a half dozen of these teams slowly working their way up through the rocks, covering one another as they went. In the distance, the Executioner had caught glimpses of men moving with heavy weapons. For a moment, at the distant end of the binocular's range, he had seen the giant.

The man was relentless. He had shadowed Bolan since the break from the jail. Skill and luck had kept the Executioner one step ahead of his adversary, but now the odds seemed to be shifting. The giant seemed to have a full platoon of highly trained and well-equipped soldiers, and his tactics were excellent. They would try to flank him and Larquette, then pin them down. After that it would be only a matter of waiting, or a single charge to overwhelm them.

The Executioner's eyes narrowed as he watched the Russians advance. He had one advantage, and that was his rifle. The big Weatherby had the power and the range over his opponents. When darkness fell, its day-night optical sight would allow him to see his opponents before they could see him. He had a few other tricks in his pack, and in the desert night he would become the hunter.

Bolan peered up into the sky. Judging by the sun it was just around 9:00 a.m., and it was already well past eighty degrees. He and Larquette would have to survive for nearly nine hours before the advantage would be theirs.

He had to slow the Russians.

He turned to Larquette, who sat conserving her strength in the shade of an overhanging slab. "Here, come and take these."

She dropped low and hunched beside Bolan. She took the binoculars and adjusted them to fit her eyes while he unslung his rifle.

"What do you want me to do?"

"Range me."

She took a deep breath and settled on her elbows. "Tell me what to do."

Bolan pointed across the hills. "Do you see that man out there with the binoculars?"

Larquette frowned as she scanned the area. "I see a couple of groups of men."

He took her chin and guided her to the spot. "That one. On the ledge. The one who's starting to look our way."

She nodded slightly, not taking her eyes off him. "Yes."

Bolan settled into a prone firing position. "Now press the button right above your right finger. There should be a red-colored readout in the bottom left-hand corner of your view. What does it say?"

"Eight hundred and seventy-three *M*."

Bolan spoke quietly as he adjusted his aim. "Eight hundred and seventy-three meters."

"Now what?"

"There's a little ravine behind us that leads back about thirty or forty yards. When I tell you, get into it fast."

The Executioner pushed off the safety and began to slowly take up the trigger's slack. In his scope, he saw the Russian's jaw drop as he came face-to-face with Bolan's rifle through his binoculars.

Larquette flinched as the huge rifle boomed beside her. As she blinked, the man she was watching seemed to be struck by a huge invisible fist and was smashed out of her field of view. Off to her right, a single shell casing tinkled to the ground, and she heard Bolan rack his rifle's bolt. She whipped her binoculars around. All through the rocks, the Russians were dropping down and taking cover. Suddenly they all seemed to be pointing guns straight at her.

Larquette was startled as a man suddenly stood and shouted. His rifle had a large tube underneath it and he seemed to look right at her as he sighted the rifle. Then he whipped it up and pointed into the sky over their position.

Larquette pointed desperately. "There! Down there!"

Bolan tracked with his rifle. His voice was steely calm. "Where?"

She desperately searched for words. "Down there! Below!" Then, with sudden inspiration, she shouted, "Seven o'clock!" She pushed the button on the binoculars. "Five hundred meters!"

The big rifle next to her roared.

The man suddenly staggered back, and the black tube under his rifle boomed and spit fire as he swayed. A moment later there was a loud boom wide to Larquette's right as the grenade detonated some fifty yards away.

Bolan spoke suddenly in her ear. "Excellent. Now move. Stay low."

She didn't have to be told twice. As she scurried away, the hills erupted into a firestorm. It seemed as if every rock in the hillsides had a black snout that spit fire. Most of the rounds fell short, but some of the longer ranged weapons managed to strike sparks off the rocks above their heads. Larquette stopped as she reached cover behind a large boulder, and Bolan suddenly rose up behind her.

She stared up at him. "So what's the plan now?"

"We git, reposition and hit them again. Force them to keep taking cover."

"What are they going to do?"

"Flank us, if they can," he replied.

"Which way?"

"Up and to the right. The terrain is rougher. We'll hit them again while they're climbing, then move to the next ridge."

"Lead the way."

11

Hal Brognola slapped down the book he was reading and rose from his chair. It was useless to pretend. He had read the same paragraph three times in a row. It was time to stop waiting. It had been two days and Bolan hadn't reported in. He knew well the nature of infiltration and deep cover. It was possible that everything was going along as planned.

But every hard-earned instinct Brognola had told him something was happening.

He came to a decision and picked up the secure phone. It answered in two rings.

"Hi, Hal. What's up?"

Brognola was silent for a moment. He had given Striker his word that he wouldn't involve anyone at the Farm. Now he was about to break that promise.

Price's voice became serious. "Hal, what's going on?"

"Something, maybe. Probably nothing." He searched for words, and he knew he wasn't fooling anybody. "I need you to do me a favor."

"Name it."

He took a deep breath. "I want you to round up Phoenix Force and assemble them at the Farm."

There was a pause as Price took this in. "Hal, most of them are standing down, taking a little R and R. Hal, what's going on?"

"Barbara, please, just trust me, and do it."

Price's voice was utterly neutral. "All right, Hal, I'll bring them in immediately, but what exactly do you want me to tell them?"

"Just tell them to come in, and be ready."

"Very well, I'll have them come in and stand on full alert." He noted the total detachment in her voice. She knew he was hiding something, and that he was hiding something about Bolan. "And how do you want them equipped?"

Brognola sighed. The damage was already done.

"Have them ready for a full assault."

THE EXECUTIONER PEERED through his scope. Even at full 8.5 magnification his target looked too small. The target was almost on another ridge entirely. Only a small gap between rock formations allowed him to see it at all. But the target had a field radio on his back, and just for a moment the giant had stood next to him before disappearing behind a ridge of rock. Bolan came to a decision.

"Range me."

Larquette locked her binoculars on the target and pressed the laser range finder.

"Twelve hundred and forty-seven meters."

Bolan's face tightened as he raised his sights. He was an outstanding marksman, but the shot was at the extreme edge of his ability and pushed the performance envelope even of his specially setup rifle. He and Larquette had momentarily eluded their opponents. To fire now would be to expose their general location. Sniper survival instincts spoke in his mind. The shot was long and risky, but it was a target of opportunity. The sniper's mantra of priorities also spoke to him—*shoot anyone with a radio.*

Bolan raised his aim. In the noon-day heat, the desert was shimmering and still. Crosswinds weren't a factor. However, at this range his bullet would drop significantly before reaching the target, and he had to compensate for that. He brought the cross hairs up until they seemed to float about a foot above his target's head. It still wouldn't be enough.

"Tell me if he moves," he said.

Larquette nodded, not taking the binoculars off her target.

Bolan eyes slitted as he raised his sights. He kept raising them until he could see only the very top of the radioman's helmet as a blur in the bottom of his scope, then the man was no longer visible in his scope. On paper it wouldn't matter. The centerline of his cross hairs stood perpendicular to the target, drawing an invisible line down to where his target's body would be. Bolan slowly let out half a breath and began to squeeze the trigger.

The big Weatherby roared as Larquette hissed in his ear. "He's moving!"

At over twelve hundred meters, it took the heavy .378 bullet nearly two seconds to reach the target. Bolan racked the big rifle's bolt to chamber a new round. He dropped his sights and saw the target turn and motion to someone out of view. As Bolan tried to calculate a second shot, the radioman suddenly staggered forward and sparks shot from the radio pack on his back. The Executioner eased off the trigger as the man fell facedown into the dust. At that angle, a follow-up shot would only drop into the rocks below the fallen man.

Larquette lowered her binoculars and stared at Bolan incredulously. "My God."

A hail of gunfire erupted from all around the hills as the Russians sought out Bolan by the booming blast of his rifle. He could hear dim shouting, and more and more fire shrieked and ricocheted off the rocks as tracers walked above their position.

Bolan flipped the rifle across his forearms and hunched backward into cover on his knees and elbows.

"Let's move."

BAIBAKOV GLARED at the smashed radio set where it lay in the dirt. Lieutenant Rybenok and Sergeant Torosyan squatted over the stricken instrument and shook their heads like horse traders examining a mare with a broken leg. Torosyan turned to Baibakov and raised his hands helplessly.

The captain turned away and stared up at the distant rock formation with folded arms. He mentally calculated the distance. It had to be at least twelve hundred meters, and he had been standing in plain sight next to Lukov only moments before the shot was fired. It was incredible. Baibakov ground his teeth with rage even as he admired the American's skill.

Baibakov turned and glanced at Lukov. The corporal sat shaken and dazed in the shade of a rock overhang. He was sweaty and pale, and he wheezed as he tried to get air into his lungs. Medical Sergeant Barsukov gave him some water, then rose and approached Baibakov. He halted and saluted smartly.

The giant nodded grimly. "Report."

"Yes, sir. Fortunately the bullet struck Corporal Lukov through the thicker elements of his radio pack and then lodged in his body armor. I believe the bullet had spent a great deal of its energy at this distance, and thus it failed to penetrate farther. The corporal is shaken and badly bruised, but no bones are broken, and I do not believe he has any internal injuries. When he catches his breath I believe he will be fit for duty."

Baibakov dismissed the medic with a nod. "I accept your report. Send me Lieutenant Rybenok."

Barsukov saluted and went to fetch Rybenok.

"Report," Baibakov demanded after the lieutenant saluted him.

"The radio is beyond field repairs, Captain."

Baibakov rolled his eyes. He had already known this, but had hoped vainly to have his suspicions proved false. Rybenok suddenly grinned and began to pull a map from his field case.

"But I think I have found something useful."

The captain looked down at the lieutenant with folded arms. "Oh?"

Rybenok was undeterred. "Yes, sir, look here." Rybenok unfolded the map and spread it on the ground. "You see, we drive this Yankee before us, but he continually retreats from high ground to high ground. He picks his shots, then retreats to his next firing position while we climb after him. By the time we reach his last position, he is hidden again and waiting to shoot."

Baibakov nodded impatiently. He was all too aware of the situation. "This is true, Lieutenant, but it cannot go on much longer. He has no water. We will drive him until he drops. Then he is ours."

Rybenok nodded. "A sound plan, Captain, but costly."

Baibakov's eyes slitted. Rybenok was treading danger-ously close to questioning his orders. "Am I to under-stand, Lieutenant Rybenok, that you have something you wish to suggest?"

Rybenok stood to ramrod-straight attention and gave Baibakov a parade-ground salute. "With your permission, Comrade Captain Baibakov!"

Baibakov sighed. Spetsnaz had always been a much more informal organization than the regular Soviet army. Using the formal Communist honorific "Comrade Captain" was shameless brown-nosing, and they both knew it. Rybenok was irrepressible, and he obviously had something to say.

The captain put his hands on his hips. "Very well, Lieu-tenant, report."

"As the captain is aware, I was in charge of security when we first ran geological surveys of the surrounding area for the tunneling project, and I am familiar with this terri-tory."

"So?"

"So, our quarry does not wish to be driven down and overwhelmed. Presumably they have some hopes of surviv-ing."

"Presumably."

"I suggest we give them a hope, and then dash it. Look at the map, sir. He must either try to get to Mexico, to the town of Crucible or to outlying ranches if he hopes to sur-vive. We have cut him off, so now he shoots and runs, try-ing to stay a step ahead of us, looking for an avenue of escape."

Baibakov regarded Rybenok dryly. "Oh? And which way shall we let our quarry escape, Lieutenant?"

Rybenok stabbed the map with his finger. "South! Look, the southeast corner of these hills fall away. They are liter-ally vertical drops. I have seen them myself, during our sur-veys. It would take rappeling gear to get down them, and glimpses we have had of the quarry do not indicate he is laden with such equipment. We will have him pinned be-tween our forces and hundreds of feet of sheer rock. He will be ours for the taking!"

"And what will prevent our quarry from skirting the drop and heading south?"

Rybenok grinned and folded his arms. "We will have another force there waiting for him."

"Major Ramzin will not like assigning more men to this mission. We are already stretched too thin, and have taken too many casualties."

Rybenok nodded sagely. "Yes, sir, this is true, but the major will do it if you say it is necessary."

Baibakov regarded Rybenok for a long moment. "Very well, Lieutenant, I accept your assessment. Take one of the jeeps and go back to base. Inform Major Ramzin of the situation. Requisition two squads. Use some of the engineers if you have to. They are combat trained and will have to hold the southernmost position only while my men make the final assault. You, Lieutenant Rybenok, will take command of the second force. I will require them ready in place within two hours, maximum."

Rybenok shot to his feet and saluted smartly. It would be his first command in the new country.

Baibakov returned the salute, then held up one huge finger. "One other thing, Lieutenant."

Rybenok looked at him questioningly. "Sir?"

The captain drew himself to his full height and Rybenok suddenly found himself standing in shade. "If I am forced to explain this operation to Major Ramzin as a failure, I will twist your head from your shoulders."

Rybenok paled, but gave the giant a weak smile. "Yes, sir."

12

The Executioner hunched down as a bullet shrieked off the rock overhang above them.

"Ready to move?"

Larquette stared at him blankly. "What?"

Bolan looked at her closely. He had been too busy running, climbing and shooting, and Larquette had stayed with him without complaining. Now that he looked at her closely, he didn't like what he saw. Her face was pale, and her breathing was shallow and rapid. He put the back of his hand against her forehead. The desert temperature was very likely a hundred degrees, if not more, and Larquette's skin was cool and clammy to the touch. Her eyes looked glassy and distant as she stared vacantly at him.

She was suffering from heat exhaustion. Unless he cooled her down, she would quickly go into heat stroke, and out here in the middle of the desert, she would almost certainly die.

Bolan pulled her deeper into the shade and took her canteen from around her shoulder. He shook it, noting it was barely a quarter full. "Drink."

She numbly accepted the canteen and took a few swallows. "We have to save—"

"Drink it. All of it."

Larquette obeyed, tilting the canteen back, then lowering it with a gasp. "It's gone."

Bolan took one of the two canteens strapped to the small of his back. It was nearly empty, as well. "Finish it."

She stared up at him guiltily and took the canteen. She gulped at the water as her thirst overrode her conscience. She dropped the empty canteen and took a deep breath.

With the water and the shade, her color was already better and her breathing was normal. Her brow furrowed as he took the last canteen and cracked it.

"We have to save some for later."

Bolan shook his head. "There's not going to be any later. We either make it to nightfall, or we don't make it at all. I have to have you walking." He held out the canteen. "Drink."

Larquette stared at the canteen, then at him. "You first."

Bolan smiled wanly. She wasn't going to have to twist his arm. He steeled himself not to gulp it all as he felt the water on his cracked lips. He took five long, slow swallows, then handed her the canteen. "Leave about a third of it. We'll need something to walk out of here on tonight."

She drank and handed him the canteen. "Now what?"

"Now you get a little rest."

"They're right behind us."

"It'll take them a little while to climb up to this position."

Bolan rummaged through his pack and pulled out a small brown package about the size and shape of a cube of butter. "I'm going to rig a small surprise for them."

BAIBAKOV WATCHED as his men poured in fire. Something had happened, and the Yankee had gone to ground. Suppressive fire from the light machine guns and the sniper teams all but kept the American's sniping to an occasional pot shot as his men crept from cover to cover. Some hundred meters upslope, Sergeant Torosyan sent Baibakov hand signals from cover.

Torosyan's hands moved in a series of rapid gestures. Enemy sighted. Covering fire in position. Assault team in position. Torosyan spread his hands. Attack?

Baibakov sliced his hand down swiftly. Attack!

Shrill attack whistles shrieked through the peaks. Every man with a rifle poured in fire at the enemy position. Torosyan rose and waved his men forward. The assault team burst from cover and scrambled up the rocky hillside as a firestorm of green tracers streaked over their heads. As the assault closed, the suppressive fire tapered off, and they fired their own weapons from the hip assault-fire position as they bore down on the enemy.

He had them.

Baibakov heard a dull roar as Torosyan and his lead men disappeared in an eruption of smoke and orange fire. The rear element of the assault team staggered and fell back from the blast. Others lay dead or unconscious as boiling clouds of dust rolled down from the hilltop and obscured them in a dense red fog. All fire ceased as the echo of the explosion rumbled and rolled through the hills with horrible finality.

Sergeant Gorchenko stood next to his captain and swallowed hard. He had come to America to find riches, and he had. Intimidating American townsfolk and riding herd on the Mexicans had been easy. Hunting an American and a woman had started off almost as a game. Gorchenko was a tough man who had risen through the ranks of Spetsnaz, but a chill went down his back in the desert heat. This was no longer a game.

It was war.

Gorchenko knew his duty and grimly turned to Baibakov. "Captain! Shall I organize a second assault team?"

Baibakov turned to his sergeant, and Gorchenko's guts turned to ice as he saw the giant's face.

"No."

Gorchenko blinked. "Captain?"

"Check the area for survivors, then group the men into formations and take them around the north side of the hill."

"But, Captain, that will take at least another half hour. If we assault again now, we—"

Baibakov cut him off with a look. "If we assault again now, we will simply run into more traps."

Gorchenko looked up at Baibakov. The fact that the man was so calm made him nervous. "So, we..."

Baibakov regarded Gorchenko expressionlessly. "So, Sergeant, we will collect our wounded as our quarry expects us to do. Then we will carefully go north around the hill and avoid further traps, as our quarry wants us to do, and we will give him his head start, just as he wants us to. Then our quarry will head south...exactly as I want him to."

BOLAN TOOK Larquette's hand as the path up the gorge steepened. He gave the sun a critical glance. It was close to four o'clock. It would be four more hours until true dark began to fall. Then he would go among the Russians to do damage and get water. But until that time, they had to keep moving. He calculated they were little more than a half hour ahead of their pursuers.

He looked back at Larquette. She had beaten the heat exhaustion and bounced back remarkably well. But now it was a question of total exhaustion. She was done in. Her rifle had become a walking stick, and her gaze never rose above the toes of her boots as she haltingly put one foot in front of the other. She needed food and water, and most of all, a good night's rest. She looked up and with obvious effort gave Bolan a haggard smile. He smiled back and squeezed her hand, but the truth was there in her stumbling gait and shuddering breath.

She wasn't going to make it for another four hours. Before nightfall he would be carrying her.

"Come on, let's see what's at the top of this hill."

Larquette didn't answer. She just took another gasping breath and grabbed his hand tighter as he pulled her up the steep, broken terrain. From the summit he could judge the lay of the land and plan their next move.

Bolan put an arm around her shoulders as they approached the top. "Just a little farther, then you can rest. I bet there's a breeze at the top." She staggered and sagged as the ground suddenly leveled out.

"I have to stop. I'm sorry, I just can't..."

Bolan gently lowered her to the ground. He took in the vista before him, and the ramifications hit him like a hammer blow. Ten feet from where he was standing the rock fell away, plunging over a hundred feet to the desert floor. It was as if someone had taken a knife and cleanly sliced away the edges of the mountains in a continuous ridge line. Mexico lay not more than a few miles across the sandy desert below, but it might as well have been a thousand miles away.

There was no way they could climb down.

Bolan glanced around. The Russians were right behind them, and they couldn't turn back. They would have to descend and try to go southeast, and they would have to move fast.

Larquette sat numbly staring out across the vista.

Bolan reached down for her hand. "Come on."

She stared without answering.

"Come on."

Her voice came out in a weak rasp. "Maybe you should go on without me."

Bolan grabbed her arm and yanked her to her feet. "Move."

She took several steps and her rubbery legs collapsed beneath her. Bolan pulled her arm, but she didn't respond.

"Patti, get up."

She spoke in shuddering gasps. "I can't."

"If they find you here they'll kill you. Get up."

She turned her head away weakly. "I don't care. Leave me alone."

The Executioner's voice became stone. "Get up."

He tightened his hold on her arm and yanked her to her feet.

"I said move."

Tears rolled down her face and she weakly clawed at his hand and wrist. Bolan ignored her efforts and dragged her behind him down the hillside. She stumbled and fell, and he relentlessly pulled her up again. Her voice broke into a shuddering snarl, and she began cursing him breathlessly in a long string of obscenities. Anger was strength. If it was enough to get her down the hill and back into the gorge, it might be enough to keep them both alive.

She shot him a look of utter hatred and began stumbling down the hill. Bolan calculated as they descended. They had lost time climbing. Now they would have to make it up. The floor of the gorge twisted southeast, and that was the only choice they had now. He hoped the Russians would waste similar time following their trail to the summit, but he couldn't count on it.

The terrain leveled out, and Larquette furiously tried to yank her arm away, but his grip was a vise and he pulled her along, forcing her to keep pace. They passed the entrance to an old mine shaft. The overhanging beams of the old entrance were bleached bone white in the sun and sagged out from the rock. He had seen a half dozen of them in the past two days. Some were little more than holes in the hillside, carved out by old prospectors. Others were more extensive and showed the use of machines. But all of them had been small private attempts. The main mine complexes were located by the big base camp. Larquette looked longingly at the shaded entryway.

He pulled her on. "Move. It's a death trap."

Her anger and her pace were flagging, but she managed to snarl a weak "son of a bitch" at him as she stumbled on.

A stream of bullets ricocheted off the rocks above them. Bolan shoved Larquette behind him and raised her rifle. He worked the lever and fired three quick shots toward the enemy rifleman's muzzle blast. He dropped behind a corner of rock as other weapons joined in.

"Go back!"

They retraced their steps as signal whistles began shrieking behind them. They would have to double back and race toward the pursuit party, and try to beat them to a path east. Bolan pulled up short as answering whistles shrieked ahead of them.

The trap had swung shut.

He handed Larquette her rifle and unslung the big Weatherby. He saw a figure a hundred yards ahead and snapped off a quick shot to keep him down. The whistles shrieked in short coded bursts, the two forces communicating their whereabouts to each other.

Bolan glanced about furiously. They couldn't go forward and they couldn't go back, and they would be killed before they could ever climb up out of the gorge again. There was literally nowhere to go. The Executioner came to a grim decision and pointed to the entrance to the old mine.

"Run."

"But you said—"

"Run!"

They broke into a halting sprint. Bolan could hear men shouting above the scream of the whistles from both ends of the gorge. A weapon broke into full-automatic fire to their left. The lines of tracer smoke flared green as they followed overhead into the cool darkness of the mine. Bolan shoved Larquette down and took a prone firing position facing the entrance.

The firing outside had stopped.

Larquette lay gasping on the ground. "I thought you said it's a death trap."

Bolan nodded grimly as he pulled a grenade out of his pack.

"It is."

13

Lieutenant Rybenok was beaming as Baibakov approached.

"We have done it, Captain! The quarry is trapped."

Baibakov looked down at the mine entrance. An occasional stream of tracers streaked through the opening to keep the Americans down and to prevent return fire. He glanced back at Rybenok. "There is no other way out?"

"None, sir. All known mine shafts were surveyed prior to our tunneling. This shaft is long and has several branches, but only one entrance, and one vertical shaft that is already partially blocked. It is unscalable, but I have men watching it."

Baibakov glanced over the gorge. Soldiers stood at the top directly over the mine.

"Any casualties?"

"None, sir. As you said, I had to requisition some of our engineers to form the team, but they fought well, using cover, and drove the quarry before them to where you and your team were waiting." Rybenok grinned. "We have them!"

Baibakov folded his massive arms across his chest and stared down at the black eye of the mine entrance. "Not quite yet, Lieutenant." A hard smile formed on the giant's face. "But I commend your tactics, Rybenok, and the performance of the men under your command. I will note these things in my report to Major Ramzin."

Rybenok snapped off a crisp salute. "Your orders, Captain. Will we mount an assault?"

Baibakov calculated. He dearly wished to kill the Americans himself and present their bloody heads to Ramzin, but he had taken many casualties already. Both the man and the woman were well armed, and the entrance to the mine would be a killing zone for his men. Firepower and numbers would prevail, but the cost in men would be tremendous, and Ramzin wouldn't be pleased. In the twisting rat hole of a mine shaft, nerve gas would be uncertain. It would take time to get the gas and chemical suits from the base, and Baibakov didn't want to wait for nightfall.

"Who among your men is the senior engineer?"

Rybenok considered. "Lieutenant Galanskov, Captain."

"Bring him."

"Yes, sir. Your orders?"

Baibakov stared down at the mine entrance. "We will bury them."

THE EXECUTIONER LOOKED up the mine shaft. The outside was a circle of light that was slowly growing dimmer. He checked the luminous dial of his watch. It was close to seven o'clock, two hours until nightfall.

Larquette leaned against Bolan as tracers streamed into the mine. The supersonic crack of their passage was deafening in the cramped space, and they hurled out green incendiary sparks as they whined off the outcroppings around them. Bolan had made a shallow redoubt out of piled loose rock. They were safe as they lay behind it and could fire from cover when the Russians stormed the entrance. Still, they were pinned down, and they weren't going anywhere.

Larquette whispered hoarsely in his ear. "Do me a favor."

"What's that?"

"Tell me you have a plan."

"We wait until it gets dark. That is, if the Russians are willing to wait that long."

"Then what?"

"I have a flash-stun grenade left. When it gets dark I'm going to toss it outside. If they're watching the mine entrance with night-vision gear, it will blind them for a few seconds."

Larquette paused. "And then what?"

"Then we shoot our way out."

BAIBAKOV STARED at Galanskov. The combat engineer was a stocky, powerful man with iron gray hair cut close to his bullet-shaped skull. He reminded Baibakov of a badger.

"Can you do it?"

Galanskov shrugged. "Certainly, Captain. The combined explosive charges brought by both teams should be more than sufficient to do the task. The question is getting the charge deep enough into the mine. It will have to be very heavy and have to go in deep. And as I recall, sir, the last man who tried hurling a satchel charge at this American was blown to bits. I do not think you will have many volunteers."

Baibakov scowled, and the impudent dwarf stared back up at him impassively. The captain knew Galanskov only by reputation, but that was formidable. In Afghanistan he had been what the Americans called a "tunnel rat." He and handpicked teams had gone down into the dank tunnels and cave complexes the rebels had hidden in and rooted them out with pistols, knives and explosives.

He shook his head. "I will not be asking for volunteers."

Galanskov scowled. "It will be suicide! One man, alone, could not deliver a sufficient charge. It would be too heavy, even if he could get close enough without being killed. And breaking the explosives into two separate charges would not be a good plan, Captain. Correct, simultaneous delivery could not be assured."

"We will not break up the charge. We will do this as you have outlined."

Galanskov put his hands on his hips. "One man, alone, cannot deliver the charge deep enough."

Baibakov loomed over the engineer. "I can, Lieutenant."

Galanskov's eyes widened as he stared up at the man. He didn't like Baibakov, nor did he care for his reputation. But as he stared up into the giant's stone-colored eyes, he realized that there was very little that Baibakov wasn't capable of.

He saluted shakily. "Yes, sir. I will prepare the charge and see to covering teams immediately."

Baibakov nodded. It was good to see this badger have some respect shaken into him.

"See that it is so."

A HAIR OF GUNFIRE streamed into the mine. The Executioner flicked the Beretta's fire selector to full-auto.

"Get ready."

Larquette pulled back the hammer of her Winchester rifle and sighted down the barrel toward the mine opening. A hand grenade bounced in from an angle and rolled along the mine floor. Bolan grabbed Larquette and pushed her down flat behind their shallow barricade. The grenade detonated with a deafening crack, and shrapnel sparked and ricocheted off the walls around them. Bolan popped back up and raised the Beretta.

A column of fire roared into the mine and everything became white-hot flame. Bolan covered his eyes and fired a burst as he shoved Larquette back.

"Go back, deep as you can!"

The jet of flame roared deeper into the mine, licking the walls and the ceiling as it sought them. Bolan felt the heat wash over him as the fire reached out. For a second the flame winked out, and a small dark object hurtled into the mine. Bolan threw himself to the ground as the stun grenade detonated. The blast rolled him over as the concussion channeled down the shaft. He shook his head to clear the thundering in his ears and the flashing lights before his eyes. As he lurched to his knees, the flame roared into life and reached for him.

Behind Bolan, Larquette's rifle cracked in rapid succession. The flame suddenly cut off, and a man with tanks strapped to his back staggered and fell forward in the mine's entrance. Dimly the Executioner heard Larquette's rifle clack empty. He waved her back in the glow of the dripping fire.

"Back! Move Back!"

As Bolan turned, the tunnel entrance darkened. A giant figure filled it, and in its hands was a bag the size of a potato sack. The Executioner raised the Beretta, and the giant spun like a discus thrower, hurling the pack into the mine.

The pack was hissing.

He fired a burst up the tunnel, but the giant was already gone. Bolan turned and charged down the tunnel. Larquette stared at him questioningly from around a bend farther along.

"Move!"

As Bolan rounded the bend, the world dissolved into overwhelming sound and light.

BAIBAKOV SAT HEAVILY in the sand and shook his head. Even outside the mine, the back blast from the charge had thrown him ten feet. Small fires burned all around him in puddles of jellied fuel. He doubted there was much left of Karkov, the flamethrower man. He looked over at the mine entrance.

It wasn't there anymore. There was nothing but a pile of huge smoldering boulders and a blank rock face covered with burning streamers of fire. Thick, oily black smoke rose in choking clouds into the sky. A huge smile began crawling across the giant's face. He had seen his opponent. He had looked into the Yankee's shaken eyes, and then he had blown him to hell.

Baibakov threw back his head, and his laughter thundered through the gorge.

Rybenok and Galanskov approached him warily. Rybenok cleared his throat. "Captain, are you injured?"

Baibakov leaped to his feet with a savage grin. "I am well, Lieutenant." He turned his gaze on Galanskov, who took an involuntary step back from the gleam in the giant's eyes. "You were correct, Galanskov. I believe the charge was sufficient."

Baibakov roared at his own joke as Galanskov swallowed.

"Your orders, sir?"

The captain leisurely stretched his arms and shook his head. "Round up the men. Collect all equipment. Ignore the fire, but I want a cursory cleanup of any evidence. You have an hour and a half until dark.''

Galanskov and Rybenok saluted. Baibakov turned back to the smoldering remnant of the mine shaft and grinned.

He had enjoyed that.

14

"Report."

Ramzin smiled smugly. "Success, Comrade."

"How was it done?"

"Baibakov blew them to bits and then dropped a mountain on top of them."

The Witch paused. "You are joking."

"I assure you, I do not jest," he replied.

"Is there any evidence?"

"No, it was done on land owned by Red Star, and it is in remote, hard country near the border. I believe there is little to be discovered."

"Very good, Major Ramzin, I commend you and your men on the performance of their duties."

Ramzin wondered how much pain it had caused her to acknowledge his victory. He would bet much that she secretly wished he had failed.

"Thank you, Comrade, you are too kind. I am sure Captain Baibakov will be very pleased."

The Witch's voice was an icicle of politeness. "I am sure he will. Now, on to business. We have another shipment to be delivered within the next day and a half. You will have everything ready?"

"Everything will be ready. You will have the new helicopter here before that time?"

"Of course, Major. However, see that you are more careful with this one."

Ramzin ignored the barb. This battle had already been won. "Everything is on schedule?"

The Witch's voice grew contemplative. "There is some trouble with our Mexican friends. I believe they want more money."

Ramzin drummed his fingers on his desk. "Perhaps I should send Baibakov to speak with them."

"Hmm . . . that is not a bad suggestion, but I believe it would be better to keep things friendly. My husband will be coming within two days to negotiate with them. However, the next shipment will come across as planned."

Ramzin scowled. He had no love for the Witch, but he despised her husband. The man was a worm. "Is that wise?"

"He knows the Mexicans. He will make things clear to them without starting a war."

Ramzin snorted. "If you say so. What of replacements for our casualties?"

"Indeed, our contacts are recruiting in Moscow as we speak."

"That is good. The base is stretched thin. I have had to use engineers for soldiers."

"Ramzin, I do not like you endangering the engineers. They are extremely important, particularly now."

"I did not like using them, either. But they are combat trained, and it was necessary. They performed well and took no casualties."

"That is good."

The major leaned back in his chair. "Do not worry, Comrade, the second tunnel will be completed on time."

THE EXECUTIONER'S EYES cracked open through caked blood and dirt. There was no difference with his eyes open. Other than a slight shift in the pounding lights dancing before his eyes, everything was pitch-black. He wiggled his fingers and toes and found they were all still where they were supposed to be. He slowly flexed each muscle in his body and found that nearly all of them ached and throbbed. Every piece of equipment still strapped to him jabbed into his body. The Executioner became grimly aware of the fact that he was very cold and that he was going to live. He had no idea how long he had been unconscious.

He lay still and shivered. In a moment he would try to summon the will to sit up and look at his watch. As he lay and listened to the ringing in his ears, he dimly heard someone sobbing a few feet away. He cleared his parched throat with effort, and his voice came out as a croak.

"Patti?"

The Executioner grunted as a human weight landed on his chest and hands found his face. Arms wound around his neck and clutched him desperately. He could feel the hot wetness of tears against his cheek. Hands stroked unbelievingly at his brow and face.

"You're alive!"

Bolan took a painful breath. "It's good to see you, too."

She kept touching his face, as if to reassure herself that he was real and wouldn't suddenly disappear. More tears dripped onto Bolan's face, and her voice trembled.

"I thought you were dead. After the explosion, I couldn't find you. The goggles didn't work, and I called and called and you didn't answer. And I crawled up and down for hours trying to find you, and when I did..." Her voice broke and her hands shook him reprovingly. "You were so cold, and you were covered with blood, and dirt, and you didn't move, and I thought you had died, and I was all alone down here in the dark, and you..."

Days of pain, exhaustion and fear finally welled up out of her and she sobbed uncontrollably against Bolan for several moments. Then she pulled herself together and started to brush dirt off him. "Are you all right?"

The Executioner sat up painfully. "I'll live." He reached into a vest pocket of his blacksuit and pulled out a small plastic pack. The top came off with a pop, and he cracked an all-weather match into life off his thumbnail. In the guttering light, he could see Larquette. Her lip was split, and her face was caked with dirt and dust. Her eyes were puffy from crying, and tears had drawn long, dark streaks down her cheeks. The majority of her hair had escaped her ponytail and hung all about in wild disarray. Bolan smiled at her in the flickering glow.

"You look awful."

Her lips twisted in amused annoyance. "Screw you, buddy."

Bolan waved the match out as it reached his thumb, and they were in darkness again. He took her hand and stood. "Do you still have the fanny pack I gave you?"

Larquette nodded and twisted it around her waist. Bolan unzipped it and pulled out a thin, rubber-armored flashlight. She stared at him sheepishly in the sudden illumination.

"You mean I had a flashlight all this time?"

Bolan shrugged and trained the light up the tunnel, and his face tightened. He didn't like what he saw. The collapse of the entrance was total. He estimated the length where the blockage started, and he knew at least twenty to thirty feet of dirt and rock lay between them and the outside. There was no way they could dig through it. He turned and played the light along the walls.

Larquette looked around unhappily. "What do we do?"

"Keep looking."

The mine forked, and Bolan chose the right-hand path, which ran a hundred feet and dead-ended. They retraced their steps and took the left bend. As they went farther into the mine, Bolan felt a draft and his feet kicked a pile of rubble on the floor. He scanned the light over their heads. A circular opening yawned above them. Bolan nodded.

"There."

THE AIR SMASHED from the Executioner's lungs as he fell heavily to the floor of the mine. His flashlight rose from the ground where it had fallen, and Larquette rushed to him.

"Are you all right?"

He had new bruises to add to the old ones, and his hands were cut from trying to slow his descent. "Nothing's broken. Save the batteries."

Bolan grimaced as the light clicked off. It was the third time he had fallen, and this time he had been unable to catch himself. The shaft above was choked and crumbling with old rock and dirt. Still more of the blockage was dangerously new, and had been generated by the explosion of the Russian charge. When he shone the light up the shaft, it was blocked thirty feet up by tenuously jammed rock and debris. However, that wasn't the worst of his problems. Fifteen feet below the jam, the walls of the shaft crumbled into dirt under his hands and boots. There was no purchase to be had. It was unscalable. Even if he was fresh and had proper gear, a vertical ascent of the shaft would be nearly impossible.

He raised himself into a sitting position, running the calculations through his mind for the hundredth time, only to have the answers stay grimly the same. He couldn't climb the shaft. Thirty feet of rock blocked the entrance to the mine, and even with the single stick of C-4 plastic explosive he had left, there was no way they could dig their way out before thirst and exhaustion finished them. Bolan searched his mind in the blackness, looking for anything he could use. He turned tools and gear he had in his pack over and over, and all of them remained grossly insufficient. His adversary was the very earth itself. It was silent and implacable. He couldn't outthink it or outshoot it. Skills that had won a hundred battles paled before the thousand tons of rock encasing them. The truth was as inescapable as the mine itself.

They were trapped.

Larquette took his hands in hers and wiped the dirt out of his cuts with her bandanna. Her hands shook as she spoke. "We can't climb out, can we?"

Bolan took a deep breath. They had been through too much together for him to lie to her.

"No."

Her voice was very small in the blackness. "Then we're going to die down here."

15

Ramzin watched the helicopter as it came in. The American JetRanger was a capable craft, but he idly wished he had a real Russian gunship. The Yankee commando wouldn't have shot down a Hind with his big rifle. The Hind was armored like a tank and armed like one, as well. The American's rifle would have been as useful to him as a pop gun, and the major's operation wouldn't now be stretched so thin with casualties. Ramzin shook his head. It would be weeks before the replacements could be smuggled in from Moscow, and they wouldn't be his own handpicked veterans. Ramzin squinted into the rotorwash as the helicopter landed. The Yankee and his woman had cost him much.

He hoped they were enjoying themselves in hell.

The major scowled as the helicopter doors slid open and the Witch's husband clambered out. The Scarecrow bent over double and held his ridiculous cowboy hat in place as he jogged out under the wind of the rotor blades. The broomstick strode up to Ramzin in his pinstripe suit and high-heeled boots and stuck out his hand.

Ramzin took the hand and pumped it twice with mild repugnance. It was as if the man had handed him a fish.

"Howdy!"

Ramzin stood at attention. "Greetings, Comrade. I trust you had a most pleasant journey."

The major had to smother a grin as the man looked at him askance. He knew the word *comrade*—anything reminding this mole of his native land—made him nervous. The man hid his annoyance, as if Ramzin had called him *pardner*.

"The flight was fine, but damn if it isn't a hot one. How are things going on your end?"

Ramzin had to give the Scarecrow credit. He was indistinguishable from an American in both manner and speech.

"It goes well. Schedule proceeds apace. Tonight's shipment will go through as planned. I am to understand you are going south to perform negotiations."

The Scarecrow frowned at him. "Really, Ramzin, you've got to work on your English."

Ramzin stared at him expressionlessly. "Yes, Comrade, exactly so."

The two men stared at each other for a moment. "Do you have someplace where I can freshen up?"

"Surely. We will be taking in the shipment soon, and afterward I will give you a tour of the facilities. In the morning I will have you flown across the border." Ramzin snapped his fingers. "Lukov, take our guest inside and see to his needs."

Lukov came forward and took the Scarecrow's bags, and Ramzin watched as they went into the compound.

He looked forward to the day that Baibakov and the Scarecrow would have a long conversation. He thought that day might come sooner than he had originally planned.

THE EXECUTIONER AWOKE. The ground was trembling. He felt Larquette's hand press on his chest as she felt it, too.

"What is it?"

The shaking grew, and Bolan felt dust rain on him from the ceiling of the mine. He turned on the flashlight, then put his hand on the wall behind them and felt the vibrations. The minilight seemed as bright as the sun after hours of total darkness. Dust drifted down in its glare as the rumbling increased. Bolan put his ear to the wall and detected a metallic rattling beneath the dull roar building in the mine.

Larquette glanced about nervously. "Is it an earthquake?"

"I don't think so."

"Then what?"

Bolan took her hand and put it against the wall. "What do you feel?"

"It's shaking."

"It's vibrating. Listen, what do you hear?"

Larquette bent and put her ear to the wall. "It's rumbling . . . and there's another sound, like an echo." She suddenly shot to her feet. "We're over the tunnel!"

Bolan ran his hand along the wall as he walked deeper into the mine. "We're close." The Executioner brought up the map of Crucible in his mind. This corner of hills was south of the mining complex, almost directly between it and Mexico. He put his ear to the wall again and inched along its surface. The metallic sound got louder the deeper he went.

He stopped. "Patti, stay here and listen."

She put her ear to the wall. "It's louder."

Bolan went down the tunnel ten feet farther, and the sound started to lessen. The shaking was dying down. "Follow me slowly, and tell me where it sounds loudest to you."

"It's starting to lessen already."

The convoy was passing them by. "Walk toward me."

They inched toward each other. Larquette stopped five feet away from him. "It got louder here for a second, but now it's fading."

Bolan stood behind her and stared at the section of wall in the small circle of light. Larquette rose from her crouch. "It's gone."

He nodded. "Stay at this spot for a moment." The soldier walked back up the tunnel to his pack and rummaged through its many small compartments. He withdrew the stick of C-4 and the remote detonator. One stick. Approximately a pound of high explosive. The question was, would it be enough? The deep end of the mine seemed to be more earth than rock, but it was aggregate, and he had no idea what lay beneath it.

It was their only chance. It would have to be enough.

Bolan took out his fighting knife and returned to Larquette. He began corkscrewing the chisel point of the Cold Steel Tanto blade into the wall. It gouged out the packed earth and rock with some difficulty. Larquette watched as he strained against the wall, slowly producing a hole.

"Is there anything I can do?"

Bolan grunted with effort. "Cross your fingers." He cursed as the point of the knife suddenly scraped solid rock.

He was approximately nine inches in. He took the C-4 and shaped it into a cone with his hands.

"Scoop up some of that dirt."

Larquette picked up handfuls of dirt as he placed the charge and inserted the fuse capsule. "Help me pack it in."

Together they packed the charge into the wall and tamped it down. They stood, and Bolan unslung the canteen. It was less than a third full. "Here, finish it."

"Why don't we split it?"

Bolan sighed. "All right."

They finished the water all too quickly. Bolan took the detonator and pulled out its antenna. "Get to the far end of the tunnel and cover your ears."

The Executioner ran his hand over the covered charge. He had shaped it to blow inward as much as possible. As a field expedient, it wasn't too bad. He walked back down the tunnel and crouched by Larquette. "Turn away from the blast."

Bolan clicked off the flashlight. In the blackness a dim red light blinked as he armed the charge. A hand slid into his and squeezed it.

He squeezed back. "You ready?"

She whispered in his ear. "Can I push the button?"

The Executioner smiled in the dark. "Give me your other hand." He took her hand and placed her finger over the firing switch. "Just flick it forward."

The hand in his squeezed tighter. "Now?"

"Now."

"VERY IMPRESSIVE, Ramzin."

The major accepted the compliment as they watched from the tower while the trucks emerged from the warehouse. It *was* impressive. Who could dream that they had dug a tunnel between Mexico and the United States? Much less a tunnel that one could run trucks through. It had been quite a feat, and his combat engineers had been consistently ahead of schedule. Ramzin had to admit there was much about America that he liked. If one had the money, any equipment and materials were yours immediately for the asking.

Even with military priority, a project like this in the old Soviet Union would have taken twice as long.

The labor had been easy, as well. Americans would have
asked questions, but there was no shortage of unquestion-
ing labor on the other side of the border. They lined up and
fought to get in the trucks and come to the border to work.
Even with the heavy earth-moving machines, there had been
an enormous amount of backbreaking hand labor, and the
Mexicans killed themselves to do it, grateful for the three
meals a day and looking forward to being taken across the
border with their families with money in their pockets.

That stuck in Ramzin's craw. He had done many things
in his time and killed many innocents in Afghanistan, but
that had been war. The order to kill the laborers when the
second tunnel was completed shook even him in its cold
brutality. Ramzin understood it all too well. They couldn't
have hundreds of illegal aliens who knew of the tunnel running around and getting arrested in the United States, but he
was glad that a man like Baibakov was here to carry out such
orders.

He had enough demons of his own without adding more.

The Scarecrow turned to him. "You say the second tunnel will be ready for business on time?"

"It will be finished ahead of schedule. Two weeks ahead
by current projections."

The Scarecrow whistled. "Damn fine work, Ramzin.
Damn fine work."

Ramzin despised the man but accepted the compliment
with pride. Worm or not, the worm was right. "Tomorrow
you will be flown to Mexico. Do you wish bodyguards?"

The Scarecrow chuckled. "Oh, I don't think that'll be
necessary, but if it makes you feel any better, you can as-
sign me two good men."

Ramzin watched as the last truck maneuvered out of the
warehouse. So far they had smuggled small things such as
guns, cigarettes, items easily distributed and hard to trace.
Soon the Witch and her bean-pole husband would establish
proper channels, and then they would begin funneling the
drugs. After that, if the pipeline proved safe, and certain
groups could produce the right amount of money, other,

more lethal commodities would be smuggled in. In the Moscow black market, if one had the money, one could obtain the materials to make nuclear weapons. Chemical and biological weapons of devastating power could be had, as well.

Ramzin shook his head. Now, with his help, the enemies of the United States could deliver such death right into the Yankee's backyards.

16

The Executioner yawned to clear the ringing from his ears and flicked on the flashlight. "Are you all right?"

Larquette rose and dusted herself off. "I thought it would be bigger."

"It was a shaped charge. Its purpose was to bore a hole." Bolan shook the flashlight in his hand as it dimmed for a moment. "Let's go see how we did."

He played the light along the wall as they came to the hole. Dirt and rock littered the floor of the mine below the ragged crater. Bolan estimated the hole was about three feet in diameter and four feet deep. As he shone the light inside, they were greeted by the dull reflection of scratched and dented galvanized metal. Larquette reached in and touched the metal experimentally. "It's warm. What is it?"

Bolan ran his hand along the pitted surface. "A ventilator shaft. Their tunnel is at least five or six miles long. They have to have ventilation or the truck drivers would asphyxiate from their own exhaust fumes before they ever reached the other side. There should be several dozen of them along the corridor.

Larquette poked it with her finger. "Can we get in?"

Bolan drew his fighting knife. "Step back." He took a hammer grip on the knife and drove it forward. Sparks shrieked off of the metal as the point punched through. He nodded with satisfaction. "I think so. Help me dig away more dirt."

Together they pried away the earth and rock around the metal, creating a hole they could both crawl through. Bolan drew the Beretta 93-R and flicked the selector to single shot.

He raised an arm in front of his face and leaned into the hole. "Cover your eyes."

The roar of 9 mm fire was deafening in the close confines of the mine. Bolan methodically emptied the clip, creating a long arcing line of ragged holes from top to bottom. He reloaded and repeated the procedure, until more than three dozen holes formed a loose four-foot circle in the abused metal. He handed Larquette the Beretta and drew his knife again.

"Here goes nothing."

Bolan pushed the knife into the top hole and ripped downward with a squealing of protesting steel. The spine of his knife was stronger than the sheet steel of the shaft, and he cut in sharp yanks, connecting each hole with the last. When he got to the bottom, he restarted at the top of the exposed metal and ripped down to draw the other half of the circle. With a last yank the jagged oblong of metal fell free. Bolan took a deep breath and wiped his brow.

"Shine the light down it."

Larquette shone the dimming light into the shaft. It was roughly five feet wide, and beyond the range of the minilight it plunged into blackness. A cold breeze that smelled of diesel fumes blew up from below and ruffled their hair. She looked back at him and shrugged. "Shall we?"

Bolan nodded. "Let's get our stuff."

They went back to their pile of gear, and Bolan bent down and examined it. The big Weatherby's optical sight had been fractured by the Russian charge, and the heavy rifle would make climbing awkward. He detached the sling and regretfully abandoned the weapon. Much of his equipment had been damaged in the blast and rockfall. His night-vision goggles had been lost in the explosion, and the lenses of Larquette's were cracked and nonfunctioning. There was really precious little left that was usable. He reloaded the Beretta and checked the .44 Magnum Desert Eagle. He secured his one remaining stun grenade and his binoculars and stood. Larquette looked up at him as she turned her fanny pack inside out. There were a few spare shells for her revolver and a battered-looking high-energy food bar.

"So we're traveling light."

"Looks that way."

Bolan looped the sling around Larquette's rifle and slung it around his back along with the empty canteen. "All right. I'll go first. Always keep two arms or two legs supporting your weight. Try not to fall on me."

She gave him a withering look and followed him to the hole. Bolan stuck the minilight between his teeth, eased past the ragged metal edges of the hole and put his boots against the shaft walls. The interior metal was unfinished, and the walls were a comfortable distance apart. He supported himself with his palms and eased downward. Four feet in, his feet met a thin metal lip where sections of the shaft joined, and he smiled in the dark. The ventilator shaft almost had its own ladder.

"All right. Follow me. Use my shoulders for support until you get set."

Bolan tensed against the cold metal walls as a pair of boots settled on his shoulders. "I'm going to ease down. Put your boots out and you'll feel an edge."

Her feet found the narrow lip, and she supported her own weight. Section by section they worked their way down in the dim glow of the fading flashlight. Bolan was more exhausted than he wanted to admit, and his shoulders ached as he took her weight between sections. The rough metal of the shaft ground against his lacerated hands as he pressed against them. As they descended, the low thrumming of the ventilation fan grew louder. Slowly the big fan blades came into view.

Bolan guided her feet to the next lip. "Stay here a minute." He quickly descended to the fan. Each blade was about three feet long and slowly turned before the entrance of the shaft. He unslung the Winchester and bent closer. The fan was moving slowly and probably ran on a continuous maintenance cycle rather than being turned off. Metal struts came up from the fan and bolted into the shaft. Bolan stuck the Winchester's barrel between the blades. The rifle rotated around in his hand, then stuck fast against one of the struts. The fan motor groaned as its blades froze and began to emit an unhappy whine. Bolan quickly unwound the rifle sling and knotted one end around one of the support struts. Beneath him the tunnel was dimly lit, and the floor was some twenty feet below. Bolan squeezed between the frozen blades, supporting himself with his hands. He grasped a strut, then put his weight on the sling.

The web held, and Bolan hung suspended in the tunnel. The webbing cut into his torn hands as he eased himself down the dangling six foot strap. He let go and dropped the remaining distance, then rose and looked about. The tunnel was wide enough to allow a truck to drive through it with a few feet of clearance on the top and the sides. Dim orange lights tracked off in both directions along the ceiling. Bolan looked up.

"Squeeze past the fan and grab the sling, then ease down it. Drop when you get to the end."

In a few moments Larquette's leg appeared and dangled between the fan blades. She hung from a strut and grabbed the sling.

"All right, just ease onto it and—"

Larquette suddenly slid down the sling out of control. She let out a yelp and caught herself near the end, then the strap slid from her hand. Bolan grunted as her weight hit him. He collapsed and went into a roll as he fell back. For a moment they lay together in a heap.

"Are you all right?"

Larquette rubbed her friction-burned hands. "Your hands bled all over the strap. It was too slippery for me to hold on to." She looked around and suddenly grinned. "We're out!"

Bolan nodded as he rose and helped her to her feet. "We made it."

She looked up and down the tunnel. "Which way do we go?"

He drew the Beretta and flicked the fire selector to 3-round burst mode.

"I remember promising I'd take you to Mexico."

RAMZIN SHOOK HANDS with the Scarecrow distastefully as the helicopter's rotors slowly began to revolve in the morning calm. "A pleasant journey. I wish you success in your negotiations."

The Scarecrow pumped Ramzin's hand. "Thanks for the hospitality. This is really quite a setup you're running. It's every bit as impressive as I'd been told. I think this little venture is going to succeed."

"Thank you. I have taken the liberty of assigning you two handpicked men of my command as bodyguards."

The Scarecrow smiled with a condescending shrug. "If you say so. Can't hurt to show a little muscle to the Mexicans. They always appreciate these things."

Ramzin nodded sagely. "Baibakov! Gorchenko!"

Baibakov ducked his head as he came out of the shack and strode to the pad. Gorchenko followed quickly behind him. Gorchenko was the second largest man on the base and as strong as an ox, but Baibakov dwarfed him. Ramzin grinned. The giant's huge frame strained against the khaki pants and oversize Hawaiian shirt he wore. A battered red-denim baseball cap covered his blond crew cut at a jaunty angle, and he wore size seventeen civilian deck shoes. Ramzin well remembered the giant's delight at discovering the American Big & Tall clothes catalog. Baibakov walked up and saluted, then turned and gave the Scarecrow a huge smile.

"Greetings, Comrade!"

The Scarecrow flinched involuntarily as Baibakov loomed over him. At six and a half feet tall, the mole wasn't used to having someone look down on him, much less someone with three to four times his body mass. Gorchenko presented himself in similar clothes and snapped the Scarecrow a smart salute. Except for their huge size, they looked like Americans on holiday, yet beneath their casual clothes each man was armed to the teeth. The Scarecrow shot Ramzin a leery look. Like most humans Ramzin knew, Baibakov terrified him.

"Really, Ramzin, do you think all this security is necessary?"

The major kept a straight face with effort. "Certainly. Your safety is paramount to the continuing success of this operation, and, as you have said, Comrade, it cannot hurt to show a little muscle. Besides, the Mexicans appreciate these things."

Baibakov and Gorchenko smiled at the Scarecrow ingratiatingly. Ramzin clapped him on the shoulder. "They will appreciate Baibakov and Gorchenko, I am sure of it."

The Scarecrow frowned. "They hardly speak much English, Ramzin, much less the local lingo."

Ramzin nodded. "True, but I believe their presence alone may be helpful to you in your negotiations."

The Scarecrow looked at Ramzin long and hard, then stared at Baibakov and Gorchenko. He flicked his smile on as if he were turning on a light. "Well, they certainly can't hurt, and they'll sure give the Mexicans something to think about. I appreciate your concern for my safety, Ramzin. I've made a note of it."

"That is good. Have a pleasant journey, Comrade. I wish you luck."

The Scarecrow tipped his cowboy hat. "Take care."

Ramzin folded his arms and watched as the three men embarked onto the helicopter. He smiled as the helicopter slowly lifted off the pad, then leaned south as it banked toward Mexico. The Scarecrow was correct. Neither Baibakov nor Gorchenko were very proficient at speaking English. However, after the war in Afghanistan, both of them had done a training tour in Cuba under Ramzin's command as tactical advisers to Fidel Castro's Trupas Especial commandos.

Both men spoke excellent Spanish, and there was nothing that would transpire at the negotiations that wouldn't be reported back to him.

Ramzin nodded with grim satisfaction as the helicopter disappeared into the morning sky.

Two could play at this game of spies.

17

The Executioner slid into the shadows and scanned the area. A padlocked gate made of storm fencing covered the tunnel entrance, and a steep concrete ramp extended upward to a large sliding corrugated steel door. Larquette crouched by his side.

"How do we get in?"

A large combination lock kept the fence shut. Bolan pulled the Beretta's sound suppressor out of a pouch in his web gear and threaded it onto the barrel. He ejected the magazine in the pistol and replaced it with the clip loaded with subsonic bullets.

"Look away."

The Beretta gave a single low hiss from the muzzle and a metallic click as its slide cycled. The lock jerked on its chain as the bullet struck it, then clattered back against the fence. It hung twisted and sprung on one end of its locking loop. Bolan unhooked it and opened the fence a crack. He and Larquette slid through, and he replaced the lock on its chain. The lock would no longer close, and a ragged hole gaped in its brass body. It would fail anything more than a casual glance, but the Executioner was betting no one would be down in the actual tunnel entrance until the next convoy came through. They walked up the ramp to the door, which had a small switch panel set in the door. Bolan put his ear to the door and was greeted by silence.

"What's on the other side?" Larquette whispered.

Bolan stood. "I'd suspect another warehouse, big enough to drive trucks into like the one on the other side of the border."

"How do we get in?"

"We push the button." Bolan pushed the green button in the panel and the door jerked and started to slide open. The Executioner spoke quietly. "Don't shoot unless you absolutely have to. My pistol is silenced, but that magnum of yours will tell everyone there's a firefight going on."

Larquette nodded and took a two-handed shooting stance as the door slid open. As the door opened up wide enough, Bolan dived through and rolled up into a firing crouch. The Beretta's silenced muzzle scanned the interior.

There was nothing.

The interior of the warehouse was a darkened cavern. The lights were off and the only light was the diffuse, early-morning sun glowing dimly through opaque, plastic wire-mesh windows set high into the walls near the ceiling. In one corner of the warehouse a set of wooden stairs led to an elevated office that overlooked the floor.

Larquette trained her pistol around the cavernous interior with a frown. "I can't believe they just left the place open and empty."

Bolan shook his head. "They didn't. They just don't expect anyone to come in from this direction. I don't think they want anyone in the warehouse unless there's an operation going on, and I'd bet there are guards outside to keep it that way."

"So how do we get out without getting shot?"

Bolan glanced up at the office. "We walk out."

"Oh, and how do we manage that?"

He looked her up and down critically. "First, you need a bath."

ENRIQUE OCHOA WATCHED the helicopter land in the red morning light. As the rotors slowed, the lanky gringo clambered out and waved at him with his cowboy hat. Ochoa smiled and waved back.

The bean pole had never ridden a horse in his life.

A large man got out after him and looked about warily. Ochoa frowned. The gringo had never brought bodyguards with him before. A third man got out, and the Mexican's eyes bulged in disbelief.

He was the largest human being Ochoa had ever seen in his life. The man was a monster. He unfolded himself from the helicopter and when he passed the turning rotor blades and straightened, Ochoa realized the man had to be at least seven feet tall, and for all his massive size he moved with the graceful ease of a jaguar. His presence dominated everything. Ochoa's bodyguards shifted nervously as the trio walked forward. The giant had the machismo of a mountain.

As they approached, the gringo replaced his wide-brimmed hat and stuck out his hand.

"A pleasure, Señor Ochoa, as always."

The Mexican took his hand. "Yes, Lyle, it is good of you to come on such short notice."

"I understand you have some financial questions you wish to discuss."

Ochoa glanced warily at the giant. He had heard the stories that had circulated among the tunnel workers of an immense Russian. The giant smiled down at him, and Ochoa had to suppress the urge to take a step back.

He spread his hands. "Yes, but let us discuss business later. Come, let us go to the hacienda. I suspect you and your friends are hungry and would like to refresh yourselves."

The Scarecrow tipped his hat. "Awfully kind of you."

Ochoa waved them to the vehicles parked by the helicopter pad. As they drove through the rolling ranch land to the hacienda, the American made small talk. Ochoa nodded his head as they spoke of the weather and his eyes drifted to the car ahead of them, where the man's companions rode. He understood what was happening all too well. He had demanded more money, and now the gringo came with giants at his side.

He suspected he was in for some very hard bargaining.

LARQUETTE STARED at herself in the small cubicle mirror.

"I look ridiculous."

The office bathroom was little more than a chemical toilet and a tiny sink, but after three days in the desert, running water was a godsend. Between that and eating the last of their food, they looked and felt almost human again. Larquette pushed at her damp hair and observed the modifications the Executioner had made to her clothes with a frown.

He had turned her khaki uniform pants into extremely short cutoffs with his fighting knife. Her uniform shirt was casually tied around her waist and the T-shirt she had worn beneath was knotted up around her ribs to show off her tanned midriff. He had cut the neck of the T-shirt into a plunging scoop, and there was very little of her figure left to the imagination.

"My butt is hanging out." Her eyes narrowed. "Everything is hanging out."

Bolan looked at her critically. "Lose the bra."

Larquette folded her arms and glared.

"Just do it."

She scowled at him. "Turn around."

He turned and looked at himself in the mirror. The blacksuit he wore wasn't exactly Russian issue, but there wasn't much he could do about that. He would have to rely on the Mexicans not knowing the difference. He had managed minor repairs with the needle and thread from his pack, but he was far from looking parade ground ready. The weapons he had strapped all over him would have to do most of his talking for him.

A bra sailed past Bolan's shoulder and landed in the corner. He turned, looked at Larquette and grinned at her. She looked like something out of a sleazy calendar.

She put her hands on her hips. "So just what am I supposed to be, anyway?"

Bolan spread his hands. "My squeeze."

She looked down at herself sourly. "I look like a whore."

"Exactly."

Larquette spread her arms. "So how am I supposed to hide a .357 Magnum in this desert-bunny outfit?"

"You can't. Take this." Bolan took his snub-nosed Smith & Wesson Centennial revolver from his ankle holster. He lifted up her uniform shirt and tucked the pistol in her waistband. "Wear it in the small of your back, like this. Keep the shirt over it."

She adjusted the little revolver into a more comfortable position, then draped the shirt back over it. She frowned at the corner where her .357 Magnum and pistol belt lay with her badge, bra and nameplate. "So we just walk out of here like this?"

"Bold as brass. You ready?"

"Ready as I'll ever be."

Bolan nodded. "Good."

They left the office and descended to the warehouse floor. Bolan went to the front door and listened. He leaned over and whispered in Larquette's ear. "I hear at least two people outside speaking Spanish. Whatever I do, just play along, and act stupid."

He took Larquette's hand before she could say anything and flung the door open.

"*¡Madre de Dios!*" The two guards jumped as Bolan strode out the door. Both men were armed with M-16 rifles. They fumbled with their weapons and looked back and forth at each other in confusion. They gawked at Bolan in his blacksuit, and at his weapons, and they stared agog at Larquette.

One of them stammered. "*Señor, qué...*"

Bolan walked up to the man and loomed over him. "*Gdeh vahsh athawjihyess messta?*"

The man stared up at him uncomprehendingly. "*¿Que?*"

Bolan scowled and scratched his chin in thought. "Mm...hacienda?"

The man brightened. "*¡Ah! ¡Sí!*" He pointed down the road from the warehouse. While the Russians had hidden their side of the tunnel in a mining operation, the southern end came out in the midst of a large cattle ranch. Barbed wire fencing stretched out across the horizon, and cows dotted the scrubby hillsides. Outlying buildings were scattered on the landscape, and Bolan could smell the charnel odors of a slaughterhouse on the wind. Approximately a mile and a half away a large hacienda complex sat on a low rise.

Bolan nodded at the man and smiled. "*Spaseeba, Comrade!*" He clapped him on the shoulder in friendly fashion. "*Dasveedanya...eh...*" Bolan frowned in immense concentration, then suddenly grinned at the guard. *"¡Gracias! ¡Muchas gracias!"*

The guard smiled and nodded happily. *"De nada."*

Bolan swatted Larquette on the behind, and she squealed admirably and ran ahead down the road. The guards laughed as Bolan grinned and gave them a wave. Larquette muttered under her breath as they walked down the dusty road. "Okay, I got the part about the hacienda, but what did you say to them?"

"I asked them where the bathroom was in Russian."

She snorted. "Do you think we fooled them?"

"They probably don't know what to think. Right now they think I just got some in the warehouse. A lot depends on whether they actually know about the tunnel or just think they're guarding a building. The fact that we're walking will seem strange either way if they stop and think about it, but with any luck they'll spend more time thinking about you."

She rolled her eyes. "With any luck. What do we do when we get to the hacienda?"

"We grab a vehicle, get out of here and contact Hal Brognola."

"That easy?"

"With any luck."

BAIBAKOV GRINNED as he reclined in a chair made of cattle hide and interwoven horns. It creaked ominously under his weight but he liked it. He liked everything about the room. The Mexican had several fine hunting rifles mounted on the wall and a number of impressive trophies. A snarling jaguar mounted in midleap dominated the left side of the room. Baibakov stared at it in admiration. The spotted beast was much smaller than a red grizzly or a Russian boar, but the predator's symmetry was magnificent. He sighed wistfully. For years he had yearned to hunt a big cat. If it wasn't for the fact that it would compromise his mission, he would very much have liked to spend hours discussing hunting in South America with this Enrique Ochoa.

The captain shrugged. It was a pity he would have to kill him before they ever got the chance.

Ochoa and the Scarecrow chatted away blithely, ignoring Baibakov and Gorchenko's existence. Gorchenko sat flopped on the overstuffed sofa by the window with his head tilted back and watched the ceiling fan slowly turn. He was the epitome of a soldier on a boring assignment. Baibakov examined the jaguar again as he listened. The Spanish they spoke was different than the Cuban he had learned. The Mexicans spoke more softly and with more musical inflection compared to the harsh speech of the soldiers he had trained with in Havana, but Baibakov understood it well enough.

The Scarecrow had already referred to him as a psychotic ape three times.

Ochoa steepled his hands and peered at Baibakov as he spoke with the Scarecrow. "Your giant seems to like my jaguar."

The Scarecrow sneered. "He fancies himself a hunter."

The Mexican raised an intrigued eyebrow. "Oh?"

"If you call slaughtering women and children hunting."

"Oh, that is too bad. There is some excellent antelope hunting on my ranch land. I had thought he might also enjoy hunting javelina with handguns."

Baibakov cringed inwardly and examined the wall clock.

The Scarecrow changed the subject. "So you feel your expenses have mounted?"

Ochoa stared at the ceiling meditatively. "Let me put it this way, my friend. In the United States you were worried about discovery if you used locals to dig the tunnel. So you had Ramzin and his combat engineers and soldiers come. A small mining concern, with foreign backing, in mines that were already considered mined out. It drew little attention. Here in my country, it is more of a question of paying people to make sure that nothing comes to anyone's attention. No one in the local government knows we have dug a tunnel between Mexico and the United States, but most of them are aware that I am doing something that is illegal. It is a question of paying them enough so that they do not particularly care what that thing might be. You understand?"

"They want more money?"

Ochoa spread his hands helplessly. "My friend, everyone wants more money."

The Scarecrow stared at him expressionlessly. "I see."

The Mexican examined his nails. "There is a problem?"

"No, I believe you may see a substantial increase in profit."

Ochoa peered at him in mild interest. "Really?"

"Yes, we will soon be expecting much more profitable cargoes, and as our partner, you of course will see your share of this."

"That is good to know, but what of my immediate expenses?"

"The situation is turbulent at the moment."

"I had heard you encountered some local difficulty, but had been led to assume that it had been resolved."

"It has, and that is part of it. We sustained casualties. We must replace men and material. But the real problem is Ramzin."

Ochoa leaned back in his chair. "Really? How so?"

The Scarecrow became agitated. "He runs his end like a military camp. He disobeys orders and dictates his own agenda. He makes veiled threats. I believe in time he intends to wrest control of the operation from us."

The Mexican put his hands to his chest. "Us?"

The Scarecrow glared. "I mean the American side of the tunnel."

Ochoa nodded. "Yes, he does seem very capable."

"He is due to be replaced with someone more tractable."

"So fine, have him killed. What is the problem?"

"The problem is that killing Ramzin is easier said than done. His men are utterly loyal to him, and they fear and respect the giant."

Ochoa sneered. "I can have the giant killed right now, and a hundred armed men down the tunnel in an hour."

The Scarecrow smiled at Ochoa sadly. "Perhaps your men could kill the giant, if they were very lucky, but God only knows how many of them he would take to hell with him in the attempt. As for your gunmen, I am sure they are adequate for pushing about peasants, but Ramzin and his soldiers would slaughter them like sheep. Then they would come across the border and lay waste to half of Sonora in vengeance. Do not ever underestimate Ramzin or his men. They are utterly dangerous."

Baibakov yawned and looked at his watch. It was the most intelligent thing he had ever heard the Scarecrow say.

Ochoa nodded. "So what do you propose?"

"We finish the second tunnel. We keep to the shipment schedules as planned. When the time is right, I will have both men killed and suitable replacements ready to step in. As for now, would, say, ten million dollars keep everyone happy?"

Ochoa smiled delightedly. "Certainly. You are most generous." He looked at Baibakov and Gorchenko. "Well, since I am not going to kill these men today, perhaps they would like some breakfast?"

The Scarecrow turned and smiled in Baibakov's face as he spoke sunnily in Spanish. "You, circus freak, are you ready for your raw meat now?"

Ochoa stared at the Scarecrow aghast.

Baibakov tilted his head and peered at the Scarecrow like a dog who has heard a sound it didn't recognize. *"Da?"*

The Scarecrow switched to Russian. "Our host wishes to know if you and Gorchenko would like breakfast."

"Yes, thank you, Comrade."

Baibakov and Gorchenko rose and flanked the Scarecrow. The giant could hardly contain himself as Ochoa led them out onto the veranda. He stared at the back of the Scarecrow's scrawny neck in speculation, wandering what kind of struggle the broomstick would put up when he killed him.

18

Bolan yanked Larquette into the bushes as the giant came out onto the patio.

Approaching the hacienda had been uneventful. Bolan had maintained a military bearing and Larquette had smiled and giggled. It was remarkably easy. Bolan's eyes narrowed as the giant stood on the veranda, stretched his huge arms and took in the morning air.

The free ride was over.

Larquette whispered in his ear. "What is it?"

Bolan pointed through the hedge.

Larquette muttered under her breath. "Just what we need, Son of Kong."

A second man came out, and by his demeanor the Executioner could tell he was a soldier. Two Mexicans with M-16 rifles followed. A tall, thin man in a Western-cut suit and an extremely well dressed man followed. They seated themselves around a table, and servants began to bring food as the men with rifles stood and watched. Larquette's hand clenched on Bolan's arm.

"What?"

Larquette gaped through the bushes. "I know him...I know both of them!"

"Who are they?"

She pointed at the Mexican. "That's Enrique Ochoa, the local crime lord. He was coming across the border and getting into trouble when I was in high school."

Bolan nodded. He knew the Russians had to have a Mexican connection. He jerked his head. "Who's the urban cowboy?"

Larquette stared at him like he was stupid. "Well that's Lyle Tyler. He must own at least a tenth of everything in Arizona. Real estate, car dealerships, shopping malls, you name it. He's a big wheel in southern Arizona. My father never could stand the man."

"You've met him?"

"Once, when I met his wife at a law conference in Phoenix."

"Who's that?"

"I mentioned her before, Anne Tyler."

Bolan's eyes flared.

Larquette nodded. "Kinda looks like a pattern, doesn't it?"

"The question is, what's he doing with a bunch of Russian Special Forces types."

She shrugged. "Ask him."

Bolan's lips tightened. "I think I'll have to."

"You know, every second we stand here staring we're asking for trouble."

"I know, but we can't grab a vehicle without being seen until they clear off the patio."

"So what do we do?"

Bolan watched Tyler and Ochoa as they spoke. After a few moments Tyler looked at his watch and gestured toward the house. The Mexican nodded and waved him in. The giant and the other soldier started to rise, and Tyler motioned them to stay seated.

Bolan took Larquette's hand.

"What's happening?"

"Tyler is going inside to make a phone call."

"So?"

"So let's go inside."

Bolan moved around the hedge toward the side of the house. He smelled food, and the side door entered into a kitchen where several women were busy cooking. The Executioner smiled and said several words in Russian while the women stared at him and frowned at Larquette's outfit. Bolan held up his hands.

"Eh . . . Señor Ochoa?"

The women pointed as one to the other side of the house toward the veranda. Bolan nodded and smiled as he and Larquette entered the hacienda. He closed the kitchen door behind them and looked around. Ochoa had a magnificent home. The living room was massively arched, and a huge window formed the entire back wall. Outside were fountains and sculpted Southwestern-style gardens. A little way off, a small hill had been leveled into a helicopter pad and a Bell JetRanger sat parked on it. Beyond it lay rolling ranch land, and in the distance Bolan could see the warehouse that formed the southern entrance of the tunnel. He took Larquette's hand as they moved across the room and entered a hallway. He jerked back quickly as a man singing a country song to himself suddenly came around the corner. He glanced back around as he heard a door open and saw a cowboy hat disappear into a room.

"Stay here and keep a lookout."

"What are you going to do?"

Bolan drew the Beretta. "I'm going to have a talk with Mr. Tyler."

LYLE TYLER SAT in Ochoa's study and pulled his secure phone out of his aluminum attaché case. He attached several wires, then connected it to his burst transmitter. He ran the test pattern and when it gave a satisfactory tone, he began punching in numbers.

His wife answered on the first ring.

"What is happening?"

"Ochoa wants more money."

"What did you promise him?"

"Ten million dollars."

There was a moment of silence. "Is that necessary?"

"He claims the people he is paying off want more money, and I believe he is only half lying in that regard. Security is always a good investment, and it is only a drop in the bucket. Also, you will be pleased to know, that when the time is right, Enrique seems perfectly willing to help us eliminate Ramzin and Baibakov."

"Very well, I agree, but money will be tight until the second tunnel is completed and the real shipments begin."

"Yes, but I believe our Mr. Ochoa is a keeper, and it will pay to keep him happy."

"How is the second tunnel proceeding?"

"Well, Ramzin is nothing if not efficient. He is two weeks ahead of schedule. We should be ready for the real cargoes in a few weeks."

His wife's voice became stern. "The last time I spoke with him, he seemed to balk at the idea of killing the workers when the tunnel is completed."

"He isn't happy about it. Ramzin considers himself a man of honor. Baibakov, on the other hand, is less squeamish, and he had an excellent suggestion during our ride over."

There was a pause. "Really?"

"Oh, yes. He thinks that instead of shooting all the workers we should just seal both ends of the tunnel once they are on their way to America and then gas them. He says it will be simpler and less messy."

"And what do we do with all the bodies?"

"He thought of that, too. We have all that earth-moving equipment at Red Star. He says we just dig a mass grave and then bury them. He says the entire project will take about a morning to complete."

His wife snorted. "Baibakov would have made an excellent Nazi."

"I gather, then, that you agree to his plan."

"Military minds do have their uses. Yes, of course I agree."

"Good. I'll have the money ready in three days."

"Say hello to Enrique for me."

"I will."

BOLAN SPOKE IN RUSSIAN. "Your pancakes are getting cold, Comrade."

Tyler snapped around and snarled back in the same language, "Idiot! I told you I did not wish to be disturbed until..."

He trailed off as he stared down the muzzle of the big Beretta's silencer. Bolan regarded him coldly. "So, you're going to kill the workers."

Tyler gaped at him.

"What did you promise them? Money and easy passage into the United States for them and their families when the work was done?"

"Listen—"

"How many of them are there? Four hundred? Five hundred?"

"Who are you?"

"Tell me, what are 'real' cargoes?"

Tyler's eyes narrowed. "You're Ramzin's little problem. The American."

"You speak excellent Russian, Lyle. Like a native."

The Executioner examined him clinically. "You're a sleeper. One of the deep-cover moles from the cold war. When were you inserted into the United States? The fifties? Early sixties?"

Tyler's knuckles whitened.

"The KGB successors would never allow a project like this. If it was discovered, it could start a war. This is a private venture, Russian Mafia, isn't it? You're going to give me names, and timetables. You're going to give me connections. Now."

Tyler sneered. "Or you'll do what? Shoot me? You'll never get out of here alive."

Bolan pushed off the silenced Beretta's safety. "I'll shoot you to pieces, Lyle, and I'll walk out of here. No one will hear a thing. An hour from now, your friend Ochoa will come into his study and find you all over the walls."

Tyler paled. "Listen, we can work something out."

"Start talking, or I start with your ankles and work my way up."

LARQUETTE NEARLY JUMPED out of her boots.

"Good day, señorita, and who are you?"

She spun around and found Enrique Ochoa looking down her T-shirt appreciatively, with two of his bodyguards. He turned to one of his men and spoke in Spanish. "She is pretty, Rujellio. Is she one of yours?"

Rujellio frowned. "No, Mr. Ochoa. I have not seen her before."

Ochoa grinned. "That is too bad for you, my friend." He switched back to English. "And what is your name?"

With an immense effort of will Larquette smiled idiotically. "I'm Patti!"

Ochoa nodded and smiled. "Ah, of course, and what are you doing hiding in the hallway, Patti?"

Larquette's mind raced furiously. She stuck out her lip and pouted. "I was promised breakfast."

A deep line of concentration drew up between Rujellio's eyebrows as he folded his arms and looked at her narrowly. Ochoa leered at her thighs.

"Oh, you are hungry." Ochoa leaned forward conspiratorially. "Did you have a long night?"

Larquette blushed and giggled as one of the cooks came into the living room and said in Spanish, "Mr. Ochoa, will you and your guests be taking coffee?"

He glanced at her distractedly. "Ah, yes, Rosa, on the veranda, thank you." Ochoa lifted a finger in sudden inspiration and turned to his other man. "Wait. Carlos, go see if the Russians want tea."

Carlos nodded and turned to leave.

Rujellio slowly shook his head as he continued to stare Larquette up and down. "Mr. Ochoa, I have never seen this woman before, and I have no idea how she got into the compound."

The cook wiped her hands on her apron and smiled. "Oh, she came with the Russian."

Ochoa frowned. "Which Russian?"

Rosa shrugged. "Why, the dark one, with all the guns."

He stared at her blankly. "The dark one with all the guns?"

Rosa nodded. "Yes."

Rujellio grabbed Larquette's wrist in a viselike fist. "Mr. Ochoa, something is wrong."

Larquette twisted and drove her boot up between Rujellio's legs with every ounce of strength in her body. He howled in agony and sagged as she yanked her wrist out of his hands. Ochoa's eyes flew wide as Rujellio crumpled to the floor moaning.

"*¡Madre de Dios! ¡Carlos! ¡Martin! ¡Andale!*"

Larquette reached behind her as she heard feet pounding down the hall. She pulled the snub-nosed Centennial revolver from the small of her back, and as Carlos rounded the corner, she leveled the front sight at his chest and fired.

"WHO IS INVOLVED in Moscow?"

Tyler squirmed in his chair. "They'll kill me."

The Executioner's voice was as cold as the grave. "I'll kill you."

The sleeper jumped at the gunshot. Bolan's head whipped toward the door. The firing signature was the distinctive crack of a snub-nosed revolver. He had heard it many times.

It was his gun.

The weapon fired twice more in rapid succession.

Tyler's chair creaked. Bolan pivoted from the waist and whipped the Beretta into line. The man had risen from his chair, and his left hand pulled a small automatic pistol from under his jacket. Bolan drilled a 3-round burst into his chest.

Tyler sagged backward, his little pistol spitting fire and sending a bullet high and wide into the wall. Sure that the Russian was dead, the Executioner turned and slipped out the door. Feet were pounding throughout the house. Just down the hall the ripping snarl of a submachine gun rang out. Bolan heard his pistol return fire. He whipped around the corner and saw two men lying on the ground. One lay dead and another was moaning. Larquette stood over them with her pistol pointing around the doorjamb into the living room. From the kitchen he could hear Enrique Ochoa screaming in Spanish and the servants screaming in general.

"The bitch shot me! Kill her! Kill her!"

Automatic fire chattered from the staircase in the living room. Larquette shrank back around the doorjamb as wood and plaster were gouged from the wall. She whipped around the jamb and fired as the burst ended, and her revolver clicking empty. She swore at the little pistol and ducked back into cover.

"Patti."

Larquette whirled and leveled the empty pistol, wild-eyed. Bolan held up his hand. "Patti, see if either of those two men are armed."

She stared at him for a moment, then blinked. "Right." She reached into the dead man's jacket and pulled out a large revolver. She fumbled in his pockets and produced a handful of loose rounds. She checked the pistol's load and nodded. Bolan holstered the Beretta and pulled his one remaining stun grenade from his web gear.

"Close your eyes and cover your ears."

He pulled the pin and tossed the grenade into the living room. The walls shuddered as the bomb detonated, and the big bay window shattered outward from the concussion.

The Executioner pivoted around the corner. A man staggered on the landing at the top of the stairs, holding his head with one hand and waving an Uzi submachine gun blindly with the other. A burst from the Beretta punched him down the steps. Another man rushed from the kitchen, firing a revolver in each hand as fast as he could pull the triggers. He sagged backward as Bolan and Larquette shot him simultaneously.

"Nobody move!"

Ochoa slowly came out of the kitchen with Rosa in front of him. He held the muzzle of a shiny stainless-steel pistol up to her head as she wept and prayed.

"Drop your guns or she is dead!"

Larquette shot Bolan a glance as she covered Ochoa.

Bolan shrugged. "Drop your gun."

Larquette grimaced as she watched Bolan drop the 93-R to the floor. He looked at her. "Do it!"

Ochoa's eyes flicked to Larquette as she dropped the pistol, and in a single fluid motion the Executioner drew the Desert Eagle and shot Ochoa between the eyes. Rosa screamed hysterically and fainted as his body fell away from her. Bolan picked up his Beretta with his free hand and jerked his head toward Larquette. "Get your gun."

Larquette scooped up her pistol and pushed fresh rounds into it. She looked around as people yelled and screamed from inside the house and out. "Which way?"

Bolan glanced through the shattered window to the helicopter up on the little hill.

"North."

BAIBAKOV AND GORCHENKO shot to their feet at the sound of gunfire. Both men pulled open their oversize shirts and drew 9 mm Stechkin machine pistols from their shoulder holsters. More shots rang out, and an automatic weapon ripped into life somewhere inside the house. The servants screamed and covered their ears.

Two of Ochoa's bodyguards stood uncertainly, fumbling with their rifles. Baibakov roared at them in Spanish.

"Come on!"

One of the men leveled his rifle at Baibakov. "Stay where you are, gringo!"

The man stumbled backward as Gorchenko shot him. The second guard stared aghast and brought up his rifle. Baibakov gunned him down before he could flick off his weapon's safety. The giant jerked his head toward the house. "The Scarecrow! His safety is our priority!"

Gorchenko nodded grimly and fell into a covering position behind Baibakov. As the giant opened the patio door, a dull roar shook the entire house and windows shattered.

Someone had started World War III.

The Russians entered the house. They passed Ochoa's study and Baibakov ground to a halt. The door was open, and the Scarecrow lay flopped back in a chair behind Ochoa's desk. His little Makarov automatic was still clutched in one hand, and the front of his shirt was riddled with bloody holes.

Gorchenko stared up at Baibakov. "Captain?"

Baibakov's eyes became unreadable. The Scarecrow had been a traitor and a worm, and he knew he was going to kill him sooner or later. But his mission had been to defend the man while in Mexico. Now he was dead.

"We go back to base and report to Ramzin."

"What about the Mexicans."

"Kill any you see."

The Russians moved swiftly through the house. As they rounded the corner, they saw two men lying in the hallway.

One was dead, the other coughing and slowly rising to his knees.

The giant shot him down.

More men lay dead in the living room, and Baibakov paused over Ochoa's body. The drug lord's eyes were crossed and staring up at the bullet hole between them. The giant looked outside the shattered bay window and his jaw dropped.

Their helicopter's rotors were turning.

Baibakov roared. "The helicopter!"

The Russians leaped out the window and broke into a sprint across the gardens. The aircraft rose slowly off the ground as it gained lift. It turned on its axis to head north, and Baibakov could see through the windscreen as the cockpit rotated into view.

It was the American commando and the woman.

Baibakov roared with rage and emptied his machine pistol into the helicopter. The windscreen spiderwebbed with cracks, and sparks shot about in the cockpit. The helicopter spun, and its turbine roared as it began to bank toward the north. Gorchenko opened fire as Baibakov slammed a fresh magazine into his Stechkin. The helicopter began to pick up speed, and the captain raised his aim to lead his shots. He pulled the trigger and emptied the pistol in a sustained burst, the tracers streaking into the helicopter's engine cowling.

Baibakov ejected the spent magazine as the helicopter roared out of range across the desert toward the United States. The pistol's grips creaked in his hand as his fist clenched. The American was alive. He had killed the Scarecrow and Ochoa. He had shot down Baibakov's first helicopter, and now he had stolen his second.

The captain pushed a fresh magazine into his machine pistol. Only one thing mattered now, and that was hunting down and killing the American and his woman.

He would follow them down to hell itself.

19

The Executioner fought the dying helicopter's controls. Something in the engine was damaged, and he was rapidly losing power. The radio and overhead controls had taken the first burst of fire, and what wasn't hanging down like wounded spaghetti lay in shattered pieces on the cockpit floor. The engine ground and whined in protest as Bolan forced the joystick up to clear the rock formations that marked the border. Larquette looked at him pensively.

"We're smoking like a chimney."

He glanced back and saw thick black smoke billowing behind them in the rotorwash. The temperature warning light was blinking red. Smoke was starting to seep into the cabin and beneath it was the unmistakable smell of overheating metal. He shot Larquette a quick look. She tried to smile at him but her face was pale, and Bolan could see her knuckles were white on the metal rim of her seat.

"We're not going to make it to Phoenix, are we?"

Bolan gritted his teeth as he hauled back on the stick. The cabin shuddered as the helicopter slid over the jagged hills. Larquette made a very unhappy noise as something struck one of the skids and the helicopter lurched. Bolan shoved the throttle full forward into emergency power.

The overheating turbine yowled in protest as the entire airframe shook. Slowly the helicopter limped higher into the sky. The grinding howl of the engine was now constant, and the smell of burning metal in the cabin was overpowering. The rocks hurtled by only a few feet beneath them.

Larquette pointed with a shout. "There!"

Off on Bolan's three o'clock, the buttes sheered away to the desert floor. He banked the helicopter to the southeast.

Larquette shouted, as if she were willing the flagging helicopter to reach the edge. "We're going to make it! We're going to make it!"

The rocks beneath reached up to embrace them as they raced for the edge.

Suddenly the rocky plateau fell away and they had altitude between them and the earth. Larquette shouted in triumph. "Yes!"

Bolan smiled grimly as he eased back on the throttle. It had been close, and they were still far from safe. Even though he eased back on the power, the turbine temperature remained in the redline. Using the emergency power had been necessary, but it had mortally strained the already damaged engine.

"I'm going to get us as close to Crucible as I can and set it down."

The desert flew past beneath them. Bolan's face tightened as he looked north. Larquette watched his face nervously. "What is it?"

Bolan jerked his head, keeping his eyes on the needles as they vibrated on red in his control dials. Larquette looked past him out the window. There against the hills was the Red Star camp.

"Do you think they saw us?"

"It's likely. We're making a lot of noise and putting out a lot of smoke."

"What will they do?"

"They'll come after us. Even if big boy hasn't reported in yet, they'll probably figure it's their helicopter and send people out. We don't want to be around when they do."

Larquette bit her lip and stared out the window. Ranches went by beneath them and miles ahead the town of Crucible was coming into view. "We should contact my friend Tom Donovan. Maybe he can sneak us out of here."

Bolan nodded. "It's our best—"

The engine suddenly shrieked in agony, and there was a tremendous clattering above their heads as something broke free and bounced around the engine compartment. The helicopter began to shake violently as the turbine continued to scream and rev out of control. Bolan released the throttle and cut the power to the engine. The engine noise slowly came to a grinding halt, and the cabin became eerily silent except for the rush of the wind through the bullet holes in the windscreen and the rhythmic threshing of the rotor blades over their heads.

Larquette looked around in panic. "What's happening?"

Bolan kept his eyes on the ground as the helicopter steadily lost altitude.

"The engine is off. The fact that we're falling is keeping the rotors turning."

"Can we land like this?"

"It'll be rough."

Larquette's face went white as the helicopter began to slowly spin on its axis.

"I don't like this!"

"Hold on!"

The ground suddenly seemed to shoot up at them, and the helicopter crunched into the sand abruptly.

Larquette looked around disbelievingly in the sudden silence. "We made it."

Bolan unhooked his safety harness and drew his Beretta 93-R. "Come on. The engine is still overheated, and we might have lost the fuel lines."

She released her harness, and they piled out of the cabin. Bolan looked east. "Town is that way, I'd say five or six miles."

Larquette stared shakily at the stricken helicopter. "I don't mind walking."

RAMZIN SHOT TO HIS FEET and shouted into the phone. "You told me the Yankees were dead, Captain! Now they have our helicopter!"

There was a long moment of silence. "I am sorry, Major. I do not know how to explain this. We blew up the mine shaft. The blast should have killed them. Galanskov assured me that there was no way to dig their way out even if they survived, and that the vertical shaft was blocked and impassable."

Ramzin shook with fury as he spoke into the phone. "Well, it appears that Lieutenant Galanskov was wrong!"

"There is more, Major."

Ramzin steeled himself. "Report."

"Ochoa is dead. So is the Scarecrow."

The major's jaw dropped. It was inconceivable. The whole operation was falling down like a house of cards. His voice went utterly cold. "How has this happened? Protecting the Scarecrow was your responsibility."

"Somehow the Yankee and the woman were in the house. The Scarecrow went inside to call his wife about the negotiations. We were ordered to stay outside. I saw no reasonable excuse to disobey. The Yankee killed him inside the house, then he killed Ochoa."

Ramzin stared at the map on the wall without seeing it as his mind whirled.

"Major, I was present during the negotiations, as ordered."

"Little good that will do us now, Comrade."

"Yes, Major. It is of no account now. However, you should know that the Scarecrow and Ochoa planned to kill us both when the second tunnel was completed."

Ramzin nodded slowly. "Well, now they will never have the chance."

There was another long pause. "Your orders, Major?"

They would have to evacuate. He estimated it would take some time before authorities could be contacted and convinced, much less mount an assault on the base. Ramzin considered his options as someone frantically banged on his door. He rolled his eyes toward heaven. How much more bad news could there be?

"Enter!"

Lukov burst into the room breathlessly. "Major! Our helicopter has been sighted. It was damaged, smoking badly. I believe it has made a forced landing some kilometers outside of Crucible!"

Ramzin calculated. They couldn't have been in the air very long. "Lukov, could they have gotten a communication out?"

Lukov frowned. "We have been monitoring radio traffic in and out of Crucible for five days. There has been nothing. Unless he had a special transmitter with him in the helicopter with its own special frequency, I do not see how, Major."

Ramzin pounded his fist on the table. There was still a chance that the situation could be salvaged. "Lukov, tell Rybenok to gather a strike team. The Yankees will surely make for Crucible and try to contact the outside. Call our old friend—it is time to make use of him again—and perhaps if we are lucky, they will go to the jail." Suddenly Ramzin grinned. "Or perhaps they will go to see our new friend, Mr. Donovan. Contact him, as well."

"Yes, Major!"

Lukov ran to carry out his orders as Ramzin returned to the phone. "Captain, return to base immediately. The situation may prove salvageable, but if not, I will need you here to help with a full evacuation of all personnel into Mexico."

The giant responded dejectedly. "Yes, Major."

Ramzin hung up the receiver and stared at the telephone with dread. Now he would have to tell the Witch that her husband was dead.

TOM DONOVAN GOGGLED at Bolan and Larquette as they stood on his porch.

"I thought you two were dead!"

Larquette smiled tiredly. "Can we have some water, Tom? It's been a long, dry morning."

Donovan bit his lip. "God, I'm sorry. Come on in."

They entered his ranch-style house, and he waved them to the couch. "What do you guys want? Beer? Soda?"

Bolan and Larquette spoke in unison. "Water."

Dononan went into his kitchen and ran the tap. He stared at the phone for a moment, then his hand reached out and picked up the receiver. His thumb hovered over a single button that corresponded to a preset telephone number that he had programmed into the automatic dialer several days earlier. He slowly pressed down, and he could just hear the muted tone of the numbers dialing. There was a click, and Donovan replaced the receiver on the hook.

He turned to the sink and filled two glasses with water and resisted the urge to throw up. He nearly dropped both glasses as a voice spoke softly behind him.

"They got to you."

It was a statement, not a question. Donovan turned and paled as he saw Bolan and Larquette in the kitchen doorway. He stood with the water glasses in his hands and stared at his feet. "I—"

"What did they do?" Bolan asked.

Donovan found the courage to look him in the face. "There was this guy, I swear, he must have been seven feet tall. He spent about an hour pulling my arm out of its socket. Then he and his buddies told me they would kill my mother and my sister. I didn't know what to do. I was just so helpless. I didn't know what to do. I just couldn't take it. I tried. God, I tried. But I just couldn't."

Bolan nodded. "It's all right, Tom. You had to protect your family." He glanced up at the clock. "How long do we have?"

"I don't know. Not long, I assume. They contacted me a few minutes before you arrived and told me to watch for you. I think they were sending men out."

"I need to use your phone."

Donovan grimaced. "They have control of the phone lines. The phones have been out for the last three days."

"Then we need a radio."

Larquette frowned. "The only shortwave set I know of around here is at the jail, and they jammed it."

"I know. I'll need a radio on a frequency they won't be jamming."

Donovan looked at him in bewilderment. "Where are you going to get one like that?"

Bolan pulled out the Beretta and checked it. He was down to his last magazine. He holstered the 93-R and drew the Desert Eagle. He looked at Tom Donovan.

"You just ordered one for me."

20

Ramzin gritted his teeth and squirmed at the silence on the other end of the phone. He had written all too many letters from Afghanistan to the families of men who would be returning to them in zinc field coffins, but he had never before told a woman her husband was dead over the phone. He knew the Witch and her husband had been planning to eliminate him sooner or later, but there was no victory for him in the stunned silence over the receiver.

The Witch's voice quavered. "How...how has this happened?"

It was the first time Ramzin had ever heard anything that resembled a genuine human emotion in her voice. He had considered the Witch and her husband incapable of such feelings, but he also knew they had been married for more than thirty years. Who could know what sort of relationship two such creatures could have, or what the end of that bond would do. The woman was a live grenade in his lap. Ramzin struggled to maintain a professional, military tone.

"He was murdered in Mexico, by the American commando."

The Witch was stupefied. "But you said that Baibakov had blown him to bits and buried him."

"That was my understanding, as well. But Captain Baibakov reports he sighted the man and exchanged fire with him in Mr. Ochoa's hacienda."

"I wish to speak to Mr. Ochoa immediately. Secure a line."

Ramzin cleared his throat. "I regret to inform you that the Americans have killed him, as well."

The silence dragged on, then the Witch's voice suddenly regained its former steel. "Very well, Major. Tell me, where are the Americans now?"

Ramzin swallowed. The woman could turn her emotions on and off like a light. "They escaped from Ochoa's hacienda in the helicopter, but Baibakov and Gorchenko managed to damage the aircraft significantly with small arms fire as it took off. The aircraft was spotted crash-landing some kilometers outside of Crucible. One of our contacts, Mr. Donovan of the citizens' committee, signaled us that they have made contact with him at his house outside of town. A strike team is converging on the house as we speak."

There was another pause and Ramzin could almost hear the wheels in her mind turning. "Very well. I believe the situation may still be salvageable. Ochoa was a drug dealer and a pimp, and he should not be difficult to replace. I, of course, will be inheriting my husband's business connections. If we can keep the woman and this commando from contacting the outside, this will only be a minor setback."

Ramzin shook his head. Her husband's death would be only a minor setback for her. Truly the woman was a witch.

"What do you suggest?"

"This is what we will do. I have already used my powers as state attorney general to put out a warrant for the arrest of the Larquette woman. Have my husband's body taken back across the border and bring it to the jail. I will make some kind of an excuse for his having been there. A business deal or some such thing. When you kill the woman, bring her body and the commando's gun to the scene. My husband was an important man and his death will be investigated. I can control that investigation, but I must at least have the vestiges of a cover story to work with."

She paused a moment. "You are sure that the Americans have not yet communicated to the outside?"

"I do not see how it is possible, and if they had, I am sure you would know of it before I do."

"Undoubtedly. I will fly down within two hours. Ostensibly to have met my husband to spend a weekend in the beautiful desert. If your men succeed, I will be ready to play the grieving widow. If they fail, and the Yankees reach the outside, we must prepare to evacuate, and that will take time. We must be prepared for that. This is what I want you to do."

Ramzin's eyes widened as she elaborated her contingency plan. He had seen the atrocities of war, and seen firsthand the ugly corruption of the KGB, but as he listened, he realized that the Witch was quite possibly the most evil human being he had ever met in a lifetime of war.

When she had finished, he responded with a tone as cold as the grave. "It will be done as you have instructed." A cold chill went down his spine as he hung up and buzzed for Lukov. There was no time to consider right and wrong. He was the commander, and he must insure his men's survival. His duty was clear. Lukov entered and saluted.

"Your orders, Major?"

Ramzin looked grimly at the area map of the base and the twin tunnel system. "Galanskov is our most senior demolition man, is he not?"

"Why, yes, Major. You put him in command of the engineers yourself."

Ramzin nodded without taking his eyes off of the map. "Exactly so. Bring him to me immediately."

"DO YOU HAVE any guns, Tom?"

Donovan looked at the Executioner nervously. "I've got an old .30-.30 lever-action Winchester, and a shotgun with some old shells."

Bolan nodded. "Get them."

He turned to Larquette, who was leaning on the back of the sofa and peering out the window with a pair of binoculars. "Anything yet?"

She answered without taking her eyes off the road. "Nope. Nothing yet."

Donovan returned with a worn Winchester rifle and a long double-barreled shotgun. He had a battered cardboard box of shells for each gun. He looked at the guns in his hands and shrugged. "They haven't been fired in a long time."

Bolan took the rifle and shells over to Larquette. "Take this. As I recall, you're familiar with one of these."

She took the weapon and frowned at it as she checked the action and began pushing shells into the loading gate. "Geez, Tom. You really ought to take better care of your guns."

Donovan shrugged helplessly. "They were my dad's, I mean, I really don't shoot that much, and..." He trailed off and watched Bolan as he broke open the shotgun and peered down the twin bores critically. The man spread his hands. "So, what do you want me to do?"

The Executioner slid two 10-gauge shells into the shotgun and snapped the action shut. He put the remaining four rounds into a pouch in his web gear. "Stay out of sight. Stay alive."

"You don't want me to help? Or is it that you just don't trust me?"

Bolan looked at him frankly. "Listen, Tom, what's done is done. I can't say whether Patti, myself or anyone else would have done anything different in the same situation. You were tortured, and it was your life and your family on the line. But you said it yourself—you don't shoot. You'll be a liability to me in a firefight. But listen. The fact that they're still after us tells me they think they can still salvage the situation. You did the job for them, and you're their contact on the citizens' committee. It's unlikely that they will want to kill you. So you stay alive, Tom. And if we don't make it through this, then you're going to have to do something."

"You mean call the authorities after you're dead."

Bolan reached down to the coffee table and wrote a number on an open section of newspaper. "Call this number. Use the name Striker. Tell the man who answers what has happened. He'll take care of the rest."

Bolan refolded the newspaper and slid it into the pile next to the couch. "Classifieds, Tom, section S."

Donovan stood and stared at Bolan bleakly. "So what do I do now?"

"Is there anyplace around here you can hide."

"The cellar."

"Go there. If they find you, tell them we threw you in there at gunpoint, or tell them you hid there and locked the door when you heard them coming. Either way, they'll probably believe you."

Donovan clenched his fists in frustration. The Executioner nodded his understanding. "I know it's gnawing at you. Hiding in the cellar doesn't seem very heroic. But it's the only chance if Patti and I don't make it. You're our insurance."

The man turned slowly without a word and went down the hall.

"Something's coming!" Larquette whispered.

Bolan went over and looked over her shoulder out the window. Two vehicles were churning up dust as they barreled down the road. He took the binoculars from her and adjusted the view. Two jeeps suddenly resolved themselves in crystal clarity.

Gun jeeps.

In each jeep a man stood behind a post-mounted 12.7 mm DSh K-38 heavy machine gun, and the windshield was lowered so that the man in the passenger seat could traverse a PKM light machine gun across the hood. Bolan lowered the binoculars.

"They'll probably split up to cover the front and the back, then tear the house apart with a cross fire from their heavy weapons. I'm going to go out the back and surprise one of them when he comes around the corner. I need you to yell to me which side of the house he chooses. Stay low, and when the shooting starts, follow me out back as fast as you can."

Her face was pale but her expression set defiantly. "Got it."

"Good." Bolan strode to the back door. He examined the terrain in the bright sunlight. The land around the house was flat scrub with little or no cover. If he was going to win, he would have to take on the Russians at point-blank range. He cocked his head as the engine noise of the approaching jeeps grew louder. The Russians would expect them to stay inside and to put up barricades. The plan was most likely to overwhelm them with superior firepower. Bolan had no illusions; their enemies' machine guns would cut through the old wooden house like tissue paper. If he and Larquette stayed inside, they would be slaughtered.

Hopefully the Russians would expect them to come out and fight.

He glanced at the long, heavy, double-barreled shotgun in his hands. A 10-gauge Magnum buckshot round threw eighteen buckshot at over thirteen hundred feet per second. At twenty yards the entire load would hit the target in a pattern the size of a dinner plate. The Executioner hoped Tom's old ammo was still good. It was going to be mighty costly if it wasn't. The engine noise became extremely loud. Suddenly Bolan heard Larquette yelling at the top of her lungs from inside the house.

"He's coming around the left side of the house! Circling wide!"

Bolan flattened against the wall and rapidly slid to the left corner of the house. He dropped into a shooter's crouch with the shotgun held in front of him. The Russian gun jeep burst into view some thirty yards from the house, and the man behind the heavy machine gun stared at Bolan in surprise and desperately tried to traverse the big DSh K machine gun.

The Executioner brought the shotgun to his shoulder and fired.

The 10-gauge recoiled brutally, and the man operating the machine gun hurtled backward out of the jeep. The driver yanked the steering wheel into an evasive turn, but the jeep was much too close and the huge shotgun was an area weapon. Bolan tracked the man's head and shoulders, and the second blast slammed the driver sideways in his seat. The jeep swerved out of control.

Bolan broke open the shotgun and stuffed in two fresh shells as the two remaining Russians dived from the runaway vehicle. The jeep plunged on and slammed violently into a tree stump and stalled.

One man hit the ground and rolled expertly. He came up on his feet and tried to bring his assault rifle into target acquisition, but the big shotgun roared and sent him sprawling to the ground before he could pull the trigger. The other man stood groggily and fired his rifle on full-auto. His shots went high and wide into the house and Bolan put the full buckshot pattern into his chest. The man tumbled back and tried to return fire.

Bolan frowned. The Russians were wearing body armor. He dropped the shotgun and drew the .44 Magnum Desert Eagle. The Russian was still reeling from the massive punch of the shotgun. As he tried to bring his rifle to bear, Bolan put two rounds into his chest. The titanium armor had never been designed to withstand a .44 Magnum solid, and the man fell heavily to the ground.

Around the house, Bolan could hear the roar of the other jeep's engine as it snarled through its gears. He broke into a sprint toward the stalled jeep as its partner came racing to its rescue. The second vehicle tore around the corner of the house, and its gunner opened fire as Bolan dived behind the stalled vehicle. The Russian heavy and light machine guns tore through the car body as the soldier threw himself prone under the wheels. The jeep shuddered and rocked on its axis under the deadly barrage. Over the roar of the weapons he could hear the vehicle grind to a halt, and he knew that the Russians were dismounting to encircle him while their machine guns kept him pinned down.

The Executioner drew the Beretta 93-R. A bullet threw up sand to his right, and he snapped off a 3-round burst from the Beretta. One of the Russians was using the corner of the house for cover. Bolan flattened himself on the ground as the machine guns drilled bursts of fire into the beleaguered jeep over his head. He scanned between the wheels and was unable to see the other dismounted Russian. He was being flanked.

Weapons opened up on all sides, and Bolan knew they were going to rush him. He tried to rise up and fire, but the machine guns tore into the body of the jeep above him. Oil and gasoline from the mauled vehicle dripped down on him as he pushed himself deeper into the wheel ruts beneath the jeep and fired several blind bursts to his right. He glanced up to see the Russian by the house charging toward him, firing from the hip. Bolan raised the Beretta and put a 3-round burst into him. The man staggered but didn't fall. The Russian's armor had held, and the Beretta 93-R clacked open on empty in the Executioner's hand. He struggled to roll over under the jeep and bring the Desert Eagle to bear as the man suddenly jerked and stumbled forward. His body jerked twice more, and he fell facefirst into the sand. More rifle shots rang out from the house.

Larquette was in the fight.

The jeep above him stopped rocking for a moment as the enemy machine guns tracked toward the house and began to tear apart the back wall. Bolan rolled out from under the jeep and rose. One of the enemy machine guns tracked back toward him and opened fire. He returned fire with the big Desert Eagle as rapidly as he could pull the trigger as he leaped into the back of the jeep that had sheltered him. The Russian light machine gunner jerked as one of Bolan's shots struck him in the shoulder, but he kept a hand on his weapon and struggled to stay on target. Bolan dropped the Desert Eagle and grabbed the twin grips of the DShK heavy machine gun. He swung the weapon on its pivot, and he and the Russian exchanged fire from jeep to jeep.

The Russian was unable to control his weapon one handed, so his burst went low and shook the battered vehicle beneath Bolan's feet. The Executioner leveled the heavy weapon with cold certainty and began cutting the other jeep apart with short bursts. His opponent shuddered as the heavy bullets tore into him, and he sagged forward over his gun. The enemy gunner desperately tried to swing his weapon back around, but Bolan cut him down before he could bring his weapon to bear. Rifle fire resumed from the house, and the jeep's driver sagged from his seat as he fumbled with his rifle. Another Russian leaped to cover behind the body of his vehicle.

The DShK's handles shuddered to a halt in Bolan's hands as he stopped firing.

Larquette shouted in the sudden silence. "Did we get them?"

Bolan kept the Russian heavy machine gun trained on the enemy jeep. "One of them took cover behind his vehicle."

"So what are you going to do?"

The Executioner put a burst into the enemy vehicle to keep the Russian honest and glanced around his commandeered vehicle. A battered-looking RPG-7 rocket-propelled grenade launcher sat in a rack behind the driver's seat. Its launch tube was dented, and it had a number of bullet holes in it from the earlier barrage. The weapon's optical sight had been smashed, but the warhead seemed miraculously undamaged. At thirty yards he doubted the Russian would be able to notice the difference.

"Patti! Put a few shots into his position, but aim high."

Larquette's rifle rang out three times in rapid succession and sparks flew off of the jeep's hood. Bolan took the RPG-7 from its rack and positioned it over his shoulder. He peered through the crushed optics and spoke loudly in Russian.

"Hey, you!"

The Russian didn't respond.

"I have an RPG-7 here. Throw down your rifle and I won't use it."

The Russian's head peeked around the rear bumper of the enemy vehicle and yanked back quickly as he saw the RPG's 85 mm warhead pointed straight at him. Larquette's rifle roared from the kitchen and shot out one of the jeep's headlights. For a moment the only noise was the desert breeze. Larquette peered out of the kitchen at Bolan and shrugged. After a moment the Russian shouted from behind cover.

"What assurance do I have you will not kill me anyway?"

"Be assured I will blow you to hell if you don't."

There was a reflective pause, then an AK-74 rifle clattered across the hood of the jeep and fell to the ground. "Very well. I am coming out. Do not shoot."

Bolan let the mangled antitank weapon slide off his shoulder, and he took the grips of the heavy machine gun in his hands. "Slowly."

The Russian moved out from behind his vehicle. His left arm was bloody and sagged at a dislocated angle from his shoulder. He stared at the heavy machine gun Bolan pointed at him and raised his good arm over his head.

"I surrender."

"Cover him, Patti. Shoot him if he moves." He released the machine gun and scooped up the Desert Eagle from the jeep. Bolan jumped to the ground and slid a fresh magazine into the pistol. It clacked into battery, and the Executioner approached the Russian. The man had short blond hair and the powerful build of a Special Forces soldier.

"Name and rank," Bolan demanded.

The man sighed heavily. "Rybenok, Constantine, Senior Lieutenant."

Larquette came out of the house with her rifle leveled at the man's midriff. She looked the Russian up and down with a hostile expression. "I thought these Spetsnaz superman types never surrendered."

The man's head jerked around and he glared at Larquette angrily. Bolan grimaced. Apparently the man knew some English.

The Russian stared at her for a moment, then returned his gaze to Bolan.

"The woman is correct. Spetsnaz never surrender. I was Spetsnaz, but no longer. My regiment was deactivated. This is not Russia. You understand?"

Bolan nodded. "You're a mercenary now. It's business. Not a war for the motherland."

Rybenok regarded Bolan and he nodded slowly. "*Da,* you understand."

"Then understand me, Rybenok. This is my homeland. You've invaded it." The Executioner raised the gaping muzzle of the Desert Eagle and aimed it between Rybenok's eyes. "Cooperate, or I'll kill you."

The Russian swallowed hard as he stared at the big weapon, but his face set defiantly. "I want your assurance that my comrades will be given the opportunity to surrender, and that they will not be killed if they do so."

Bolan's gaze narrowed. Rybenok was a brave man. He nodded and lowered the pistol slightly. "I'll give them one chance. After that, the base will be taken unconditionally, by force."

Rybenok took a deep breath. "Very well. I will cooperate."

21

The Witch stared expressionlessly at the body of her husband. He had taken seven rounds through the chest, and the result hadn't been pretty. He lay partially wrapped in a plastic sheet on the table with his Western clothes hanging about his shrunken limbs in bloody folds. In the rigor of death, he truly looked like a scarecrow. The Witch jerked her head at Ramzin.

"Take it to the jail."

Ramzin nodded to Baibakov and Mosiev, and the two men wrapped the plastic sheet around the body and carried it out. The Witch turned to Ramzin.

"Where is his gun?"

He frowned and pointed. "It is there, on the desk."

The Witch strode over to the desk and picked up the little Makarov. She checked the pistol, one eyebrow rising when she noticed two rounds had been fired from the magazine. She slammed the magazine back into the gun and handed the pistol to Ramzin butt first.

"Have it reloaded and bring me a spare magazine. Bring me some rubber bands, as well."

Ramzin blinked. "Why, yes." He jerked his head. "Lukov."

He handed the pistol to Lukov, who took it out of the room. The Witch examined the area map on the wall. "Send in Galanskov."

The major buzzed his intercom. "Get Galanskov." He clicked off the intercom and folded his arms. "Your plan troubles me."

The Witch turned from the map and regarded him. "I am sure it does. Do you have a better one?"

"No, but it is the Devil's own work that we are doing."

The Witch shook her head disgustedly. "Perhaps you would rather have your men die in vain fighting the entire Arizona National Guard, or languish in an American prison for twenty years. They are much nicer than the gulags of home, Ramzin. They have television and weight-training facilities. You and Baibakov would feel right at home. It would be just like boot camp."

Ramzin's lips curled back in a snarl as he loomed over her. "Do not mock me, old hag. You are not in a suitable position."

The Witch's lips skinned back from her teeth, but she didn't retreat. For a moment she seemed about to say something, and then she bit it back. Her gaze narrowed. "Listen to me, Ramzin. You and I, we need each other. You have some money here at the base, I know, but you realize I still control several million dollars in offshore bank accounts. You have no connections in Mexico. I do. Without my husband, I am somewhat vulnerable. Together, you and I can set up business in any country in South America. There are many groups south of here who will pay handsomely to use my connections in Moscow, and make use of you and your men's expertise."

Ramzin said nothing.

The Witch looked him up and down and nodded. "Oh, you are a capable man, Ramzin, and your men are well trained. Perhaps you really could shoot your way out of here, but then where will you go? Cuba? You need my connections, and I need you and your men. You must do your duty, Major. However painful it is to you. You must swallow your honor, think of your men and do what must be done to insure our survival. Agreed?"

Ramzin took a deep breath. "Very well."

There was a knock on the door and Galanskov entered the room, followed by Lukov. Galanskov stood at attention while Lukov turned to the Witch. "I am to give these to you."

He handed the Witch her husband's Makarov and a loaded spare magazine. She slipped the magazine in her pocket and checked the pistol's load. "The rubber bands?"

Lukov straightened. "Ah." He reached into his pocket and produced several thick rubber bands. The Witch took them and wound them around the pistol's grips, then tucked the pistol into the small of her back under her coat. Ramzin and Galanskov looked at each other as she shifted back and forth for a moment to make sure the pistol rode securely.

She nodded in satisfaction and turned to Galanskov. "I trust it is done?"

Galanskov grimaced distastefully. "Yes, I have done as I have been ordered. The charges have been set as directed, and the workers are being moved under guard from the barracks both here and in Mexico." Galanskov looked as if he wanted to spit. He gave Ramzin an accusing look. "Everything will be ready as specified within the hour."

The Witch nodded. "Good. What of your strike team, Major?"

Ramzin looked at Lukov and the man's face tightened. "They have not reported. They cannot be reached on radio. I fear the worst, Major."

"Have communications picked up any signals coming out of Crucible?"

"No, Major. We have been scanning continuously and detected nothing."

Ramzin calculated. "Very well. Perhaps there is still a chance. Have the men watching the jail be ready. Contact that idiot Severn again, and make sure he and the men I gave him are ready, as well."

Lukov saluted. "Yes, sir."

The major turned to Galanskov. The two men stared at each other for a long moment, and Ramzin could tell that Galanskov didn't see him in the same way anymore. He knew that the demolition man had killed many men in his time, but now he was being ordered to commit an atrocity. Ramzin knew one other thing, as well, that the Witch was right. There was no time for morality now. Now it was a question of survival. He was still the commanding officer, and he stared Galanskov down until the engineer blinked.

"Do you question my orders, Lieutenant?"

Galanskov gritted his teeth and stared straight ahead. "No, Major."

"Good. Then make sure everything is ready, and then you and Captain Baibakov will prepare the men for possible evacuation on my order." Ramzin took a deep breath and let it out slowly. "Then bring me the detonators."

Galanskov saluted woodenly and left the room.

"HOW MANY MEN does Ramzin have?"

Rybenok looked out the window as they drove Tom Donovan's minivan toward town. His left arm had been bound in a sling across his chest and his right hand was tied to it. Larquette drove with Donovan beside her in the passenger seat while the Executioner sat in the back with the Russian. Rybenok looked out into the desert and sighed.

"You and the woman have thinned our ranks a good deal. I suspect Ramzin can probably muster at least one full-strength platoon, and perhaps a thin second. There is also several score of combat engineers. They will fight if necessary, as well as some other technical-support personnel."

"Will Ramzin surrender?"

Rybenok frowned. "It is not in his nature, but he will not allow his men to die senselessly. He saw too much of that in Afghanistan. If he sees no way out, I suspect he would surrender. But Ramzin is a fox. You would do well not to underestimate him."

"His men will surrender?"

Rybenok shrugged. "If Ramzin orders it."

"What about the giant?"

The Russian's eyebrows rose. "Ah, yes, Captain Baibakov."

"What about him?"

Rybenok smiled at the Executioner bleakly. "Pray that you see him before he sees you."

"I'll keep that in mind."

"See that you do. You have made yourself a capable enemy."

Donovan spoke from the front. "So why are we going into town? Isn't this a bit dangerous?"

Bolan looked at his watch. "I have to communicate with the outside and get help. Unfortunately the Russian radio was torn up in the firefight and we lost the power supply. I think I can hook it up through the radio at the jail and transmit on a frequency they won't be jamming. It's our best shot."

Donovan glanced at the Russian nervously. "So why are we keeping him around? Is he a hostage, or what?"

Rybenok snorted. "I believe my comrades might very well shoot me if it was required to get at you. Keeping you from communicating is a matter of survival. In this situation, I have no illusions about my expendability."

The Executioner looked out the windshield as the town of Crucible became visible. "I gave him my word. As long as he doesn't try anything, I'll do what I can to keep him alive. As for keeping him with us, it's safer than letting him wander around by himself."

Donovan nodded, but he still looked unhappy about the situation.

In the afternoon heat, there were few people on the streets of Crucible. As they entered town, the few that were about looked at Donovan's minivan and then gawked openly when they saw who was driving it. Larquette shook her head. "I think there's going to be trouble."

Bolan leaned over her shoulder. "What do you see?"

She pointed down the street toward the jail. "See the cruiser parked outside? That's Ken Severn's." Larquette smiled dryly. "My loyal deputy."

The Executioner pointed at the vehicle next to it. "What about the van?"

Larquette shook her head. "I've never seen it before in my life."

Donovan looked at Larquette in embarrassment. "Er, Patti, Ken's kind of the new chief."

The minivan shrieked to a halt. Larquette turned on Tom and gave him a withering look. "Don't tell me you and the citizens' committee appointed him, Tom. You didn't. Tell me you didn't."

"No, we didn't appoint him or anything, it's just that... Well, he was the only law around after you disappeared, and he just sort of assumed the job and no one opposed him."

"So, what? You all just assumed I was dead?"

Donovan squirmed. "No, Ken addressed the citizens' committee. He showed us a federal warrant for your arrest."

"For what?"

"Drug trafficking, conspiracy and suspicion of murder."

"And just who am I supposed to have murdered?"

Donovan avoided her gaze and studiously looked out the window. "Your father."

Her knuckles went white on the steering wheel. She turned and stared bloody murder at Rybenok. "My father was assassinated by a goddamned Russian mercenary."

The Russian stared at her coolly. "No, that is not correct."

"So just who the hell *did* kill my father?"

Rybenok shrugged. "Why, his deputy, Severn, of course. Ramzin has the pistol with his fingerprints on it. The act committed him to our cause, and the evidence helps insure his loyalty."

Larquette looked down at the steering wheel for a long moment, then peered out the window at the jail. When she spoke her voice was icy calm. "Has he sworn in any deputies of his own?"

"Well, no. None that I know of."

The Executioner glanced critically at the unmarked van parked next to Severn's cruiser. "You said he had a federal warrant. Where did he get it?"

Donovan shrugged. "There have been some federal agents hanging around the jail, and backing him up when he's interviewed people."

"How do you know they're federal agents?"

"Well, Ken said they were."

Larquette stared out at the jail. "Tell me, Tom. How much English do these federal agents speak?"

"I only saw them once. They don't say much. They just stand around in suits behind Severn. They—"

Bolan cut him off. "How many?"

"Four, I think. Maybe five."

"They're going to be waiting for us, probably on a high state of alert since Rybenok never called in," Bolan stated.

Larquette continued to stare expressionlessly at the jail. "So how do we do this?"

"We have to draw them out of the jail. Patti, I want you to park in the front and hold Rybenok here as hostage."

The Russian sighed. "I am afraid I will not make a very good shield."

Bolan nodded. "No, but if it's just Patti and Tom they may try to talk them out of it and keep you alive."

Donovan looked up with a start. "What?"

The Executioner handed him one of the AK-74 assault rifles he had taken from the Russian jeeps. "Tom, you have to back up Patti, understand?" He pointed at the rifle's action. "It's loaded, and the safety is off, so keep your finger off the trigger unless you have to fire. If something happens, put the front sight on a bad guy and pull the trigger. Keep pulling the trigger until they fall down. Got it?"

Donovan nodded.

Larquette looked at Bolan. "What about you?"

The Executioner slung an AK-74 rifle across his back and pulled a PKM light machine gun from behind the seat. He wrapped the end of the 50-round ammo belt across his forearm and checked the action. Larquette snorted. "Well, I knew you took that thing off the Russian jeep for some reason."

As she checked the load in the revolver she had taken from Carlos and shoved Rybenok's confiscated bayonet into her belt, the Executioner pointed at the bank outside. "Let me off here, and give me thirty seconds. When you get to the jail, park across the street and get out. Keep Rybenok in front of you. When they come out, I'll flank them." He slid the door open and stared at the Russian. "If you do anything to warn your friends, you're the first person I'll kill."

Rybenok stared at him blandly. "I do not doubt it."

The midday heat hit Bolan like a wall as he left the interior of the air-conditioned minivan. He held the PKM machine gun in the assault position on his hip as he rounded the corner of the bank and jogged down the alley to the back street. He turned around the corner, and two teenagers gaped at him as they sat on a stoop drinking soda in the shade. They paled as Bolan smiled at them and ran on. He passed one cross street, then a second, and he knew the jail would be on the next block.

Bolan paused at the corner of the jail. A new security door replaced the one that the Russians had blown off its hinges. As he paused, he heard car doors open across the street. A voice rang out from the front of the jail.

"Stop right there, Patti! That's far enough!"

Bolan slid to the corner and glanced around the edge of the jail building.

Larquette and Donovan were across the street. Rybenok stood bound and stone-faced a few paces in front of them while they pointed their guns at his back. On the steps of the jail stood a tall, lanky man in a khaki police uniform and a Stetson hat. He was flanked by two pairs of armed men in dark suits and sunglasses. They had dressed the part, but Bolan knew most federal agents didn't have military crew cuts, and no United States government agency issued Russian-made 9 mm Stechkin machine pistols. Severn stood on the steps with his service revolver drawn.

"I have a federal warrant for your arrest. Drop your guns and surrender peacefully."

"Why don't you throw down your weapon and surrender, Kenny?"

Severn sneered. "Oh? What's the charge?"

Her gaze narrowed. "How about impersonating a police officer?"

Severn's face turned mean and his voice lowered. "We can do this easy, or we can do it hard, Patti. Surrender and we can maybe work out a deal. If you don't, my friends here will cut you to pieces. You don't stand a chance."

Larquette looked at him icily. "Well, Ken, that's more of a chance then you gave my dad."

Severn flinched. They stared at each other for a moment then Severn spoke quietly to the men around him.

"Kill them."

Bolan rounded the corner and leveled the Russian machine gun.

"Freeze."

For a moment everything was utterly still. The Russians stood motionlessly, staring down the barrel of one of their own PKM light machine guns. Severn gaped. Bolan's voice was cold as he spoke in Russian.

"Drop your weapons. Do it now. Or I'll kill you."

The closest Russian stared at the PKM's muzzle through slitted eyes and slowly let his machine pistol fall from his hands. Bolan shifted his aim to the man next to him. "Now you."

The first Russian blurred into motion. His hand slapped the small of his back and withdrew a small automatic pistol. Bolan heard the click of the safety coming off as the man brought the pistol to bear. The PKM thundered in the Executioner's hands as he put a 6-round burst into the man. The Russian staggered back from the trip-hammer blows of the machine gun, and Bolan drilled a second burst into him to put him down. The rest of the Russians brought their pistols to bear as Larquette shoved Rybenok to the ground and brought her rifle to her shoulder. Severn threw himself down as weapons began firing in all directions.

The second Russian's machine pistol chattered at Bolan. He felt a punch in his shoulder, but the small subsonic bullets were no match for the Executioner's armor. A stream of green tracers drew smoking lines into the Russian's chest as Bolan hammered him down with the PKM. Larquette's rifle roared from across the street, and the third Russian staggered. Bolan finished him with a burst as bullets tore into the concrete around him in a hail from above.

There was a man on the roof.

The Executioner swung the PKM to his shoulder and aimed the light machine gun like a rifle. The smoking trail of a tracer seemed to draw a line straight at him, and he felt the wind of the bullet's passage by his head. He put the PKM's large battle sight on the man's chest and squeezed the trigger.

The Russian jerked as the bullet hit him. On full auto the PKM was almost uncontrollable when fired from the shoulder, but Bolan had put the first round dead on before the machine gun's recoil made his sights climb off the target.

The PKM spit out its last round and ran dry.

He threw down the spent machine gun and swung the AK-74 rifle into action. The remaining Russian on the steps had cut down Tom Donovan with a burst through the legs and was whirling on the Executioner with grim determination. The burst went high as Bolan dropped into a crouch and fired the assault rifle from the hip. The AK-74 snarled on full-auto as Bolan put a 5-round burst into his opponent. He rose out of his crouch as the Russian fell in a heap.

For a moment all was silent.

"All right, drop it!"

Bolan turned his head. Across the street, Rybenok lay quietly on the ground, and beside him, Tom Donovan lay clutching his wounded legs. Larquette lay unmoving on the ground with her rifle and pistol kicked away from her. Severn stood over her with his revolver drawn.

"My next shot goes right between her eyes."

"Do it and I'll cut you in two."

The click of Severn's revolver was very loud as he cocked the hammer and smiled. "She'll never know the difference."

In his peripheral vision, Bolan saw motion on the ground. He kept his gaze locked on Severn's. "Give it up. You'll never get out of here. Even if you do, you have no place to go."

Severn sneered. "Mexico is nice. I have some friends who are moving there real soon."

Bolan shook his head. "The Russians will kill you, Severn. You're a liability to them. The only way you get out of this alive is to drop your weapon, now."

"The only way she gets out of this alive is if you drop yours."

Bolan shrugged. "All right." Severn's eyes widened as the Executioner opened his hands and let the AK-74 clatter to the ground.

Severn's sneer turned triumphant. "Well, now—"

Bolan lunged to his right and slapped leather for the big Desert Eagle on his hip. Severn snarled and swung up the cocked revolver as the pistol cleared its holster. The deputy screamed suddenly as Larquette plunged Rybenok's bayonet into his calf up to the hilt. His shot flew wild as he staggered, and the .44 Magnum roared in Bolan's hands. As Severn crumpled back against the minivan and collapsed to the pavement, Larquette dropped the bayonet and fell backward. Bolan raced to her side.

She had been shot low through the left shoulder, and this time it wasn't a grazing wound. She lay pale and sweating on the ground with a pool of bright red blood spreading beneath her. Her breathing was shallow and rapid. Bolan tore a field dressing from his web gear and pulled Rybenok into a sitting position. He slashed the Russian's wrist free from his sling with his fighting knife and pressed the field dressing into his hand. "She's going into shock. Apply pressure to the wound. I have to see about Donovan."

Rybenok nodded and pushed the dressing against Larquette's shoulder with his good hand.

Bolan turned to Donovan. He had taken a bullet in each thigh, and he was bleeding profusely. He gritted his teeth as he looked up at Bolan. "How bad is it?"

The soldier pulled another dressing from his gear. "You'll have some interesting scars, Tom, but your friend missed the femoral arteries. You'll live."

The Executioner whirled as he heard movement behind him.

An older, dark-haired woman with a large medical bag stared aghast at the Desert Eagle. A young man and woman who were her spitting image stood behind her. The muzzle didn't move as Bolan spoke.

"Who are you?"

She kept her eye on the pistol. "I'm Sheree Redbird. I run the clinic down the street. This is my daughter Peggy and my son Matt." They stared at Bolan nervously.

Donovan spoke tiredly. "I can vouch for her. She's on the citizens' committee. Her daughter is studying to be a nurse. Matt is an intern."

Bolan nodded. "Take care of them." He pulled Rybenok to his feet, and Sheree Redbird frowned.

"That man needs medical attention."

"I need him."

She stared him down unflinchingly. "He's a mess. He needs medical attention, now."

Bolan softened his tone. "I need him for five minutes, or you're likely going to have more dead and wounded people here than you've ever seen. Please see to Tom and Patti first."

She bit her lip, then bent over Tom. "Matt, go back to the clinic and get a gurney. No, get two."

Bolan jerked his head at Rybenok. "Come on."

As they walked to the jail, one of the Russians sprawled on the steps moaned. Bolan turned. "There's a wounded man over here."

Redbird nodded without looking up.

The Executioner and Rybenok entered the jail. Rough repairs had been done since the Russian assault, but holes still riddled the walls and furniture. A large Russian field radio and a cellular phone unit sat on a desk next to the police dispatch console. Bolan pulled up a chair for Rybenok and handed him the field radio's handset.

"Get me Major Ramzin."

22

Lukov burst into the shack.

"Major! A radio communication from Lieutenant Rybenok!"

Ramzin shot to his feet. "Patch me through to him, now!"

He picked up his receiver as Lukov ran back out. There was a moment of static and the line cleared. "Rybenok! This is Ramzin. What is your status?"

Rybenok's voice was weak but clear. "There is a man here who wishes to speak to you, Major."

"Put him on."

A deep voice came through his receiver. "Major Ramzin."

"This is Ramzin. To whom am I speaking."

The voice answered him in Russian. "Your opponent."

Ramzin's blood turned cold but his voice remained even. "What is it you want?"

"Surrender. Now. It is over, and you have lost. Have your remaining men stockpile their weapons and stand down in their barracks. Then wait for the federal authorities. I promise your men will be treated fairly and no reprisals will be taken."

"What is the status of my men holding the jail?"

"One of them is badly wounded but still alive. He is receiving medical attention. The rest are dead."

"Ah. And the strike team I sent against you at Mr. Donovan's home?"

"Dead. Rybenok was still alive, but wounded, and I allowed him to surrender. He will receive medical attention, as well."

Ramzin paused. "That is kind of you."

"Surrender, Major. It is over."

"Not quite."

Bolan's voice became cold and grim. "I can have air strikes flown in against your base within thirty minutes, Ramzin."

Ramzin drummed his fingers against the desktop.

"I think not. It is my belief that you are a single agent, and that you are working alone. Your story will have to be processed through channels and verified. To stop me you must be able to plug my escape route to Mexico, and to do that you must have the cooperation of the Mexican government. That will also take time. Even if you bomb the base without permission, your superiors will fret over the decision to start an international incident to capture some smugglers. I believe that I have some time. However, I will concede that you are a remarkable man, and perhaps you truly can carry out your threats. Still, I strongly recommend that you do not. For that matter, I recommend that you do not contact anyone for at least forty-eight hours."

"Oh?"

Now it was Ramzin's voice that became cold and grim. "As you have probably already ascertained, we have been using extensive Mexican labor in digging our tunnels. I have moved the laborers from their barracks into the second tunnel, which is not yet complete. In the second tunnel, my engineers have set a nuclear demolition charge. If I am hindered in any way, if I meet resistance on either side of the border, I will remotely detonate the charge and five hundred Mexican nationals will be vaporized. The mountain itself will be their headstone. Do you understand?"

There was a long silence.

"I understand."

Ramzin clicked off the receiver and punched his intercom. "Lukov! Jam all our frequencies now!"

Lukov's voice came back confused. "Our frequencies, Major?"

"He has one of our field radios! Jam our frequencies! Now!"

"Yes, sir!" Lukov clicked off, and Ramzin punched the button for the barracks. He needed to speak with Baibakov.

LIEUTENANT GERALD LOFTIN of the United States Army Signal Corps sat in the listening room of Fort Huachuca and stared at his console in surprise.

"Er, Captain, I have an anomalous transmission here."

Captain Barbara Ann Blesskany looked over the lieutenant's shoulder. "What is it?"

Loftin stared at the console with raised eyebrows. "It's a weird one. A voice transmission, in English but on a Russian military frequency from a Russian field radio. I've never seen anything like it here."

The captain read the screen and suddenly frowned. "The Justice Department? Let me check the books." Blesskany pulled one of a dozen binders as thick as a New York telephone book from a shelf and flipped through it rapidly. She found a page and ran her finger down a long column of codes. Her finger stopped near the bottom and tapped meditatively on the clearance.

"I'll be damned."

Loftin peered quizzically at his commanding officer. "What should I do?"

Blesskany shrugged. "Get me a priority line to the Justice Department in Washington."

HAL BROGNOLA JUMPED as the secure phone rang. He grabbed the receiver. "What have you got, Barbara?"

"I thought you might like to know that Fort Huachuca just got a coded priority message for the Justice Department over a Russian military frequency."

He rubbed his eyes tiredly. "Fort Huachuca? I don't understand."

"Fort Huachuca, Hal. In Arizona. It's the center of the United States Army Signal Corps."

"What was the message?"

"Well, following the current Justice Department Emergency Code Prefix, with your security numbers attached, the message was, 'Flash Priority—Crisis Crucible—Send Able—Send Phoenix—Gadgets UXB-HALO—Striker.'"

Brognola shot to his feet. "Barbara I need a plane fueled and on its way to Phoenix International Airport five minutes ago."

"Not a problem."

RAMZIN STOOD behind the communications console with Baibakov.

"Lukov, you have jammed the frequencies?"

"Yes, Major. Nothing can get through."

"Could our friend have sent out a message?"

Lukov frowned. "He would have had a ten-second window to do so. However, that assumes he was totally familiar with our equipment and had someone near enough to transmit to with a field radio. We were not monitoring all of our own frequencies, but we did not pick up a transmission. His message would have had to be very brief. If it got through at all."

Ramzin bit his lip. "It does not matter. He knows what I will do if I am interfered with. However, keep monitoring all frequencies." He turned to Baibakov. "Have our observers keep watch and get the rest of the Mexicans into the second tunnel. Have everyone else prepare to evacuate."

The Witch spoke from behind Ramzin as Baibakov left. "Everything is according to plan?"

"The strike team failed, as did our pawn Severn and the men I gave him. However, I believe your plan will work. I do not believe we will be seeing the Arizona National Guard or hundreds of federal agents. Even if our friend contacts his superiors, I think the idea of five hundred hostages and nuclear devices will keep them from taking any action until it is much too late. My only fear is having to fight our way across Mexico."

"That is already being taken care of. Money is moving out of Moscow to smooth our passage."

Ramzin let out a deep breath. "That is good."

The Witch looked at Ramzin critically. "The plan still bothers you?"

"The plan bothers me, and this American bothers me. He gave in too quickly."

The Witch shrugged. "What can he do?"

"The man is a supremely capable warrior. I do not trust him to lie down quietly and let us escape."

BOLAN STRODE into the infirmary with Rybenok in tow.

Sheree Redbird sat on Larquette's bed and looked up as he entered. The chief smiled and Bolan noticed she was pale but looked stronger.

"How is she?"

Redbird tapped her pen on a chart absently. "Well, she lost a lot of blood. She was already suffering from exposure and exhaustion, and it was enough to drop her into shock. It seems she had already been shot once a few days ago, and I had to stitch that one up correctly." Her black eyes peered at Bolan speculatively. "Though, I have to admit, I liked the field dressing. It was expertly done."

Bolan smiled. "I'm American Red Cross certified."

The doctor snorted. "Well, her other shoulder will probably require some rehabilitation, but it was a clean wound and didn't break any bones. She was lucky."

Bolan jerked a thumb at Rybenok. "He's all yours."

Larquette spoke as Redbird went over to Rybenok and led him to a table where she began carefully unwrapping his sling. "So what's up?"

"Trouble."

Larquette sagged back into her pillows tiredly. "I take it our friend Ramzin isn't going to come out quietly."

"No, he's not."

Her face set angrily. "Well, I say it's time we set the United States Marines on the son of a bitch."

A small grin ghosted across the Executioner's face. "Normally I'd agree with you, but he has five hundred hostages and a nuclear demolition charge."

Larquette's jaw dropped. "Where'd he get an atom bomb?"

"Not an atom bomb. A nuclear demolition charge."

She stared at Bolan incredulously. "Well, what do you do with a nuclear demolition charge?"

The Executioner shrugged. "Dig great big holes. Destroy bunkers."

Her eyes suddenly narrowed. "Or collapse tunnels."

"That too."

"So what do we do?"

"Ramzin has put all the non-Russian laborers into his second tunnel. He says that if he's interfered with, he's going to drop the mountain on top of them."

"And you think he'd do it?"

Bolan's face set. "I know he's going to."

"You mean he's going to do it anyway?"

"Left to his own devices, I don't believe Ramzin would kill all the workers. But he's going to blow up the base and the tunnels behind him when he bugs out. The workers have to be in the tunnels to keep his threat viable, and they're not going to waste time evacuating potential witnesses when they leave. I believe your friend Anne Tyler and whoever is backing her have no qualms about blowing up civilians."

"But we can't just let them all be killed!"

Bolan nodded. "We're not."

"But how? You said if Ramzin sees anyone coming he'll blow the whole place!"

"He will."

Larquette looked at him quizzically "Then how?"

Bolan squeezed her hand. "I called some friends, and with a little luck, Ramzin will never see us coming."

23

Jack Grimaldi spoke into the C-130H's intercom. "Two minutes, gentlemen!"

In the belly of the big transport, the Stony Man warriors came to alert as the warning light flashed briefly. Elements of Able Team and Phoenix Force had been rounded up as quickly as possible, and Gary Manning was nominally in command until they contacted Bolan. He surveyed his team.

Carl "Ironman" Lyons ran a rag over his Atchisson Assault 12 magazine-fed automatic shotgun a final time. He rose and attached the weapon to his jump rig and stood impatiently. Striker needed them and he was ready to go.

Rafael Encizo turned to David McCarter. "Are you ready to catch some air, my friend?"

McCarter put down his copy of *Autosport* magazine and peered up at the jump light. "Too right."

The two men rose and checked each other's straps a final time. Gadgets Schwarz and Rosario "Politician" Blancanales stood and inspected each other. Blancanales carried an M-16 rifle with an attached M-203 grenade launcher, and various grenades hung about him on bandoliers like strings of lethal Christmas ornaments. Manning looked at Schwarz. Gadgets preferred the quiet kill, or better yet, to let his technical genius do the work from a distance. But for this mission a Heckler & Koch MP-5K submachine gun accompanied his usual bag of tricks and silenced Beretta pistol. The five men finished inspections and turned to Manning. The big Canadian looked at the grim-faced men before him in silent appraisal. They were festooned with weapons and in their blacksuits and body armor they looked ready to storm hell itself. They pulled on their jump helmets and oxygen masks and coolly observed the jump light as they adjusted the air flow from the bailout bottles.

Manning nodded toward the cargo door as warning lights flared to life, and the airframe shuddered as the hydraulics opened the fuselage to the frigid wind outside. The Stony Man team filed to the open cargo-bay door. The Sonoran Desert was a swirling patchwork of red and brown thirty-six thousand feet below them. On the ground it was nearly a hundred degrees, but up in the C-130's gaping belly it was well below freezing. Manning watched the distant earth below. They were jumping in blind, with no knowledge of the drop zone, the situation or the expected resistance. All they knew was that Mack Bolan needed them, and that was enough.

The thirty-second light came on, and Manning braced himself. As jump master he would go last. They lined up in three rows of two, and the plane shuddered as Jack Grimaldi held the big transport as close to stalling speed as he dared.

Grimaldi's voice came across Manning's headset as the green jump light came on.

"Go! Go! Go!"

Manning shouted at the top of his lungs. "All right! Let's go!" He gave his companions a final thumbs-up.

"And remember! Officially we're still on vacation."

Even Lyons grinned.

Six of the most dangerous men in the world plunged into space.

MACK BOLAN SCANNED the sky and spotted six small smudges gliding down toward the outskirts of Crucible. He clambered into the cab of Larquette's Jeep Cherokee and drove westward out of town. Looking up through the window, he could see the smudges turn into the dark gray rectangles of parafoils descending in lazy spirals out above the flats. Past them, two cargo chutes with torpedo shaped jump containers drifted down to crunch into the sand of the desert floor.

Bolan stopped the Cherokee and got out as the parachutes veered and began to steer in his direction. The lead parafoil pulled up almost to a stall and dropped the jumper directly in front of Bolan. The silenced British L-34 Sterling submachine gun strapped across the jumper's chest told Bolan immediately that it was David McCarter. The other five jumpers descended in rapid order behind him.

The Briton pulled off his jump helmet and looked at Bolan with a cocked eyebrow. He took in the big man's torn and bloodstained blacksuit and the sun-darkened skin of his face. Bolan's body armor had a number of ragged holes punched in its outer shell, and he carried a Russian AK-74 assault rifle loosely in his hands. McCarter gave him a grin.

"Been having a jolly good holiday, I see."

The others finished folding their chutes and formed a loose ring around Bolan. Manning nodded at the Executioner as he slipped the jump cover off of his M-14 sniper rifle. "What's the situation?"

"A foreign crime syndicate has dug a tunnel between the United States and Mexico. Approximately five hundred hostages are being held in a secondary tunnel. The opposition has at least one nuclear demolition charge and is threatening to detonate it if they're hindered from withdrawing into Mexico."

Lyons snorted as he unslung his automatic shotgun. "So who's the opposition?"

Bolan stared at Lyons frankly. "At least one full-strength platoon of Russian Spetsnaz troops, elements of a second, and support by an indeterminate number of combat engineers and specialist troops."

"A platoon of Spetsnaz here?"

Bolan nodded. "Here, and getting ready to bug out as we speak."

McCarter shrugged and unclipped his submachine gun. "Not bloody likely."

Bolan turned to Schwarz. "I need you to take out the charge, Gadgets."

Schwarz nodded. "It shouldn't be too difficult. A demolition charge probably won't be very sophisticated. The problem, of course, will be to get to it before they decide to detonate." Gadgets paused. "They're going to detonate anyway, aren't they? Whether they get away or not."

Bolan's voice was stone. "I believe so."

Manning finished checking his weapon. "What's our plan?"

The Executioner pointed at the ground. "We come up underneath them."

RAMZIN BARKED his commands. "Lukov! Report!"

"Everything proceeds, Major. Galanskov and his team have the hostages secured in number two tunnel and await orders. Captain Baibakov has the base mobilized and has troops ready to cover withdrawal. All nonessential personnel have gone to the warehouse, and the convoy is preparing for departure."

"Good. Continue to keep me updated until departure."

The Witch spoke behind him. "What of our assets here?"

Ramzin turned. "All portable assets have been mobilized. What of our move across Mexico? Do you have your end covered?"

The Witch smiled. "My husband had friends in Mexico, and it is amazing what a few million dollars in the right hands will do. I expect little trouble in Mexico. It is a very large country, and much of it is lightly populated. A temporary base is being set up for us in the mountains between Sonora and Chihuahua. It will be a hard drive, through rough roads, but I expect we can reach it in seventy-two hours if we push. I was at this hacienda once with my husband some years ago. It will serve."

Ramzin nodded and folded his arms. His one fear had been that of being caught in the open by hostile Mexican authorities and overwhelmed. He wouldn't be happy until they had reached this hacienda in the mountains, but at least now he dared to hope.

There was no sign of any activity by the Americans. No planes had been spotted. No word had come from the Witch's spies in the Arizona state government that anything was known, much less being done about the situation in Crucible. It seemed that even the Yankee commando had blinked at having the blood of five hundred hostages on his hands.

The plan appeared to be working.

He looked down at the twin detonators sitting on his desk. The blood would be on his hands. Ramzin's father had fought the Nazis in the Great Patriotic War to Defend the Motherland. He had been one of the liberators at the death camp in Treblinka, and seen the Nazi atrocities first hand. A cold wind blew through Ramzin's soul, and he wondered what his father would say to his son now. Ramzin's resolve suddenly stiffened. He knew exactly what his father would tell him. He had told it to him a hundred times, from the train station that had first taken him to officer training school to the departure gate that had sent him off to the war in Afghanistan: be brave, do your duty, keep your men alive.

Ramzin turned to the Witch. "Have all your affairs in order and prepare to move."

THE EXECUTIONER GAVE the vertical shaft a final glance and stepped back. "All right, Gadgets, blow it."

Schwarz pressed the red button on his remote detonator. "Fire in the hole!"

There was a muffled boom as smoke and dust fountained out of the shaft. Manning tossed a coil of rope into the hole, and it fell away down into darkness. He handed the other end to Lyons, and the Ironman quickly fired a climbing spike into the surface of the butte with a piton gun and knotted the rope to it. He tugged on the rope to test it and gave Bolan the thumbs up.

Blancanales squatted on the lip of the hole and peered down the shaft. A circle of yellow light shone into the darkness below. "We've got a clear passage to the floor of the mine."

Bolan jerked his head at Lyons. "Carl, take point."

The Ironman clipped the rope to his harness and positioned himself at the lip of the shaft. He took the rope in one hand and held his automatic shotgun across his chest with the other. Without a word, he rappeled backward and disappeared into the mine. Seconds later the rope went slack, then jerked twice. Bolan clipped himself onto the rope and laid the M-4 Ranger carbine that his team had brought him across his chest. They had also thoughtfully brought him more grenades, .44 Magnum and 9 mm ammunition than one human being could reasonably be expected to carry and still be able to walk.

He kicked back from the edge of the hole and rappeled into the vertical tunnel. The explosive charge had broken away the rocks and loose scree choking the shaft and had left a chimney wide enough for a man to rappel down without bumping the sides. Bolan slid down the rope in three stops and dropped lightly onto the pile of rubble on the floor of the mine. Lyons squatted a few yards away with his weapon trained down the mine. The Executioner unclipped and jerked the rope twice. He pulled his night-vision goggles over his eyes and stepped forward as McCarter came down the rope.

Bolan glanced around his former grave. The walls were still scorched and stank of vaporized explosive and flame-thrower fuel. Dozens of empty shell casings littered the floor. Manning was the last man down the rope, and he pulled his goggles over his eyes as the team assembled around Bolan.

The Executioner led them to the hole he had blasted a few days earlier. Gadgets examined it, then grinned. "A little sloppy." He ran a device around the jagged metal edge of the ventilator and pointed the device's antenna downward. "There doesn't appear to be any active alarms or surveillance. This shaft leads to the primary tunnel?"

Bolan nodded as Encizo uncoiled a second rope. Lyons fired a piton into the wall opposite the hole and attached the rope to it. Blancanales wrapped a field dressing around the rope where it lay against the ragged edge of hole in the ventilator and covered the padding with tape. Ironman gave the rope an experimental yank and nodded satisfactorily.

"We're a go, Striker."

Bolan clipped himself in and entered the ventilator. With the aid of a rope, the descent was simple and he quickly reached the fan. Larquette's Winchester was still jammed between the blades, and the sling of his sniper rifle still dangled from a support strut. He couched above the fan and listened intently. In the distance he could faintly hear noises and the echo of an occasional shout. He locked his ankles around the rope and hung his head past the ventilator fan.

Everything was clear in both directions. The noises were coming from the United States side of the tunnel. He dropped the loose coils of the rope and quickly slid down to the packed earth of the tunnel floor. Bolan crouched for several long seconds and listened. After a moment he pulled up his night-vision goggles and let his eyes adjust to the orange glare of the tunnel lights.

He tugged twice on the rope, and one by one his team silently slid to the tunnel floor. They moved swiftly down the corridor in a short L formation, with Bolan, Lyons and Blancaneles in the front. As they moved closer to the American side, the noise became louder and Bolan recognized the shout of "Halt! Stay back!" in Russian.

The Executioner held up his fist and the team halted and dropped to the ground. He pulled out the range-finding binoculars the team had brought him and trained them down the tunnel. The underground corridor was a straight shot, and Bolan adjusted the gain on the binoculars as shapes resolved in his view. The shapes were two gun jeeps, parked in front of what appeared to be an access door set into the side of the tunnel. Two men stood in the backs of the jeeps and leaned casually on the grips of post-mounted DShK heavy machine guns. A third man sat in the passenger seat of the nearest jeep, apparently manning the radio.

Bolan pressed the laser range finder and the readout told him six hundred and forty-two meters, a little over half a kilometer. He looked back and jerked his head at Gary Manning, who moved forward on knees and elbows with his M-14 sniper rifle cradled across his forearms. Bolan handed him the binoculars, and Manning looked down the tunnel.

"Three targets, Gary. I suspect there are more Russians in the side tunnel. Probably guarding the hostages. I need those three taken out, quick and silent."

Manning shook his head. His M-14 was an extremely accurate weapon, but it was a semiautomatic battle rifle, chambered for the powerful .308 NATO cartridge. He could take out the targets quickly, but it would make a lot of noise.

A rifle like the M-14 was extremely hard to suppress, much less silence.

"Get me Gadgets' Heckler & Koch, and I can do it. But I'll have to get close."

He nodded and signaled Gadgets forward. Schwarz silently hunkered in between them. Bolan handed him the binoculars, and Gadgets scanned the situation. The Able Team warrior peered down the tunnel, then handed the binoculars back with a shrug.

"Gary should use my weapon."

Bolan and Manning looked at each other. You could never overestimate Gadgets Schwarz.

Manning took the submachine gun and handed Schwarz his big rifle. He examined the weapon in his hands. The German Heckler & Koch MP-5 was undoubtedly the most sophisticated submachine in the world. Its closed bolt action and precision manufacture allowed it riflelike accuracy past two hundred yards under ideal conditions. Its suppressor was built into the gun itself instead of being threaded onto the end of the barrel. When the gun fired, it spoke barely above a whisper.

"Your call, Gary," Bolan said. "How do you want to play it?"

Manning unfolded the weapon's collapsible buttstock as he calculated. "I'll have to get within a hundred yards to make it work. But if they manage to get off a shot, we're blown. I'll need you and Gadgets to back me with your Berettas if it gets hairy."

Both Bolan and Gadgets had sound suppressors on the end of their Beretta 93-R pistols, and they drew their weapons. The Executioner signaled to the others, and they crept close.

"We're going to take the sentries. Keep a hundred yard interval behind us and stay low. If you hear gunfire, come in hard."

He turned to Lyons. "Carl, if it hits the fan, I want you to take out those cables along the ceiling." Bolan pointed up at the exposed bundle of wiring that tracked the length of the tunnel. "Hit that transformer box. With any luck that will kill the lights. All of you have your night vision ready."

Lyons nodded, and the rest of the team powered up their goggles but kept them ready on their foreheads.

The Executioner, Manning and Schwarz detached from the group and began to creep up the tunnel. The overhead lamps threw regular, evenly spaced pools of orange light in the tunnel, and the warriors silently stuck to the shadowy fringe along the walls. They crept on interminably, until it seemed they were so close that the Russians couldn't help but see them.

Manning held up his fist and came to a halt. They were within a hundred yards. He peered down the sight of the submachine gun at his targets. Luckily the jeeps were parked tandem and sat squarely under one of the overhead lights. He looked at the big guy, then Schwarz. Both held their silenced pistols ready. If Manning couldn't get all three before they could react, Schwarz and Bolan would pour in suppressed fire from their weapons, hoping to get a hit and prevent the Russians from firing their weapons or sounding the alarm.

Manning placed the MP-5's sight on the man in the far jeep. The machine gunners were the priority. If they got off a shot, it would sound like a cannon firing in the confines of the tunnel. He adjusted his aim a hair and took a breath. His target was motionless, leaning in bored fashion against his machine gun. Manning slowly let out half of his breath, then began to squeeze the trigger.

24

Lieutenant Galanskov shouted angrily and waved his hand in a cutting motion as one of the Mexican laborers edged along the wall of the tunnel toward the service entrance. "Get back!"

Galanskov didn't speak Spanish, and the Mexican didn't speak Russian, but as the corporal behind Galanskov swiveled the big DSh K heavy machine gun, the meaning was very clear. The laborer's eyes widened, and he moved back into the press of his comrades behind him. His eyes never left Galanskov's face.

The lieutenant settled back on the jeep's seat and kept his hand close to his machine pistol. He was a decorated combat engineer, not some snot-nosed private from Siberia to be pulling guard duty on a bunch of peasants. But guard duty was the least of what bothered him. If someone was going to mind a nuclear demolition charge, he was undoubtedly the most qualified man on the base. It was the eyes of all those men staring at him in fear that gnawed at him. Galanskov had designed and built these tunnels, and these men had worked for him. They had nearly broken their backs, working, sweating and bleeding in ceaseless nonstop shifts to finish the tunnels on time. They had done so without complaint, all in the hopes of seeing the promised freedom and opportunity of the United States.

Now he was going to blow these men into their component atoms.

Well, *he* wasn't going to do it. Ramzin had the detonators, but there was cold comfort in that.

Galanskov watched the laborers walk about nervously, jammed into the dead end of the unfinished second tunnel like sardines. They knew very well that something was wrong. Only the heavy machine guns of the jeeps kept them in check. The engineer glanced unhappily at the charge where it lay against the wall.

It was the size of a large suitcase and covered with green webbing. It was a fairly small charge, only ten kilotons, but it would bring down everything within a kilometer. The timer was set for twenty-five minutes after activation, plenty of time for him and his men to drive to Mexico in the jeeps and escape once the convoy had passed. The laborers, however, would never be able to hike out in time. Even if they managed to run several miles down the tunnel and escape the fireball, the blast would be channeled down the corridor like a fire hose of superheated rock and air. They would be incinerated instantly.

"Halt, damn you! Halt!" Corporal Zubarev shouted and swiveled the heavy machine gun as the laborers in the front were pressed forward by those in back. The throng halted as Corporal Sviridov swiveled his weapon from the second jeep, as well.

Down the access tunnel, Sergeant Bridilov shouted from the second pair of jeeps guarding the entrance to tunnel number one. "Is everything all right, Lieutenant?"

Galanskov craned his neck around and snarled, "Everything is fine!" He looked at his watch. He would have to check in with the base in another minute. He looked up and his face split with rage. One of the poor bastards had a rock in his hand. He would have to shoot a few of them to keep the rest quiet. Galanskov pointed a condemning finger at the man, and the DSh K swiveled on its mount behind him. The man dropped the rock and desperately tried to move back into the throng, but the press was just too close.

"That one! Shoot him and the men around him!"

Galanskov jumped at the sudden sound of an automatic weapon tearing into life somewhere behind him in the first tunnel. With the hard won instincts of a tunnel rat he grabbed his machine pistol and rolled out of the jeep as the tunnel lights cut out.

THE EXECUTIONER MOVED through the darkness with Manning and Schwarz on either side of him. The big Canadian had taken out the three men in the jeeps within three seconds of the "Everything is fine!" Then, from down in the access tunnel, where they couldn't see, had come the shouted order in Russian, "Shoot him and the men around him!"

Bolan had made a cutting motion with his hand, and Lyons had ripped into the overhead lighting transformer with his automatic shotgun. The Executioner raced down the tunnel and his night-vision goggles flared as bright light suddenly shone forth from the access tunnel.

Whoever was inside had lights.

Bolan pulled a flash-stun grenade from his belt and roared at the top of his lungs in Spanish, "Get down! Down if you want to live!"

From inside, a heavy weapon ripped into action and tracers streamed out of the tunnel entrance.

The Executioner crouched and tossed the grenade around the corner. The explosion was horrendous in the confines of the tunnel. Bolan took the corner low. The concussion had shattered the searchlight mounted on the gun jeep, and a man leaned drunkenly on the heavy machine gun and blindly tried to get his bearings. Four other men weaved and groped in the dark with weapons in their hands, two in the jeeps and two on foot. One man crouched and fixed his bayonet to his rifle, trying to discern what was happening in the inky blackness around him.

The Executioner knew from experience that the man couldn't hear anything through his ringing ears, or even know direction after the stun grenade had hit him. Bolan strode up to the Russian, keeping himself out of line with the man's rifle barrel and gave him a heavy buttstroke to the chin with his carbine. The man fell back as if he had been shot.

Bolan pointed at the man on the heavy machine gun, and Manning jumped into the jeep and brutally yanked him backward, spilling him to the ground. The Russian landed badly, and as he groped in the dark, Schwarz walked up to him and smashed the knife edge of his hand into the side of the soldier's neck. The third Russian gagged and folded as Bolan rammed the muzzle of his carbine into the pit of his stomach.

The fourth was crouched and groping for the weapon he had dropped when the grenade exploded. Manning butt-stroked him with his borrowed submachine gun and gave an affirmative thumbs-up. The rest of the team stormed in, and Bolan gave them the all-clear signal as Manning and Schwarz bound the incapacitated Russians.

The Executioner looked past the jeeps and saw the hundreds of men lying on the floor. Bolan reached into one of the jeeps and turned on the headlights. The men looked dazedly into the sudden glare, and a few rose warily to their knees. Bolan shouted in Spanish, knowing most had been partially deafened by the blast.

"We have come to rescue you. Get up slowly, then move forward slowly. We are going to get you out."

The men stood and began to come forward, some helped by others. Bolan turned to his team. "Rafe, Pol, get me a quick head count and see if any of them are injured. The rest of you spread out and find the charge."

A voice spoke from behind them in Russian. "Do not move."

McCarter slid his eyes down and to the right of the vehicles, and Bolan followed the subtle movement.

There was a Russian under the jeep.

The man peered out grimly from where he had wedged himself between the jeep's large, all-terrain tires. He brandished a machine pistol in one hand and the other was awkwardly held back out of sight.

The Russian jerked the muzzle of his Stechkin at Bolan. "Drop your weapons."

Bolan regarded the Russian. "No."

"I will kill you."

The Executioner shrugged. "Maybe, but my men will kill you, regardless."

The man nodded. "Perhaps, but none of them will live to see daylight."

"You have the charge under there with you?"

The man nodded. "Surrender. Throw down your weapons."

"You are willing to die?"

The man stared at Bolan without blinking.

Bolan pointed back into the side tunnel. "You are willing to sacrifice your men?"

The man looked over to where his four men sat bound against the wall of the tunnel. He was obviously surprised to see them still alive.

The Executioner lowered the muzzle of his carbine. "Surrender. You and your men will be well treated."

The Russian looked at his men, then over to where the laborers stood milling apprehensively. Finally his gaze rested back on Bolan. For a moment the man didn't move, then he tossed his machine pistol a few feet away and began to crawl from under the jeep. As he rose, he pulled a large rectangular package with him. The Russian stood and dusted himself off. He was a short, powerfully built man and he held himself ramrod straight.

"I am Senior Lieutenant Vitali Galanskov. I surrender."

Bolan nodded. "Go and sit by your men."

He switched over to English. "Schwarz, check him and tie his hands."

As Schwarz patted down Galanskov, the radio in the lead jeep squawked. Bolan turned and looked at Galanskov. The Russian sighed.

"I am supposed to check in regularly. I am late."

Bolan crooked a finger at Schwarz. "Bring over Lieutenant Galanskov."

The Executioner sat in the jeep and picked up the transmitter.

RAMZIN PUNCHED the transmitter's button a second time with mounting unease.

"Galanskov! You are overdue! Report!"

There was a small burst of static and a cold voice came over the receiver. "It is finished, Ramzin. Surrender."

Ramzin's blood went cold. Baibakov's knuckles cracked and went white as he drew himself to his full height. The Witch stared at the radio set incredulously.

The voice spoke again with the surety of command. "Surrender. It is over."

Ramzin keyed his transmitter. "What of my men who were in the tunnel?"

"Two are dead, one is badly wounded. Several are injured but alive. Lieutenant Galanskov is alive, and I have accepted his surrender. The injured will be cared for." There was a long pause. "You cannot escape through the tunnel. I can hold it indefinitely against your men. You no longer have hostages. Reinforcements will arrive soon. If you force me to take the camp, many of your men will be slaughtered. Surrender. Now."

Ramzin took a long slow breath. "I will give you one opportunity. Release Galanskov and his men. When he tells me that you and your men have been secured, I will instruct him to march you and the laborers out of the tunnel before I collapse it behind my convoy. I give you my word on this."

"That is not going to happen."

Ramzin picked up one of the remote detonators from his desk and pushed the arming button.

"Then die."

25

Mack Bolan's gaze turned to stone as a green light began blinking on the nuclear demolition charge's control panel.

"Gadgets, I need you."

Schwarz leaned over and regarded the charge with great curiosity. Galanskov stared at it in horror.

Schwarz scratched his chin and nodded. "Well, it's armed, all right."

"Can you stop it?"

Gadgets looked at Galanskov. "It will be easier if he helps. Your Russian is better than mine, Mack. Ask him whether he wants to be blown to bits."

Bolan turned to Galanskov. "Can you stop it?"

Galanskov stared at the charge as if it were a giant spider that had dropped in their midst. He suddenly looked up at Bolan. "Stop it? Do not be a fool! We must get out, now! The charge is set on a twenty-five minute timer. Using the jeeps, your men and mine can be out of the tunnel and to safety before it detonates. We must flee, now!"

Bolan turned his gaze to the laborers as they stared uncomprehendingly, and Galanskov's gaze followed his. Bolan's voice was iron.

"That is not an option."

"You will kill us all!"

"You're wasting time."

For one long moment the Executioner and Galanskov stared at each other. The Russian sighed heavily and resigned himself to fate. "Very well." He jerked his thumb at Schwarz. "This man has some expertise in these matters?"

Bolan nodded. "A little."

Galanskov snorted. "I do not doubt it." He nodded at
Schwarz and they squatted on their heels with the nuclear
device between them. The two men began to speak to each
other in a rapid-fire jumble of Russian and English technical terms. Bolan leaned over Schwarz's shoulder.

"What've we got?"

Gadgets tapped his chin with his finger. "It's a pretty
standard Russian nuclear demolition charge."

Talking to Gadgets about technical matters was like pulling teeth. "The situation, Gadgets, quickly."

"Well, it's a fairly primitive, uranium 235, gun-type nuclear charge. Which means when it goes off it's going to
slam one piece of fissionable uranium into another and we
are going to have a nuclear explosion. It's a dial-a-yield,
which means you can select an explosive yield from about
three to ten kilotons, and our friends have it cranked up to
ten."

Galanskov looked up and spoke in crude English. "*Da*,
ten kilotons."

Schwarz nodded. "That's about a kiloton or two shy of
the bombs at Hiroshima and Nagasaki, and it's going to go
off in twenty-two minutes."

The Executioner folded his arms across his chest. "So
what are you going to do about it?"

Gadgets shrugged and peered at the charge's casing.
"Well, that's the rub. It's a nuclear demolition charge, not
a warhead or a bomb, specifically."

Bolan nodded and waited for more.

Schwarz began tapping his chin again in meditation.
"Well, you see, a bomb or a warhead is generally pretty
straightforward. You fire it off in a missile or drop it out of
a plane, and it does its job. If you know what you're doing,
disassembling one or disarming it shouldn't be too difficult. But a nuclear demolition charge is something your men
use on a battlefield. Generally you put one in place to destroy an underground command bunker, or a tunnel or
something big, deep and fortified, and then you get the hell
out of there. In that kind of situation, you don't want the
enemy coming up and disarming it after you bug out, so you
make it tamperproof."

"And?"

Gadgets sighed. "And our friend Galanskov has done an excellent job of tamper-proofing his charge. To disarm the charge I have to get inside it, and if I try to get inside it, it goes off. He has put sensors on the four bolts that hold the casing together. If I try to unscrew the bolts or cut them away, I'll break a circuit and the charge will detonate instantly."

"How about cutting into the casing?"

"Well, that's one way, but Galanskov has rigged an intrusion sensor inside."

Galanskov spread his fingers outward in an explosive gesture. "Boom."

Bolan stared hard at Gadgets. "So you can't disarm it?"

Schwarz tapped as his chin a moment. "Yeah, but not in our given time frame."

"So what are you going to do about it?"

Schwarz shrugged. "I believe I'm just going to have to blow it up."

Bolan looked at him and cocked an eyebrow. "Oh?"

Gadgets steepled his fingers. "I think that if I use some C-4, I can blow up the charge and make it detonate low order. We'll still have limited fission, but because the fissionable masses won't have slammed together correctly, the explosion will be much smaller—maybe a kiloton, maybe less."

"And?"

"And everything for several hundred yards will be blown up. The mountain itself will collapse over the blast area and contain the radiation. A mile or two down the tunnel, everything should be all right. That is, if everything goes correctly, which I can't promise you. But—"

Bolan unfolded his arms and cut him off. "Do it."

He turned to Encizo and Blancanales. "Find out who among the workers were foremen and put them in charge. Tell them to get their men as far down the tunnel as fast as they possibly can, and not to stop until they get to Mexico. Tell them to take the Russians with them."

The two men began to address the laborers, and some of them raised their hands and stepped forward through the throng. Bolan turned to Lyons. "Take the radio and get topside. Contact Jack and let him know we're going to need up close air support, and I need it ten minutes ago. Then get back here as fast as possible. You have fifteen minutes."

Lyons jumped into one of the jeeps without a word and peeled off in a screech of tires toward the team's entry point down the tunnel. Bolan turned to Manning and McCarter. "If the Russians are going to blow the tunnel, then they'll have sealed off their side. Take any explosives that Gadgets isn't using and rig a jeep."

Manning nodded. "We're going to assault?"

The Executioner pointed north. "Right now Ramzin expects us to be running toward Mexico for our lives. He'll be busy getting ready to bug out himself. He's not expecting to get hit from underneath."

THE WITCH WAS NEARLY spitting with fury. "Blow up the tunnel? Are you insane? You have cut us off!"

Ramzin shook his head. "No, this American is correct. The tunnel is narrow. He can hold it for hours, perhaps days until help arrives. Let him have the tunnel. Let it be his grave."

She looked at him in cold anger. "And what is it we are to do now? Hold the base against the United States Marines?"

"No, before the tunnel was completed, some men and materials had to be smuggled across the border through the mountains. There are paths there that the trucks can manage. It will be long and risky, but we can still get into Mexico."

"You are a fool, Ramzin. How are we to get across undetected? A whole convoy? The American authorities are probably already on their way."

"Yes, undoubtedly. That is why we will require a diversion."

The Witch's anger switched gears and she peered at Ramzin. "What kind of diversion?"

"A ten-kiloton surface blast on United States soil should be ample to divert their attention from some lonely mountain passes on the border. It should keep them busy for days.''

"You have another charge?"

Ramzin held up the second detonator. "Of course."

"You are going to blow up the base behind us."

"You are correct. The entire American early-warning system will go mad when their satellites detect a surface nuclear explosion. Once in the passes, we will be in no danger. We will have a mountain between us and the charge when it goes off, and no one will be looking for us. They will have too many other things to look at and think about. Once in Mexico, however, we will require your resources to get to safety."

The Witch calculated. "I do not see that being a problem. Once we are across the border I will alert my contacts to the change in plan. We should still be able to proceed through northern Mexico disguised as a Mexican army convoy. The way has already been paved. I trust the markings on the trucks are in place?"

Ramzin glanced at Baibakov, and the giant nodded. "More than an hour ago."

The major nodded in grim satisfaction and put the detonator in his pocket. "Good. We leave in half an hour. Have the men ready."

JACK GRIMALDI STOOD in the control tower of Fort Huachuca with his escort-liaison, Warrant Officer Steven Anderson. The base commander hadn't known what to think when Grimaldi had flown into his base in an unmarked C-130 with more top-secret security clearances than he had ever heard of. He wanted the man watched. Anderson had almost forgotten about his mission. The mysterious guest knew just about everything there was to know about military aviation, and they had spent the past hour in deep, arcane, aeronautical conversation. Anderson enthusiastically pointed at an AH-64D Apache helicopter gunship out on the pads. He was the Apache's gunner and was very proud of his aircraft. The gunship sat on its pad bristling with missiles and rocket pods.

"That's Stella. We're going to take her through a demonstration run for some South Korean military-procurement types. She took out four tanks and two armored vehicles in the Gulf. She's got all the latest target acquisition sensors, I mean everything, and all the latest upgrades, as well." He gazed down lovingly. "She's one sweet machine."

Grimaldi whistled as he looked at Stella. The armored attack helicopter was remarkably ugly. Her only beauty was in the totally stark functionality of her lines. She resembled an overgrown, utterly hostile prehistoric dragonfly. The tower communications officer spoke as the two men stared in the dreamy camaraderie of the air at the lethal machine below.

"Mr. Grimaldi, I have a flash-priority communication for you, code name Striker."

"Thanks." Grimaldi took the handset. "Go ahead, Striker."

"This is Ironman."

"Go ahead, Ironman."

"We need close air support ASAP." Lyons tensely gave Grimaldi the situation. Grimaldi's eyebrows rose as the nature of the threat and where it was hit home. His face tightened.

"I'm already inbound, Ironman. When I come, you pop green smoke. Anything else I see, I'm going to trash."

"Understood. Ironman out."

Grimaldi handed the communications officer the handset. "I need to speak with the base commander immediately. This is a military emergency."

The officer gawked at Grimaldi. Fort Huachuca never had military emergencies. "Right away!"

Grimaldi turned to Anderson.

"Get your flight suit on. We're taking Stella for a ride."

26

The Executioner stared up the ramp through the remains of the chain-link fence that guarded the entrance to the tunnel on American soil. The final door was corrugated iron, similar to the entrance on the Mexican side. There had been no traps when he and Larquette had stolen into Mexico, but he was taking no chances.

He nodded down the tunnel to Manning. "Hit it."

The big Canadian rammed the jeep's accelerator to the floor, and the vehicle leaped forward in a screech of tires. He gave Schwarz the sign, and Gadgets hit the detonator on the preemptive explosive he had attached to the Russian nuclear charge. The jeep tore up the ramp, and Manning jumped out and rolled behind the shelter of the concrete ramp's edge.

Bolan heard a dull rumbling and felt the earth shake beneath his feet. Two and a half miles behind them hundreds of thousands of tons of dirt and rock were shifting to fill the empty space the nuclear charge had created with its miniature atomic fireball.

The jeep slammed into the corrugated door, and the ten pounds of C-4 high explosive detonated. There wasn't time to worry about whether Gadgets had attained a low order explosion with the nuclear charge. The team's own smaller explosion was the more immediate danger, and Bolan and the rest of the Stony Man warriors crouched as shards of metal and scrap from the jeep flew over their heads in lethal, burning arcs. Bolan shouted over the ringing in his ears as the metal fragments fell and clattered to the floor.

"Move!"

The Executioner raised his M-4 carbine to his shoulder and triggered its 40 mm grenade launcher, sending a white phosphorus grenade arcing through the smoking wreckage of the door to explode in the warehouse behind it.

The team stormed up the ramp. Lyons drove the second gun jeep and it ground up the ramp in low gear. Its bumper slammed into the wreck of the jeep blocking the way and pushed the blackened hulk before it into the warehouse. Encizo stood behind the heavy Russian machine gun mounted in the back, and Blancanales manned the lighter weapon mounted on the hood in front of the passenger seat. Both weapons blazed into life as they gained entrance to the warehouse.

Bolan jogged to where Manning crouched by the ramp and handed him his sniper rifle. "You all right?"

The big Canadian shook his head to clear it and grinned as he took his weapon. "Never felt better."

Bolan grabbed his hand and hauled him to his feet. "Good. Let's get moving."

RAMZIN STOOD on the running board of one of the trucks and gave last-minute instructions to its driver. He turned as a low rumble echoed through the desert air and the very mountain behind the base seemed to groan and shake. Dust slowly shook off the mountainside like shuddering tufts of red smoke, and small avalanches of rocks and gravel rattled onto the desert plain.

Ramzin checked his watch curiously. The explosion was five minutes early, and much smaller than he had anticipated. He looked back into the center of the base. The main warehouse should have been ripped apart by the venting of the blast through the tunnel, and a pillar of superheated air and dust should have rocketed into the sky like a geyser.

The warehouse sat squatly in the middle of the base, apparently unharmed. Ramzin and Baibakov stared at each other.

An explosion boomed hollowly inside the warehouse and the corrugated walls shook and the high-set, narrow windows shattered. It was followed almost immediately by a smaller and higher-pitched blast.

Ramzin's blood turned to ice as he realized the absolute worst of his fears were coming true. There was only one thing left to do, and that was to save his men. He turned to Baibakov and a feral snarl split his face.

"Captain, take the convoy and get it to Mexico. I will take two squads and fight a delaying action."

Baibakov stared at his commander in horror. "Major, we must—"

Ramzin's face was a rictus of rage. "Do you question my orders, Captain Baibakov?"

Baibakov snapped to attention. "I obey your orders without question, Major!"

"Then get my men out of here." Ramzin slapped the side of the truck. "Squads one and two! Fall out!"

Heavily armed men began to leap out of the truck and fall in behind Ramzin. As the last man leaped out, the major shouted to Baibakov. "I will catch up with you once our backs are safe!"

Baibakov nodded as he leaped into another truck.

Ramzin pulled a spare AK-74 rifle and a belt of spare magazines from the abandoned truck and jerked his hand at his men.

"Follow me!"

THE APACHE GUNSHIP roared across the desert at 190 miles per hour, armed with eight Hellfire antitank missiles and two 18-round pods that fired 70 mm rockets. The aircraft's M-230 chain gun was fully loaded with 1,200 rounds of 30 mm shells, and the airframe shuddered as the helicopter streaked across the sky under full emergency war power. In the distance, Grimaldi could see the rugged rock peaks that marked his destination. He took the aircraft down a hundred feet and checked his bearings. The red rocks swept toward them as he kept the throttles full forward.

Warrant Officer Steven Anderson spoke into the intercom from the weapons officer's station in the forward cockpit. His commanding officer had told him he was to do whatever this mysterious pilot told him to, and that it was a matter of national importance. The XO had told him this while Anderson was yanking on his flight suit, and the old man hadn't elaborated further. His face had said "Don't ask," and Anderson didn't question orders. Now that they were up in the air he was getting a little nervous. "Er, Mr. Grimaldi, what exactly is our mission?"

"Close air support," Grimaldi replied as he adjusted course slightly.

"Oh. Supporting who?"

"United States citizens."

Anderson considered this. "Against what?"

"Enemies of the United States."

"I see." Anderson decided to try a different tack as they suddenly swept low across the rocky hills. "What kind of resistance are we expecting?"

Grimaldi's voice was terse across the intercom. "Heavy. Automatic weapons, heavy machine guns, possible missile threat. I suggest you begin countermeasures now."

Anderson didn't have to be told twice, and he armed the switches on the ALQ-144 jammer. To the human eye, nothing happened, but in the infrared spectrum, blinding pulses of infrared light streaked in all directions. Anderson flicked on the Longbow ground attack radar and immediately got feedback.

"Mr. Grimaldi, multiple moving targets on radar!"

"Where?"

"Moving into the mountains, away from the target area."

"All right, arm all weapon systems. We're going in."

"THEY'RE COMING, MACK!"

Bolan clambered into the jeep behind Lyons and took the handles of the DSh K heavy machine gun. "Which way?"

Blancanales was peering through a hole he had punched in the warehouse wall with his knife. "Due west, from the edge of the compound. At least one squad, probably two."

Bolan turned to Gadgets, who was busy on the opposite wall. "Blow it!"

Schwarz moved away from the wall where his long, thin rope of flexible charge was attached in a ten-foot hoop the shape of a giant mouse hole. He punched the detonator as he got out of range. There was a hissing crack and a shower of sparks as a section of the corrugated iron wall was instantly cut away and fell in a warbling clatter.

The warehouse had been empty on entry, but they could hear the grinding of the trucks and jeeps outside, and they knew that their entrance had been heard. Bolan racked the bolt on the heavy machine gun as Encizo grabbed Gadgets's arm and pulled him into the jeep. The Executioner slapped Lyons's shoulder.

"Hit it!"

Bolan crouched behind his weapon as the jeep barely cleared the jagged top of the hole they had cut and shot out into the sunlight. Behind him, he heard Blancanales and McCarter open fire from the opposite side of the warehouse to get the opposition's attention.

"Ironman! Take her around, northern side!"

The jeep's gears ground and dust sprayed out behind them as Lyons took the jeep around the warehouse's northern corner. Encizo shifted his grip on the light machine gun mounted on the hood as they barreled around the final corner.

The Russians were moving from cover to cover, engaging the front of the warehouse, where Blancanales and McCarter were holed up. From behind a parked bulldozer, a rocket-propelled grenade hissed from its launcher and slammed into the side of the warehouse, sending its lethal payload of molten metal and superheated gas inside. Several Russians were firing automatic weapons from behind a thick tube of rolled metal siding.

The heavy machine gun thundered in Bolan's hands as he sent burst after burst into the siding. The rolled metal would stop small arms fire, but it was no match for the machine gun, and the Russians fell under its withering fire. Sparks screamed off the bulldozer as Encizo engaged it with his light machine gun. The RPG team crouched behind the heavy vehicle and reloaded. Bolan shouted at Schwarz and released the heavy machine gun. "Take it! Ironman! The dozer!"

As the jeep sped ahead toward the bulldozer, Gadgets manned the heavy machine gun and engaged targets off to their left. Bolan pulled a grenade and leaped from the vehicle as it pulled past the bulldozer. He pulled the pin as he rolled and as he came up he lobbed the grenade over the bulldozer's thick shovel blade. There was a sharp snapping explosion as the grenade went off, and the Executioner sprinted around the vehicle's south side to keep it between him and the rest of the Russians.

Two bloodied Russians lay behind the bulldozer. One moaned weakly, and the other lay facedown over his RPG launch tube and didn't move. The jeep pulled behind the cover of the bulldozer as a swarm of small arms fire began to shriek against the heavy vehicle. Bolan unslung his M-4 carbine and flipped up the grenade launcher's sight.

"Where?"

Encizo leaped out of the jeep and took the light machine gun with him, wrapping the dangling belt of ammo around his left wrist. "One group, fifty meters, behind those concrete pilings."

Bolan remembered the pilings. Tracers had streamed from them. He raised the grenade launcher in a high arc and fired. A few seconds later he was rewarded with the dull boom of the grenade and screams of pain. The Executioner shucked a high-explosive grenade into the smoking breech of his launcher.

"Rafe, we need cover."

Encizo flopped down between the treads of the bulldozer and began to fire short bursts into the pylons, while Bolan, Schwarz and Lyons burst from behind the vehicle. Schwarz dropped behind a metal drum and added to the covering fire as Bolan and Lyons charged. Bullets chewed into the ground by the Executioner's feet, and he fired the M-203 off to his left. The two men dived behind a pickup truck as tracers streamed into the truck's body.

Bolan slid a grenade into his launcher as Lyons fired a burst from his automatic shotgun over the hood of the truck. "They're moving, Striker."

The soldier nodded as he adjusted the ladder sight of his grenade launcher. "They'll flank us if they can."

Lyons pulled a white-phosphorus grenade from his belt, yanked the pin and hurled the bomb off to the right. Streamers of white smoke and burning phosphorus arced up into the air. Bolan's head jerked up as he heard the whooshing sizzle of a rocket.

"Incoming!"

They threw themselves flat as the RPG round struck the truck and detonated. The pickup rocked violently on its chassis and flames shot out from under the hood. Bits of burning metal flew into the air. Bolan stood and fired a burst through the dark smoke. Return fire raked the pickup's charred and burning hulk.

The Executioner spoke quietly into his throat mike. "Gary, we need you. We're pinned down and they've got an RPG. Our cover is deteriorating rapidly."

Manning's voice spoke in Bolan's earpiece. "I read you, Striker. Targets acquired. Hold tight."

From the roof of the warehouse a heavy rifle boomed three times in rapid succession. Some of the fire pinning down Bolan and Lyons dropped off, and the Executioner saw the sparks of bullets striking metal on the edge of the warehouse's roof.

Manning's voice spoke through the radio. "RPG team down, Striker, but the rest of the boys know I'm here."

"Roger. Get out of there before they start lobbing grenades."

"I'm gone," Manning replied, and the radio went silent.

Bolan heard the hollow thumping of grenade launchers and smoking trails arced toward the roof of the warehouse. The Executioner fired off a grenade of his own toward where the smoking arcs had originated. Blinding white flowers of white-hot phosphorus bloomed on the roof of the warehouse, and ribbons of the burning element drifted down across the battlefield. Lyons fired a burst from his automatic shotgun and dropped behind cover as Bolan spoke into his mike.

"Gary?"

There was no reply.

"Gary, do you read?"

A voice panted into Bolan's earpiece. "Here, Striker. Things got a little hot. I'm rappeling down the far side. Will engage targets of opportunity."

"Roger that." Bolan spoke to McCarter. "Get out of the warehouse. You're being flanked."

"Roger that, Striker, but we're already flanked."

Another RPG exploded into the side of the warehouse and the hollow thuds of grenade launchers boomed not far away.

Bolan glanced about and spoke into the mike. "Gadgets?"

The concrete pylons exploded in a thundering ball of orange fire. Bolan risked a glance over the top of the truck and saw Schwarz crouched some yards away from the pylons behind several cement-filled drums. Bullets shrieked off of the drums but no more grenades boomed from behind the pylons.

"Gadgets?"

"I'm okay, Striker, but that was the last of my C-4, and I'm running out of options out here."

"Sit tight, we'll get to you."

"Roger that."

Lyons fired another burst and dropped behind the truck. "They've stopped their initial attack."

Bolan nodded. "Yes. They're going to get sneaky on us now."

The Able Team leader slid a fresh magazine into his automatic shotgun. "What's the plan?"

The Executioner glanced at his watch. "Pop green smoke."

THEY HAD BARELY GOTTEN a half mile from camp when Baibakov leaned out the cab of the truck and stared upward in alarm. A helicopter was rapidly descending out of the pass ahead like a thundering monster from a nightmare. Its olive-drab contours were all slants and angles, and it was loaded with weapons. There was no way it was a police helicopter or border-patrol observation craft.

It was a gunship.

Baibakov grabbed the CB radio from the dash and roared into the mike. "We are under attack! Break formation! Now!"

The lead jeep of the convoy opened fire with its heavy machine gun. The helicopter was coming straight on, and yellow flashes sparked off its fuselage as the heavy bullets struck it. The gunship dived into the fire and a missile burst into life below one of its stub wings and roared off its launch rail. The jeep broke to the right but the missile slanted to follow. The driver desperately swerved to the left, and the missile jinked its trajectory.

The gun jeep blew apart in a ball of orange fire.

The vehicles began dispersing in wide swerving arcs. The men in the jeeps swiveled their heavy guns and fired on the helicopter, but the gunship ignored the machine guns and swooped among the trucks and jeeps. A swarm of rockets hissed from one of the helicopter's pods, and a truck shuddered and lifted up off its axles as it was rocked by multiple explosions. The vehicle jolted up onto two wheels, then fell over on its side, where it lay burning. There were no survivors.

Baibakov cursed as he reached behind his seat. "Halt the truck!"

The giant kicked open his door as he drew a long, slender launch tube from the back of the truck. He grabbed the cabin's outside railing and vaulted onto the roof. He crouched as the helicopter tore apart a jeep with its chin-mounted automatic cannon. The gunship was too heavily armored. It would take a miraculous hit or extensive cumulative damage with machine guns to bring it down, and Baibakov and his men had time for neither.

The captain rose and shouldered the SAM-7 surface-to-air missile. The helicopter was flying away from him, a perfect angle for the tail-chase profile of the heat-seeking Grail missile. The giant tracked the helicopter through the optical sight and activated the infrared seeker. The indicator light blinked and held as the missile's seeker achieved a lock-on.

Baibakov took a breath and fired.

The Grail missile hissed out of the launch tube, and the second stage of its rocket engine fired. The missile rapidly accelerated to Mach 1 and shrieked toward the gunship. The missile's seeker became extremely unhappy. It had been unhappy the moment Baibakov had turned it on. Its computer mind knew nothing of the Apache gunship's ALQ-144 jammer. To its heat-seeking eye, but no gunship, there was only a strobing pattern of incredibly bright infrared flashes. It knew something was there, but it couldn't achieve a genuine lock. It was like trying to stare at something that was flying straight out of the sun. The Grail flew into the blinding pattern, and suddenly it was clear. It was a contact weapon and its fuse had slammed into nothing. There was nothing ahead of it in its narrow cone of observation. It flew for another thousand yards and sought another target until it ran out of fuel. Its rocket motor burned out, and it began to fall back to earth.

Baibakov roared at the driver of the truck. "A missile! Another missile!"

It was incredible. The missile had flown right at the gunship and missed. The helicopter hadn't even moved. Now, however, it moved. The gunship swung about on its axis and its nose pointed at Baibakov in judging accusation.

"Another missile!"

The helicopter's stub wings were almost engulfed in flame as rockets hissed out from underneath them and flew straight at Baibakov. His last thought was to drop the launcher and unsling his rifle when his world exploded in a storm of sound and orange fire.

WARRANT OFFICER Steven Anderson swallowed hard. "That was close."

"Yeah." Grimaldi swung the helicopter around. Two jeeps and one of the trucks were heading back to the base as fast as they could, and they looked like they might make it. The rest of the vehicles were either knocked out and burning or didn't move. The survivors had stopped firing and some had sought cover. One jeep lurched and smoked as it tried to move. One man drove the beleaguered vehicle while another leaned bloodily over his mangled heavy machine gun. A third man slumped unmoving in the passenger seat. Grimaldi dropped the Apache almost right on top of them. The jeep ground to a halt, and the driver stared at the gunship as it hovered twenty feet in front of him.

The Stony Man pilot spoke into the intercom. "Aim the cannon at him."

The Apache's chin-mounted cannon was linked to the gunner's helmet sight, and as Anderson turned his head and looked at the jeep in front of them, so did the smoking muzzle of the gunship's cannon.

The Russian stared up at the helicopter and squinted against its rotorwash. After a moment he raised one hand, slowly removed the jeep's keys with the other and tossed them into the dust. Grimaldi grinned.

"Real smart fella."

"What now?" Anderson asked.

The Russians weren't going anywhere. Their vehicles were out of commission, and they had wounded to attend to. The authorities or a contingent from Fort Huachuca could sweep them up later. Striker needed them now. "We're heading for the base. What is our weapons status?"

Anderson checked his screen. "Two Hellfires, fourteen rockets, 750 rounds of 30 mm."

Grimaldi grinned and shrugged. "Well, that ought to do the trick." He pulled the gunship into the air and dropped the nose toward the mining base. "What do you say we go meet the home team?"

27

Ramzin's face was contorted into a snarl of rage as he crouched in the drainage ditch and fired his rifle. The American commandos were good. Too good. Two of the them were behind the burnt-out truck, and another was pinned down by the pylons. Others—he didn't know how many—were still in the warehouse. He could hear fighting and explosions beyond the base where the convoy had been headed, and he gritted his teeth. His plan was swiftly going to hell. The radio was in the truck, and he had no time to go back and find out what was going on. He had hoped to delay the Americans on the base, then make a strategic withdrawal. Once clear, he would blow them to hell while he and his men lost themselves in the mountains. Now they were holding him here in a stalemate as each side pinned down the other. Time wasn't on his side, and he couldn't afford to play games. He had to take these Americans, and he had to take them quickly.

Ramzin figured he had at least fifteen able men left. It would have to be enough. Degederov lay wounded beside him. He was shot through the legs, but he still lay tenaciously behind his RPK-74 light machine gun and fired bursts into the enemy positions. The major grinned in savage defiance. Degederov was Spetsnaz. They were some of the most well-trained and dangerous soldiers in the world. They would break this stalemate, and they would break it now.

"Degederov, give me your weapon."

The man nodded and Ramzin pulled the RPK squad automatic weapon to him. It was essentially a strengthened AK-47 assault rifle, with a heavy barrel, a bipod and a

75-round drum magazine. Ramzin looped the sling over his shoulder and handed Degederov the detonator for the second nuclear charge, and his rifle.

"Do not let this fall into enemy hands."

Degederov nodded and grimly took the detonator and the rifle. Ramzin loosened his CZ-75 pistol in its holster and took a high-explosive grenade from his belt and pulled the pin. He hurled the grenade over the lip of the drainage ditch toward the pickup truck the Americans were using for cover. Ramzin took a deep breath and leaped up out of the ditch. He pulled the RPK machine gun into the hip assault position and roared at the top of his lungs.

"Follow me now! Attack!"

His men rose from their positions and rushed forward, hurling grenades and firing on the run. The RPK snarled in Ramzin's hands as he led the charge. Tracers streaked from their weapons in a smoking hail of gunfire.

It would end now. One way or the other.

"HERE THEY COME!" Lyons roared as he slammed a fresh magazine into his weapon.

"Here they come!"

Bolan tossed the hissing smoke grenade behind them, and green smoke coiled up into the desert sky. Similar plumes floated up from the warehouse and Gadgets's position. Bolan and Lyons's cover was being shot to pieces under the Russian assault. It appeared the Russians weren't going to be sneaky, after all.

They were going for it.

The Executioner slapped the muzzle of his M-4 carbine over the pickup's battered hood and fired the M-203 grenade launcher blind. The weapon recoiled savagely from the defensive munition, and the 40 mm buckshot round sprayed into the charging enemy. Bolan dragged the weapon back and rolled to the truck's left fender. The carbine chattered on full-auto and he heard the methodic hammering of Lyons's automatic shotgun from the other side of the truck.

The Russians came on. It was an assault that would have overwhelmed normal opponents, but the men from Stony Man were some of the most well trained men on the planet.

They didn't panic. They aimed and fired, and the charging Russians fell.

Bolan tossed aside the spent carbine and brought up his Beretta 93-R pistol in one hand and his .44 Magnum Desert Eagle in the other. A big man led the charge with an RPK light machine gun, firing from his hip. The Executioner put a burst into him from the Beretta, but the man didn't fall. Instead, he coolly dropped to one knee and brought the light machine gun to his shoulder and sighted directly at Bolan.

The Desert Eagle roared in the Executioner's hand and the .44 Magnum round defeated the Russian's armor and slammed him backward. A second round toppled him. Above the snarl of the assault weapons, Bolan could hear the rapid booming of a heavy rifle, and he knew that somewhere Manning was firing his M-14 sniper rifle as fast as he could acquire targets. From the warehouse, McCarter and Blancanales fired lethal bursts into the Russian advance. Gadgets Schwarz's silenced 9 mm submachine gun was felt but not heard.

The Russian assault broke as Encizo joined the fight with the stolen jeep's heavy machine gun. The enemy stopped charging and dropped prone, some providing covering fire while others rolled or crawled for cover.

Bolan rose and peered quickly across the hood of the truck. His stomach tightened as he saw two jeeps and a truck tearing at dangerous speeds into the compound. He knew that would be enough to turn the tide. Ammunition was running low and his team was running out of time. The men from Stony Man wouldn't be able to stop a second assault. Bolan glanced into the sky as he slipped a fresh magazine into the Beretta.

Something that resembled a smoking fire hydrant streaked out of the sun, and the lead jeep blew apart in a ball of orange fire. Men dived desperately from the second jeep into a drainage ditch, and a moment later the jeep was blown to pieces as another missile roared in from above and struck it. More men jumped from the truck and scrambled for cover in all directions. The air thundered and dust blew up in red clouds as a helicopter gunship swooped out of the sky. The truck driver leaped from the cab of his vehicle, and the chin of the gunship erupted in fire as its cannon roared to life and chopped the truck into a smoking ruin. The helicopter rotated and flew toward Bolan and the plume of green smoke behind him. The Executioner couldn't see the man's face through the windscreen and his tinted helmet as the gunship whirled overhead, but he knew the thumbs-up the pilot threw him. Grimaldi had brought the cavalry. The helicopter rotated to face the Russians, then climbed up into the air to gain more altitude. The cannon spoke again, and the Russians hurled themselves to the ground as the gunship drew a smoking line across the compound.

Bolan shouted to Lyons. "Get back to Rafe! Bring out the jeep!"

Lyons ran back to the bulldozer. Moments later the jeep ground out from behind its cover with the Able Team leader behind the wheel and Encizo manning the big gun. The muzzle of the DShK swung to cover the Russians who lay in the open. Above the battlefield, the helicopter rotors beat the air like thunder. The enemy lying in the open looked at one another. From cover, others cradled their weapons in the lull and prepared to sell their lives dearly.

The Executioner stood from behind cover and holstered his weapons as dozens of Russians trained their weapons on him. He walked forward slowly with his hands open and knelt before the man who had led the charge. The man was still alive, and he peered up at Bolan with calculating gray eyes. He had been wounded in the shoulder and in the side. The shoulder wound was clean, but the wound in his abdomen would kill him soon if he didn't get medical attention. Bolan knelt beside him.

"You are Ramzin," he said in Russian.

The man grimaced against his pain. "Yes, I am Ramzin."

"Order your men to surrender, or the gunship will cut them to pieces."

Ramzin's eyes rolled up to look at the helicopter orbiting the camp. Too many times in Afghanistan he had been in the armored gunships and devastated helpless men armed only with rifles and machine guns. He nodded bitterly. He had lost. His last duty now was to his men.

"Help me to my feet."

Bolan took Ramzin's arm and gently pulled him up. The Russian's breath hissed from between clenched teeth, and he leaned heavily on the Executioner's arm. The major took a deep breath and wheezed as he tried to bark out a command. He tried to shout again, but couldn't seem to fill his lungs with air. Finally he grasped the sling of the RPK around his shoulder and with great effort he shrugged it off. The weapon clattered to the dusty ground. Ramzin glared about at his men, then sagged. Bolan lowered him to the ground, then shouted above the rotor noise in Russian.

"I have accepted your commander's surrender! Throw down your weapons. You will be well treated. There will be no reprisals."

A Russian stood slowly and looked at Ramzin where he lay. The man's shoulders sagged, and he shook his head as he tossed his rifle to the ground. After a long moment another rifle dropped, then another. More soldiers clambered out of the drainage ditch, tossing their weapons before them. Others threw their weapons aside but stayed by their wounded comrades.

McCarter and Blancanales emerged from the burning warehouse with their weapons leveled. Gadgets rose from behind the blackened and battered concrete pylons. Ramzin spoke at Bolan's feet. "My men. Many need medical attention."

Bolan looked at him squarely. "They'll get it."

Ramzin nodded. "Good. That is good." He closed his eyes again.

A shrill voice shouted across the compound. "Drop your weapons!"

All eyes turned as Anne Tyler stood up in the drainage ditch. She held a Makarov pistol in one hand and a small metallic box in the other.

"Drop your weapons now!"

Lyons raised his shotgun. "You drop yours, lady."

Bolan held up his hand and Lyons lowered the shotgun. The Witch walked forward and glared at the Executioner. Her hair was disheveled, and her face and clothes were smudged with smoke and dust. Her eyes glittered clear and bright, and her thumb lightly tapped the remote control in her hand.

"You know what this is, I assume."

He nodded.

"Then you will have your men drop their weapons. I will take Ramzin and two men in that jeep your men are sitting in. You will guarantee us safe passage to the Mexican border, or I will obliterate the entire compound."

Bolan shook his head. "No one is going anywhere."

The Witch trembled with anger, and she stepped closer. Her voice dropped low. "I am an old woman. My husband is dead by your hand. I am not going to spend my remaining years languishing in an American prison. I will destroy you, your men, my men and myself, and I will be glad of your company in hell."

The Executioner stared into Anne Tyler's eyes and he had no doubt of it. They stood fast and regarded each other.

Manning's voice spoke quietly in Bolan's earpiece. "Striker, take one step to your left and I can take her out. One step and I'm green light. You make the call."

The Witch slid her thumb on top of a black switch, and her voice came from between her teeth in a hiss. "You have one second to decide, you son of a bitch."

Gunfire erupted at Bolan's feet. The Witch jerked as round after round struck her. She staggered backward as the bullets hit her mercilessly, and the detonator tumbled out of her nerveless hand and fell to the red dust. She collapsed to the ground as the CZ-75 pistol in Ramzin's hand clacked open on an empty chamber.

The major sagged back and rested the pistol across his chest. He shook his head wearily and looked up into the sky.

"I never liked her very much."

EPILOGUE

"Ramzin shot Tyler?"

Bolan sat on one hip on Larquette's bed in the clinic.
"Yes. Apparently he didn't appreciate her idea of nuking his
men in a last act of defiance." Bolan looked off into the
distance. "He was a formidable opponent and a good commander."

Larquette smiled at him. "You respect him, don't you?"

He met her gaze. "I don't respect what he was doing. I'm
sorry to see such a capable man turn to crime. But in his own
way, he remained a man of honor. He'll still have to pay for
his crimes. So will his surviving men." He grinned at her
suddenly and changed the subject.

"What about you?"

"Well, I'm chief of police these days. But I was appointed by committee, so I guess there'll have to be an election."

"I think you might win."

She looked at him slyly. "Oh?"

He nodded. "Yeah. In town they're calling you Patti
Earp. Not every town has a chief who shoots it out with
armed Russians on the steps of the jail. You and Tom are
heroes."

Larquette blushed bright red and looked at her toes. After a moment she looked back up at him. "What about
you?"

"There may be repercussions. I broke some rules."

Her eyebrows slanted together. "Screw the rules. You
stopped a Russian invasion. You got the man who murdered my father. That ought to count for something."

Bolan shrugged. "Well, there is that."

Larquette glanced at him long and hard. "I don't know who you really work for, and I don't suppose I'll ever get to know your real name, either. But I bet somewhere along the line you had to swear something about defending the United States against enemies both foreign and domestic. If I were you, I'd keep my chin up."

The Executioner couldn't help but smile. "I also swore something about upholding the Constitution. I think I may have violated Ramzin's civil rights."

Larquette laughed. "I'm a lawyer, trust me. I think the case is arguable."

"I'll keep that in mind."

"You do that." Her face became serious, and she reached out and took Bolan's hand. "I want you to know, if this does get you in trouble, I'll swear in court that I deputized you."

Bolan squeezed her hand. "You're a very remarkable woman."

"You're a very remarkable man," she replied.

Manning leaned into the infirmary. "The bus is leaving, Striker."

She peered up at him. "Striker?"

"Doesn't really matter, does it?"

"No, I guess not."

The Executioner placed a hand on her shoulder. "Take care of yourself."

He turned and walked out of the infirmary. Outside, the team was waiting by his Bronco. They had a five-mile drive to the airstrip. McCarter sat on a bench and drank a Coca-Cola. The general store had an antique machine that dispensed soft drinks in old-fashioned bottles, and the Briton had become totally enamored of it. Bolan jerked his head toward the truck.

"You ready?"

McCarter rose. "Very ready. I believe this is going to be a terribly exciting debriefing."

The Stony Man warriors loaded into the truck and headed toward the airstrip and home.

It's blood sacrifice time on the
California proving ground

STONY MAN™ 22
SUNFLASH

Nuclear power is destroying life and peace on the
planet. A power surge and worldwide nuclear accidents
have destroyed lives, while antinuclear demonstrations
threaten violent civil unrest. After discovering the explosive
combination of a Red Chinese satellite, a New Age politician
and a race to control a new power source, the Stony Man
teams fear they may be running out of time.

In Deathlands, past and future clash with frightening force

JAMES AXLER

Keepers of the Sun

The gateways are secret installations from the predark days, which Ryan Cawdor and his band of warrior survivalists use as escape routes. In KEEPERS OF THE SUN, Ryan and his group emerge into a world ruled by the samurai code. Here Ryan faces a new threat that could destroy the only home he knows.

A new dark age has dawned with the hope of a promised land. But in the Deathlands, hope is not enough.

**An old enemy develops a deadly
new train of thought...**

THE

Destroyer

#103 Engines of Destruction

Created by
WARREN MURPHY
and RICHARD SAPIR

The railways have become the fastest—and surest—way
to get from here to eternity. Could the repeated sightings
of a ghostly samurai swordsman be linked to the
high-speed derailments that are strewing the rails with
headless victims? Suspecting the train terror is merely a
decoy, Remo Williams and Master Chiun become
involved, only to find they may literally lose their heads
over an old enemy.

**Don't miss out on the action in these titles featuring
THE EXECUTIONER®, ABLE TEAM® and PHOENIX FORCE®!**

SuperBolan

#61438	AMBUSH	$4.99 U.S.	☐
		$5.50 CAN.	☐
#61439	BLOOD STRIKE	$4.99 U.S.	☐
		$5.50 CAN.	☐
#61440	KILLPOINT	$4.99 U.S.	☐
		$5.50 CAN.	☐
#61441	VENDETTA	$4.99 U.S.	☐
		$5.50 CAN.	☐

Stony Man™

#61896	BLIND EAGLE	$4.99 U.S.	☐
		$5.50 CAN.	☐
#61897	WARHEAD	$4.99 U.S.	☐
		$5.50 CAN.	☐
#61898	DEADLY AGENT	$4.99 U.S.	☐
		$5.50 CAN.	☐
#61899	BLOOD DEBT	$4.99 U.S.	☐
		$5.50 CAN.	☐

(limited quantities available on certain titles)

TOTAL AMOUNT	$
POSTAGE & HANDLING	$
($1.00 for one book, 50¢ for each additional)	
APPLICABLE TAXES*	$_____
TOTAL PAYABLE	$_____
(check or money order—please do not send cash)	

To order, complete this form and send it, along with a check or money order for
the total above, payable to Gold Eagle Books, to: **In the U.S.:** 3010 Walden Avenue,
P.O. Box 9077, Buffalo, NY 14269-9077; **In Canada:** P.O. Box 636, Fort Erie, Ontario,
L2A 5X3.

Name:_____

Address:_____ City:_____

State/Prov.:_____ Zip/Postal Code:_____

*New York residents remit applicable sales taxes.
 Canadian residents remit applicable GST and provincial taxes.

GEBACK11A